THE BLUESTOCKING'S BARGAIN

CLAIRE DELACROIX

DEBORAH A. COOKE

The Bluestocking's Bargain
The Ladies' Essential Guide to the Art of Seduction #5
By Claire Delacroix

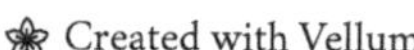 Created with Vellum

THE LADIES' ESSENTIAL GUIDE TO THE ART OF SEDUCTION

REGENCY ROMANCES

The Ladies' Essential Guide to the Art of Seduction is a series of Regency romances. In each story, a marriage in dire straits is rescued by the lady's consultation of Miss Esmeralda Ballantyne's incomparable volume of amorous advice. Over the course of the series, Esmeralda matches wits (and more) with the resolute Duke of Haynesdale, who is determined to stop her endeavor, no matter the price.

1. **The Christmas Conquest**

2. **The Masquerade of the Marchioness**

3. **The Widow's Wager**

4. **The Hellion's Heart**

5. **The Bluestocking's Bargain**

6. **The Duke's Desire**

THE BLUESTOCKING'S BARGAIN

CHAPTER 1

London—September 1817

Miss Patience Carruthers liked to collect facts as much as she liked to collect books. She found pleasure in knowing things, the more things the better. In fact, it was her considered opinion that the vast majority of people did not know nearly enough—or read enough—to be relied upon to function well.

The rakehell Arthur Beckham was a good example. Despite his charm, his remarkable good looks, and his determination to win her approval, he was incapable of shaking her convictions. After all, the man's reading habits were woefully inadequate. If he would just pause for breath, Patience would tell him so.

"Clearly, the book," Arthur said with an engaging smile "is wrong." He pushed a volume across the counter that he was returning along with the other volumes his mother had borrowed earlier in the year.

Patience bristled, confident that she was unaffected by that smile. "Books, sir, are not wrong simply because an individual does not care for their content. Books provide an infinite variety of entertainment value as well as a wealth of factual information. Those books that appeal to one person may not appeal to another, which explains the inventory of libraries and bookstores..."

She could have continued at some length in this vein, but the well-attired gentleman on the other side of the lending counter at Carruthers & Carruthers opened the book in question, presenting its contents to her. Patience had already noted that it was a leather-bound edition of *Childe Harolde* and surmised it was one of their lending copies, given that it was being re-turned with a number of other such volumes. But when the book fell open in Mr. Beckham's gloved hands, she immediately saw that it had been savagely mutilated.

She gasped, as loudly as if he showed her a child with a fatal knife wound.

The block of pages had been rudely sliced from the inside of the case, the edges left so ragged that there were threads of linen binding visible. The endpapers were torn, as well, a travesty since they had been of fine marbled paper, perhaps from Florence. The volume that had been sloppily stitched into the case for the poem had a disreputable look about it. It was much smaller than the original block had been, which meant that the ravaged binding was exposed at the top and bottom of the spine. The paper was cheap and thin, and the pages were scuffed as well as discoloured around the edges. It was either a very well-thumbed volume or one that had been left in inappropriate circumstances for some extended period of time. The very prospect of a book being so abused was a shock to Patience and she gripped the lip of the counter, as well as falling into a horrified silence.

What had happened to the poem that had originally been inside this case?

Surely it had not been discarded?

Surely the man before her had not destroyed the original volume? If so, he was even more reprehensible than she had imagined.

Patience raised her horrified gaze to his and Mr. Beckham raised a hand, almost retreating a step. "I assure you that it was like this when we opened the package of books. I am not responsible for this book's state, Miss Carruthers." His dark gaze bored into hers with startling intensity. "I give you my word of honor."

Patience had no notion of the merit of his word of honor, though he made the declaration with such vehemence that she could not remained unmoved. She was only slightly relieved, for the damage could not be repaired.

"The book remains wrong, however," he said and held it a little closer to her.

Patience's gaze slid over the text and she retreated a step, appalled when she understood the content. The words printed there formed no part of the poem *Childe Harold* and were, in fact, lewd in the extreme.

But then Arthur Beckham was notorious in so many ways.

She glared at him, as he continued to watch her, eyes twinkling. (They were very, very dark and she dared not look into them for long, lest she tumble into those alluring shadows and forget herself utterly. Doubtless he relied heavily upon his very pleasing countenance to lead innocents astray. She would not join their ranks.) "Do you see my meaning, then?" he asked.

"That book does not belong in that case."

"And yet, here it is." Mr. Beckham closed the book

and shook it at her. "I must say that I never expected to receive such a volume from Carruthers & Carruthers."

"But…"

"My mother left an order of books to be borrowed for our trip to Venice," he continued smoothly. "And this volume was included in the parcel, though its contents were not as expected. Fortunately, I discovered the truth before my mother or younger sister became aware of it."

Patience had a sick feeling then, for she recalled an instance that she had dismissed at the time. Her older sister Catherine had been annoyed about a book disappearing in the spring, a book that she insisted did not belong to the bookshop. Had it not been a copy of *Childe Harold*? Patience thought perhaps it had been.

She had packed Lady Beckham's order. She remembered that well. Was she responsible for the inclusion of this volume? She had to be.

And Mr. Beckham appeared to have guessed as much.

"I will see the matter resolved, sir." She reached for the book with an unsteady hand, examined it upon all sides, then checked the endpapers front and back. There was no stamp declaring that it belonged to the bookseller. In fact, what remained of the endpapers were marbled with a thread of gold, an expense her father only undertook for particularly important books and never for those to be lent.

Which meant that either Mr. Beckham played a jest upon her, having presented a book that had not originated in her father's place of business—and that meant he might be lying about his role in the desecration—or this was Catherine's missing book.

There was no logical cause for Mr. Beckham to tease her. Patience was certain they had never spoken before, though—of course—she knew who he was. And she, perhaps foolishly, trusted his word. He seemed very earnest in this moment and she was tempted to believe he told the truth as he knew it.

She stole a glance to find him watching her closely, as if he could not anticipate what she might do and was interested to find out. Patience's heart fluttered, as it never did, for such action would be irrational—but then, she was not accustomed to having very handsome and eligible young men study her so avidly.

She was glad she had worn her better dress on this particular day, which made no sense at all.

She shook her head. It was Catherine's book, then, and the mystery of why her sister had such a volume in her possession could wait for a later interview.

Patience held fast to the book and smiled politely. "I thank you for bringing this error to my attention. I will ensure that the necessary corrections and repairs are made."

"That is all you mean to say?"

"I cannot imagine what else I would say. It appears that no one was inconvenienced by the mistake, and by your own admission, there is no cause to send apologizes to your mother or sister."

"But I was grievously affronted." The wicked glint in his eyes hinted otherwise.

Patience gave him an icy look. "But a glance, sir, apprised me of the book's content, and given your reputation, I hardly expect the content was a shock to you."

He grinned. "Was it a shock to you, Miss Carruthers?"

"I hardly see that the reply is of any import at all."

"Oh, but I see it as a very worthy question." He leaned closer and she could not avert her gaze from his cursed confidence—or those eyes dancing with mischief. What would he say? He lowered his voice to a whisper that she found inappropriately seductive. "I must wonder whether you included that volume on purpose."

Patience retreated a step. "To what end, sir?"

"To provoke me into thinking of you." He tapped the counter with a fingertip. "Perhaps to create this very opportunity for discussion."

Patience felt her mouth open and close again. She had no reply to such an audacious suggestion.

Mr. Beckham nodded with a surety in his own notion that was irksome beyond all. "Perhaps you wished to speak with me. Many young ladies do. I assure, you, Miss Carruthers, that I am yours to command." He consulted his pocket watch as she was amazed by his high opinion of his own charms. "For the next seven minutes. After that, I will be obliged to attend my mother." He closed the watch and returned it to his pocket and regarded her, his pert expression reminding her of a sparrow keeping track of a particularly tasty crumb.

"I did no such thing," Patience said. "Though I am reluctant to confess as much lest you be overly disappointed in the measure of your own allure."

He laughed, a loud and merry sound that made more than one patron turn to look. Patience felt her color rising. "*Touché*, Miss Carruthers. You put me in my place for making assumptions about your interest."

"If I did include the book, it was by accident, though I have no recollection of so doing."

"Then I should take it back, as perhaps it does not belong to Carruthers & Carruthers."

Patience tightened her grip upon the volume. "We did have a report of a lost book of this title in the spring. I shall see it returned to its rightful owner."

"May I witness that exchange?"

"To what purpose?"

"I imagine, Miss Carruthers, that you blush most emphatically." His gaze swept over her, an appreciative

gleam in his eyes. "You are so fair. It must be bewitching to watch, and I cannot imagine that you could return that volume without a blush or two."

"Oh!" Patience felt her cheeks heat. "You are audacious beyond all, Mr. Beckham."

"I know." He grinned, then touched the brim of his hat. "Perhaps that is unlike other young men of your acquaintance."

"You have no notion…"

"Why else would I surprise you so?" He gave a dramatic sigh. "I suppose that you have a very proper betrothal arrangement, to a very proper clerk who is a very suitable match for the proper daughter of a proper bookseller and publisher, and as such, is not a man to make such improperly bold suggestions." He lifted a brow, which made him look disreputable indeed. The twinkle in his eyes did not mitigate the impression at all. "Perhaps you peruse such volumes with him?"

"I have no betrothed," Patience said crisply. "I yearn for no man to take my hand within his, for I have books for companionship."

"A book like that might keep you awake long into the night. It did as much for me."

What was in that book? Patience wished she'd had more than a glance, but she wouldn't open it while Mr. Beckham was still watching her. The deed would give him far too much satisfaction and he was already insufferably convinced that he could guess her every impulse.

It would have been so much more satisfactory if he had been mistaken.

She lifted her chin. "Everyone should be so fortunate as to be kept awake at night by a good book," she said, not expecting his loud guffaw. Evidently, she had surprised him, for he strove to cover his amusement, though her father gave him a stern look from the back of the shop.

"And what of love, Miss Carruthers? What of that siren's song drawing destined partners together forever?"

Patience gave him the look he deserved for promoting such nonsense. "Love is a fleeting inducement and one unworthy of trust. If more people were sensible of its perils…"

"Then there would be far fewer people," Mr. Beckham concluded cheerfully. "Do you not wish for children, Miss Carruthers?"

Patience felt her color rising. "That is a most inappropriate query, sir."

"And yet I remain intrigued by your reply." He watched her with an intensity that heated her to her toes. Patience knew she should feel fortunate that reckless young men seldom engaged in such conversations with her, yet she felt curiously invigorated by his attention.

She could not even think of a suitably dismissive reply. His eyes twinkled as her flush deepened and she swore the man was going to laugh.

"What a delightful honor to provide your amusement," she said tartly.

"Oh, I am the one honored, Miss Carruthers. Did you know that you blush in the most beguiling way?"

"Sir!"

He leaned on the counter between them. "I am, in fact, utterly beguiled."

Patience was very aware that this exchange would be drawn shortly to a close, one way or the other. She spoke clearly, so others could hear. "The poetry section, sir, is to the right of the pillar there, while historical sagas are on the opposite wall. I trust you will find something similar to *Childe Harold* in one location or the other, or another volume to snare your interest."

"What about more books like that one?" he asked and she glanced at him. "The one that is actually inside the binding." He dropped his voice to a dangerous whisper and he watched her closely as he spoke. "*Harris's List of Covent Garden Ladies*."

Goodness. Is that what it was? Patience could not hide her shock at the prospect of holding a copy of that guide of courtesans and whores. She glanced down at it, curious indeed. Were its contents as scandalous as they were reputed to be?

"Aha! You know it! There is nothing, in my view, so refreshing than an educated lady."

"Statistically, very few young women benefit from the advantage of a formal education in our society," Patience found herself saying. When agitated, she invariably provided unwelcome statistics. "While young men, particularly those of the upper classes, routinely have tutors at a young age then attend school. Many even proceed to university to complete their educations, leaving their sisters to take dancing lessons from a governess."

"My sister studies French, German, Latin and Italian but tends to neglect her dancing lessons."

Patience thought she might like his sister.

"But you change the subject, Miss Carruthers. Have you read the volume in question?" Mr. Beckham murmured wickedly, the words recalling her to the situation. "If not, I could summarize it for you."

"We do not lend or sell such volumes, sir," she said crisply. "This work clearly does not belong here and I thank you for doing your part in seeing it reunited with its rightful owner."

He looked left and right, then leaned over the counter, the very image of devilry. "Will you read it first, Miss Carruthers? We might arrange to meet and compare observations on the text."

Patience barely resisted the urge to cast the book at him—but then he might abscond with it and keep it, which meant she would have no opportunity to read it herself.

Or return it to Catherine.

How had Catherine even come to have such a work in her possession?

"You make the most scandalous suggestions, Mr. Beckham. I do believe several moments have passed, perhaps even seven, and I would not detain you from your engagement with your mother. Good day." Instead of turning to the next customer, Patience retreated into the back of the shop, where the printing presses were running noisily.

She told herself that she was not truly hiding from an aristocrat overly convinced of his own merit, but that there was no other way to terminate the conversation. Mr. Beckham seemed oddly determined to speak with her at length.

In fact, she glanced back to find his gaze still locked upon her. He lingered at the counter for long moments, apparently awaiting her return. The man must believe himself to be irresistible. He certainly had a rare ability to disconcert her, a talent possessed by very few.

He was unlike other persons of her acquaintance.

He had simply surprised her.

Patience glared at him, then retreated into her father's office when the audacious rogue winked at her.

She peeked out a moment later to see the back of Mr. Beckham's impeccably tailored dark blue jacket as he left the bookstore. Goodness, his shoulders were broad and she could not help but like that he was so tall. He was handsome even from the rear and even better, he would not see her looking at him. She watched as he tipped his hat to a pair of ladies entering the shop, then caught her breath when he suddenly glanced back one last time. The corner of his mouth lifted in a smile when their gazes caught and her heart skipped in the same moment.

It was as if he had known she watched him.

Of course, such a notorious rake would expect her to be fascinated by him.

Patience saw no reason why Mr. Beckham should learn that his expectation was correct. She began to turn away, but halted when she spied a street urchin tug on the hem of Mr. Beckham's jacket. She paused to watch, certain he would ignore or dismiss the child, but instead, his smile broadened. He reached into his pocket as he spoke to the boy and she imagined from his expression that his tone was kindly. She saw the glint of a coin as he gave it to the boy, then the boy's delighted smile, then she turned away from the view.

So, Mr. Beckham had kindness in his heart. The knowledge should not influence her view of him—even though it did. Patience reminded herself that now that he had his moment of amusement, she was unlikely to ever see or speak to him again.

It was less than a satisfactory prospect, which meant only that the man stirred irrationality within her. Patience was better with his absence than his presence, to be sure.

She returned to the office, closed the door, then sat on a stool considering the book she had retrieved from him. *Harris's List of Covent Garden Ladies*. She had heard of the scandalous volume, of course, but no one ever specified in her presence what might be found within its covers. She opened it at a random page and felt her eyes widen.

It was a list, including the names of courtesans and women whose favors could be hired, with addresses, descriptions—and prices. Oh! Patience snapped the volume shut, certain she was blushing all the way to her toes.

If he had been able to pursue her to her father's office, Mr. Beckham would have gained his wish to see her cheeks burn crimson, of that there could be little doubt. Patience would not be disappointed that he was gone—though she could not help but strive to guess his reaction.

It was easy to imagine how he would laugh and how his eyes would glimmer and how utterly handsome he would appear—with his gaze locked upon her, as if she were fascinating herself. A young lady might become treacherously accustomed to such attentions. Patience had spoken to him for a matter of moments and the man had beguiled her as easily as any adoring young maiden. She could only hope he had not guessed his effect upon her ridiculously agitated heart.

Doubtless he had forgotten her already. She had been only a moment's diversion for him.

She sighed despite herself. Hers was not the life that thronged with male admirers and she did not regret that as a rule. There were books, after all.

Like this one.

What a veritable education it might offer.

Patience eyed the book, knowing her father would be outraged if he learned that she had glimpsed within it, certain that Catherine would forbid her the merest glance, and knew this was her sole chance to learn its secrets. Lest she think the better of her impulse, she quickly opened the book and began to read about Mrs. G—frey.

"This lady may be about thirty, rather plump, she has however every requisite to make an agreeable bed-fellow, every nerve during the preludes to enjoyment, seem trembling alive to all the refined sensations, and every part about the

frame is blessed with that corresponding aptness that cannot fail of producing the most desirable effects, neither has the too frequent use of the most bewitching spot rendered it the least callous to the joys of love..."

Patience yearned for a pencil to introduce some punctuation to this torrent of praise, then frowned and read it again

What did these comments and descriptions mean, exactly? Where was the lady's most bewitching spot? Did all women have one or just Mrs. G—frey? It sounded like a body part, but Patience had studied the anatomy books available for lending and knew that none of them catalogued a 'bewitching spot'. It also sounded like it could be worn out with frequent use, which was even more confusing. Body parts, in her experience, did not fray to nothing like velvet ribbons and silk slippers.

There was, of course, no one she could safely ask for explanations—save the gentleman who had just returned the book. Mr. Beckham alone knew that Patience had it in her possession. And likely, he would be amused by her questions.

She did not doubt that he had read it from cover to cover, more than once.

She was certain he knew the answers to her questions.

She wondered if he had acted upon its contents, following a reference to a specific address.

Perhaps he was already acquainted with some of the ladies documented within, and could compare his own assessment with that of the guide. At the very possibility of such wicked indulgence on the part of someone with whom she had actually spoken, Patience was certain she was blushing to her very toes.

She also wagered that Mr. Beckham would know a great deal more than she did about Mrs. G—frey's bewitching spot, whether he was acquainted with the lady in question or not. She peeked at the book again to learn more.

"...she still feels all that torrent of rapture, the mutual dissolution of two souls in liquid bliss can possibly afford, meets the coming moment with uncommon ecstasy, and asks the speedy return."

It might as well have been written in Greek—save that Patience could read Greek with some skill. This volume's prose was incomprehensible at intervals, but oh so very intriguing. She sensed that there were forbidden secrets hidden behind the words, and the only thing Patience liked better than a book was a secret. There had to be a code to decipher its meaning.

It suddenly became quite busy at the lending counter and she heard Prudence call her. She sighed and reluctantly hid the book away, knowing that her older sister would not be forthcoming but that it had to be returned. It probably was fortunate that she was unlikely to cross paths with Mr. Beckham anytime soon.

Perhaps she could find some other helpful reference here at the bookshop or at home in the library kept by her father. Patience most certainly would look.

ARTHUR WAS NEVER late for any appointment, particularly one with Lady Beckham. Not only was her generosity responsible for his many comforts and amusements, but he liked his mother. Their relationship had always been amiable: she was fair in all matters and he strove to be the son she expected him to be. Fortunately, Lord Beckham, the lady's own father, and all of her brothers had been wastrels of the worst order, so no amount of indulgence within Arthur's capabilities could result in the loss of her affection.

He saw no reason for concern in being summoned for an interview at a precise time. Lady Beckham was nothing if not organized—indeed, it was her custom to schedule as much of her day as possible, often weeks in advance.

He allowed himself to review his interview with Miss Carruthers as the carriage made its way through the congested streets of London. She was entirely different from the two types of women Arthur tended to meet. On the one hand, there were the females to be found in gambling dens, theatres and establishments of lesser repute, who were invariably wise in the ways of the world and its foibles, painted, and generally willing to oblige a gentleman's desires. The company of these women might provide amusement and entertainment, but they were not worthy of serious attachment.

Any of them would have been familiar with that scandalous volume and its contents, and likely known the location in its pages of a reference to themselves, or even recited it from memory. Such worldly women, in Arthur's experience, were impossible to shock.

In contrast, there were the debutantes and daughters of the aristocracy, each and every one seeking a husband. They were universally young, meek, and dull. Some were desperate to be chosen; others believed the entire merit of their lives would be measured by their husband's rank; yet others saw the marriage mart as a competition and one in which they were determined to triumph. There was one lady in particular whom Arthur found scheming and unattractive, but he avoided Miss Felicia Grosvenor like the proverbial plague. With any luck, she had forgotten about him while he was in Venice. He dared to hope she might even be married by the time their paths crossed again.

But Miss Patience Carruthers did not fit into either category. (Neither was she a relation, which he supposed was a third category of female but one only slightly more interesting than eligible young ladies.) She was unwed, yet she declared herself to have no interest in matrimony. She was not to be found in those establishments where he sought entertainment in the evening, nor was she painted or dressed to display her virtues. Her gown had been a simple and serviceable one of navy blue with white trim. Her fair hair had been drawn back in a style that was almost austere, given its lack of dangling curls and fetching little ribbons, but her prettiness could not be disguised.

She had magnificent eyes of silvery grey, thickly lashed pools that could be serene in one moment and flashing like a storm at sea in the next.

Best of all, she possessed no guile. Her thoughts had been easily read, her reactions immediate—a sign of cleverness, to be sure—and her company a delight. She amused and provoked him, a most welcome combination. He could not anticipate her, which was even more enticing. Was she kind? Arthur suspected she might be. Her family was respectable, to be sure, her father and uncle running the largest publisher and bookseller in London. Arthur liked that Miss Carruthers was both polite and well-read, that she was opinionated and expressed herself well. He had not been joking about her blushes. She flushed more perfectly than any lady he had ever seen, the rosy hue lighting in the midst of her fair cheeks and spreading slowly to suffuse her face. It was as if this concession to mortal flesh surprised even her.

He already enjoyed both teasing her and challenging her, simply for the pleasure of watching her reactions. Better yet, he had no doubt she would take satisfaction in chastising him for a view she found inadequate.

He smiled at the prospect, resolving that he would have need of many more books in the near future. Anything to enjoy the company of Miss Carruthers at regular intervals.

He also fancied she might be one of the few people of his acquaintance who would tell him the truth. Not only did she appear to have no ability to deceive, but she also seemed enamored of honesty itself. Arthur found himself drawn to such candor, and for more than its refreshing novelty.

All in all, he was content to be back in London again, particularly as Miss Carruthers was unlikely to leave town soon.

His excellent mood did not last long. His sister Amelia, an imp all of ten summers of age, hissed at him when he was removing his hat in the foyer. She was hidden in the side corridor, one of her favorite places to eavesdrop. Arthur looked left and right as if to ascertain he was not watched. This amused Amelia mightily, so he habitually performed the rite. He was well aware that the door to the drawing room was closed and their butler, Stevens, had already vanished. He then crept into the side corridor, as if meeting a fellow spy, and flattened his back against the wall.

"The lark sings at dawn," Amelia whispered, her typical confirmation of his identity—though she could see him clearly.

Arthur suppressed his smile for spying was solemn business. "The crow calls at sunset," he replied in an undertone, looking around the corner again.

"The sparrow chirps at noon," Amelia confided.

"And the bats fly at night," he whispered and Amelia flung herself at him. He caught her in an unexpected hug.

"Bats are not part of the code," she chided as he set her on her feet.

"But they should be."

"It should be the owl," she insisted.

"The owl flies at night?" Arthur shook his head. "The owl hoots at midnight," he proposed and his sister's delight in that suggestion was clear. They had a new code, then.

Then she looked around the corner, before reaching up to whisper in his ear. "*He* is here." Her eyes shone, undoubtedly because she was in possession of valuable information.

"Who?" Arthur mouthed.

She mimicked their uncle's manner, sticking her nose in the air and drawing down the corners of her mouth as if she were a bad-tempered fish. Arthur barely kept from chuckling at her antics. It was true that they shared a dislike for their mother's much younger brother, but they strove to hide as much in company, particularly his. Alone together, they mocked him mercilessly.

"Why?" he mouthed and she drilled a fingertip into his chest.

"You. He wants *you*."

This made no sense at all and Arthur shook his head in confusion.

Amelia, though, nodded wisely. She drew a fingertip across her throat then feigned choking from a garrotte, her dramatic expectation making Arthur smile. She could not make him fear the earl.

"He just wants money. Again," he said, for that was undoubtedly true. Lady Beckham's brother was the biggest wastrel in London. Arthur pointed up the stairs. "Your French verbs are waiting."

"I have to listen!"

"You will be caught."

"Then you must promise to tell me."

"I will tell you what you deserve to know, no more and no less." For this offer, she stuck out her tongue at him." Go." Arthur leaned down to hold her gaze. "I promise I will tell you all. You know that I always do."

She smiled and rubbed her hands together. "You are powerless when faced with my relentless questions."

Arthur laughed, because it was true.

She crossed her heart with a fingertip, and only when Arthur had done the same did she dart away. He stood, amazed at how silently she could move through the house. She must have every creaking stair memorized.

Maybe she *was* a spy, or had a promising future as one. There could be no secrets wherever Amelia resided, though he wagered her governess was unaware of great swaths of her charge's life.

He checked the knot of his cravat in the large mirror in the foyer, giving Amelia time to retreat before he entered the drawing room. He caught a glimpse of her face at the top of the stairs and saluted her, marching toward the drawing room even as he heard her giggle.

What could Reynaud want?

"Mother," he said as he entered the room, bowing to Lady Beckham. He could not fail to note that she looked agitated, which was not her custom.

She had not invited her brother, then. What did Reynaud want from her? His frequent requests for funds did not typically trouble her. Arthur immediately felt the urge to defend the lady and did not take a seat, standing before her and almost between the siblings.

Reynaud Tattinger, Earl of Fairhaven, turned from his place at the window to nod a greeting. The product of an impulsive second marriage on the part of their father, he was more than twenty years younger than his older sister, and only a few years older than Arthur, her oldest son. The earldom had fallen to him, and their respective ages meant that Arthur had no expectations of inheriting the title. Reynaud had not married as yet, but he undoubtedly would and there would be a veritable army of sons between Arthur and the earldom. He had made his peace with the situation long before.

"I thought you had become lost in the foyer," Reynaud said tartly. "It is not so large as that, Arthur. Have you mislaid every last increment of intelligence?"

There was something about the earl that provoked a sensible man into hiding his assets, lest they be appropriated or put to the service of the Earl of Fairhaven. He was not an unattractive man, with his fair hair and chiseled features, but there was a pettiness about his uncle that Arthur disliked.

Arthur made an elaborate bow. "My cravat, sir, had to be tidied before I could face Mother," he said lightly. "I find it quite impossible to get the knot exactly right without my valet." He turned to Lady Beckham. "What do you think, Mother? Will it suffice?"

That lady, to Arthur's relief, had a welcome gleam in her eye. He knew she was glad of his presence. "A little asymmetrical, dear boy. Do come here."

He bent and allowed her to adjust his cravat, winking at her when his uncle could not see his face. Her eyes twinkled as her smile was restored.

To be sure, Lady Beckham could be as demanding as her brother. The Tattingers were a fiercely stubborn lot. Arthur liked to think of himself as an exception.

Lord Fairhaven cleared his throat, then took a seat opposite his hostess. "I have no time for such fripperies and nonsense," he said sourly. Lady Beckham poured the tea and Arthur delivered a cup to his uncle before accepting his own. "I have come on an errand of importance, and I will not be put aside."

"I do not believe anyone has attempted to dissuade you from doing as much, Reynaud," Lady Beckham said, offering a plate of iced cakes.

"But you have delayed me. My time is of the greatest importance, as you would understand if you had any obligations at all, Yvonne."

Arthur watched his mother straighten. A lady of great activity and instigator of many initiatives for the welfare of others, she did not take well to any suggestion that she was idle.

The earl was living dangerously.

"I did not realize you had obligations, Reynaud," she said, her tone seemingly mild. Arthur heard the current of steel beneath her words though. "Have they taken to scheduling appointments in the gaming hells?"

The earl, astonishingly, sputtered, a dull red rising up the back of his neck.

"Oh, you have come to entreat me for funds again," Lady Beckham said with surety. "I regret, Reynaud, that I can no longer indulge you or your profligate habits. If you cannot pay your gambling debts, you should not incur them."

Arthur moved to stand by her side, bracing himself for a tirade from his uncle.

"Just because you married well, Yvonne, does not mean you are my superior," the earl said bitterly. "You were fortunate in your match, that is all, and you were fortunate because Father saw to it…"

"I was fortunate in my match because my husband was not a fool," Lady Beckham said crisply.

The earl's disdain was clear. "He was as inveterate a gambler as I."

"Yet he had the good sense to die before he had exhausted his inheritance. You might have taken a lesson there, Reynaud."

The pair glared at each other.

"And you have a son," the earl concluded, his gaze flicking to Arthur.

"You might take a wife if you desire offspring," Lady

Beckham said before she sipped her tea. She looked wise and implacable, perhaps because the uncertainty of this encounter had been removed. The earl wanted money and she had already refused him. Arthur guessed that his uncle would leave shortly. "I do understand a successful result requires the participation of both parties."

"Save for the Madonna," Arthur noted.

"One event only in the history of the world," his mother said. "A miracle and a gust of wind. To my knowledge, no ladies since have endured such good fortune." She smiled at her brother, who glowered at her.

"I did not come for advice, Yvonne."

"Then why did you come, Reynaud? I assure you that we were quite content in your absence." Lady Beckham sipped her tea, her expression angelic. "I can also assure you that I have no funds to spare for your debts."

"That is not it."

"Then what *is*?"

The earl sighed. He rose and paced the width of the drawing room and back, as Lady Beckham and her son exchanged a glance of confusion. The earl dropped onto the settee opposite Lady Beckham and fixed her with a look.

The look.

Arthur, and undoubtedly his mother, immediately understood that the earl had a problem, one that presumably only they could repair.

That was not the most reassuring realization, given past incidents when the earl had donned with the same pleading expression.

If it was not money he wanted, what else could it be?

Nothing good, in Arthur's view.

"There is a small situation," the earl confessed heavily. "Which requires a happy resolution, an occurrence you can assure."

"Me?" Lady Beckham asked.

"You," the earl said, looking at Arthur. "You have to wed anyway, and making this match will set everything to rights."

Arthur retreated a step, putting distance between himself and any suggestion of marriage. There were limits to his duty to the Tattinger family.

"Reynaud," Lady Beckham thundered. "What have you done?"

CHAPTER 2

The book might have been made of lead for the apparent weight of it in Patience's bag. She was certain that everyone in the shop knew that she carried the scandalous volume and that even passersby in the street could sense that it was in her possession.

She wanted to read it from cover to cover.

She wanted to know how it had come to be in the shop at all.

She knew that the only person who could unravel the mystery was Catherine. This, in itself, defied belief as Catherine was the oldest and the most responsible of all three Carruthers sisters—but Catherine had been the one to proclaim her copy of *Childe Harold* to be missing when the Beckham's order was packed. Perhaps it belonged to her husband.

Either way, Catherine knew the truth. The book had to be returned to her, and Patience only hoped she might gain some details in exchange.

When she left the shop, Patience did not go home. It was simplicity itself to ask Quinn, the family driver, to take her to Trevelaine House to visit her sister instead. Catherine was expecting her first child in December and now that her pregnancy was evident, she spent less time in the bookstore. It was completely reasonable that Patience would visit her. She even chose some books for her sister and bought some sweets from the confectioner shop next door to the bookstore.

She had never been able to read in carriages, unlike her sister Prudence who could read anywhere, but for once that did not vex her. She was thinking of Arthur Beckham and considering herself fortunate that her family did not mingle overmuch in society. She had found herself almost overwhelmed by the attentions of such a handsome young man, particularly one so inclined to make mischief. Had she encountered a number of such men in succession, each determined to charm, tease or provoke her, there is no telling what she might have done.

Actually, there was no uncertainty. Patience would have done what was right and proper—most likely, nothing at all but return home with her chaperone—there was a family jest, after all, that Patience suited her name while Prudence did not.

"I suppose that you have a very proper betrothal arrangement, to a very proper clerk who is very properly a suitable match for the proper daughter of a bookseller and publisher, and is not a man to make such improperly bold suggestions."

She heard Mr. Beckham's words again, and saw him, leaning over the counter, the light glinting in his dark hair. His confidence was alluring, to be sure, and his conviction that he was right as irksome as his surety that he was irresistible. Patience wished heartily that she might have been the one to prove his charm less than he believed it to be, but to herself, she could admit that she had been beguiled.

She had always imagined that an older brother might tease a sister thus, but there was something in Mr. Beckham's manner that had not been brotherly.

No, there had been an admiration and an awareness,

an *interest* that had been the reason she could not simply turn away from him. She was surprised to realize how much she had enjoyed his attention. She had not been certain what he would say, and that had intrigued her.

Had he been flirting with her?

If so, he had been teasing her, of course. Such a man, a handsome rakehell with every asset at his fingertips, would court the favors of a lady who was his social equal. An heiress, perhaps, the cherished daughter of an aristocrat, a beauty so indulged that she never had to mend her petticoats or lengthen the hems of her older sister's discarded dresses. The Carruthers were comfortable, but their father was frugal.

The fact was that Patience had never concerned herself with marriage or her prospects. Books were her companions, and they were far more reliable than most people. When she was younger, the family conviction had been that Catherine would wed first, but her older sister had not succumbed to a nuptial vow early. It had only been three years since the Duke of Haynesdale had arranged Catherine's match to Rhys Bettencourt.

Why had he done as much? Patience had never considered the choice, though now she wondered. Catherine had been old for marriage even then—to be wed the first time at twenty-three years of age was somewhat astonishing, to wed so well might be a miracle. At any rate, the duke was unlikely to arrange a match for Patience—there had been no suggestion of that eventuality.

Contrary to Mr. Beckham's convictions, there was no clerk paying his attentions, proper or otherwise. If there had not been one thus far, Patience doubted one would appear when she was so long in the tooth as to be one-and-twenty.

How curious that the situation had not troubled her before Arthur Beckham teased her.

It was the nature of having sisters, she decided, to dislike any sense that she was missing something. Was she missing something by not entering the matrimonial state? This book suggested she might be—but Mr. Beckham's provocation made a more compelling case.

Patience wanted to know.

As the carriage made its way through the streets, she considered her own eventual fate. Remaining unwed did not trouble her, unless she considered the likelihood of her father departing this world before her. What then?

Childbirth did increase the possibilities of a woman's death at a comparatively young age, but without a husband, Patience was unlikely to bear a child. Given her robust good health, she would likely survive her father.

It was easy to anticipate the rest. The bookselling and publishing firm would pass to her uncle, her father's younger brother and the other Carruthers of the firm's name, and thence to his sons, now thirteen and eleven years of age. Even if Uncle Richard was survived by his brother and Patience's father, her cousins, Michael and Thomas, would still ultimately inherit the business.

And that would mean that an unwed Patience would be beholden to either or both of those hoydens for the rest of her days. She closed her eyes briefly at the prospect. Catherine would ensure her comfort, she was certain, if her sister did not succumb to the risk of childbirth herself. If she did, heaven forfend, and her husband remarried, there might not be a welcome for Patience at Trevelaine House.

Patience gripped her bag, thinking somewhat more favorably about the prospects of marriage than she had to date, and purely on the basis of its financial repercussions. She looked out the window at the numerous people going about their business.

Where did one find an eligible partner, preferably one with sufficient finances to support her desire for books? How she wished one could place an advertisement, as Wentworth did when they had need of a new housemaid.

Perhaps Catherine could help.

~

THE EARL'S tale was surrendered in fits and starts, as was characteristic of his reluctant confessions. Lady Beckham had to order a second pot of tea to sustain them while he wound his way to the heart of the issue, and Arthur thought the sun might set upon another day before they heard the damning details.

Of course, his uncle was lacking in funds. That was the defining situation of the man's existence.

Of course, he had exhausted all potential sources of loans. (Arthur knew this meant his uncle did not like the offered terms.)

And yet, *and yet*, the earl could not resist the tables—this was followed by an eloquent soliloquy about the siren's call of the dice, etc. which need not be recounted again—and so he had gambled. He had lost so many times that he knew his luck was due to turn—by his telling, the change in his fortunes was a virtual certainty.

Arthur rolled his eyes and turned to face the window, wondering whether the earl would ever learn that there were no certainties in gambling—save perhaps, for the older man's inevitable losses. It was all mathematics, but the earl had never troubled to learn as much. Worse, he failed to have the ability to walk

away from a game, even when he was losing disastrously.

The only time to remain at the tables was when one was winning, to Arthur's thinking.

Of course, the earl had taken a most uncommon wager, one he was convinced he would win handily. He presented this detail with conviction, as if they could only agree with him.

Lady Beckham and Arthur again exchanged a look.

The earl paused for breath and mopped his brow with his handkerchief, his manner revealing the truth of the situation.

"But you lost," Arthur guessed, needing no foresight to know the result of the tale.

The earl hung his head in apparent shame, a regret that must have nearly reached its limit. Arthur had to assume the game had ended some twelve hours ago or more. "I did."

"I will not lend you any more money," Lady Beckham said. "And I will not give you any outright, either. Drink your tea, Reynaud, and if you are that broke, put a biscuit in your pocket for your dinner. That is all you will have of me."

"I did not bet mere money, Yvonne. I told you it was a most unusual wager."

The glance exchanged by his companions this time was wary.

"What were the stakes, Uncle?" Arthur asked, his uneasiness growing.

The earl looked between them, smiled as if that would make a difference in their reactions, then blurted out the truth. "You."

"Me?" Lady Beckham demanded, her voice rising in outrage.

"No, no, Yvonne. Arthur here. Does he not need a wife? Is his marriage not past due?" The earl chortled as if he had contrived a merry solution, but no one shared his amusement. "I have done all of us a favor, in fact, by seeing that question resolved!"

When his laughter faded, a deadly silence claimed the drawing room. Lady Beckham set aside her tea, the cup rattling precariously in the saucer as she put it down.

"Reynaud," Lady Beckham said, a torrent of fury in that single word, then pinched the bridge of her nose. She visibly struggled for mastery of her emotions.

Arthur said something markedly more pithy, a single word which made his uncle's eyes widen. "Who?" he demanded then, his voice like a bark.

"Miss Felicia Grosvenor."

This time, Arthur swore with a fluidity that left his uncle visibly astonished. "I do apologize, Mother," he said tersely, but she waved away the offense.

"I think you are entitled to such a view, frankly. Reynaud should never have acted so rashly."

Arthur put down his cup and marched to the window to glare at the passing traffic. There was very little of it, but he had to contrive a scheme for his own escape. He would do a great deal for Lady Beckham—he had done a great deal for her, and he had personally benefitted from the arrangement—but this, this was out of the question.

"She is the very ideal of femininity," Reynaud insisted, a plea in his voice.

The very suggestion of that young lady being considered to have merit, never mind the prospect of her becoming his wife, set Arthur's teeth on edge.

"According to her father," he said crisply. "Whose view is not without bias."

"Who must resort to a *wager* to find her a spouse," Lady Beckham said with a click of her tongue. "What does that tell you of her eligibility, Reynaud?"

"You are harsh, Yvonne…"

"You should wed her yourself then," Arthur retorted but his uncle only laughed.

"Me? I will wed a lady of lineage or no other."

"Who are these people?" Lady Beckham snapped, putting out a hand. "Bring me the Burke's, Arthur."

Arthur shook his head and did not move. "You will not find them there." He felt his mother's horror.

"Thomas Grosvenor," the earl said, the surname making Arthur turn to face him. "And his daughter, Felicia."

"Is he in trade?" Lady Beckham's perspective was unmistakable.

"Worse, Mother. The lady in question is ambitious, grasping, conniving, untrustworthy, unattractive and gauche," Arthur supplied. "She could not possibly be rich enough to induce me to take her hand, and I gather my view is shared by the vast majority of eligible men in London, perhaps in all of England." He took a sandwich that he did not want and bit it in half savagely, taking the opportunity to glare at his uncle. "I would not have put it past her to have contrived this scheme with her father, or her father—for she must have come by her dishonest nature honestly—to have fixed the cards and *cheated* to ensure his victory."

"Oh!" Lady Beckham gasped.

"But my honor…" the earl protested.

"Your honor is of no relevance to me, sir." Arthur spoke with a vehemence that he knew surprised his companions. "I could never wed Miss Grosvenor, for I would be driven to madness in less than five minutes in her company."

He met Lady Beckham's horrified gaze, and knew their thoughts were as one.

"Oh, *that* girl," she said softly. "I remember her now."

"There is nothing for it," the earl said, striving to

sound hearty. In truth, he was perspiring mightily. "The wager has been made and lost, and you must keep the bargain, Arthur. Perhaps she will become more attractive to you in time."

"Impossible," Arthur said and finished his sandwich with an emphatic bite.

"Reynaud, you cannot expect Arthur to bind his life to that of a woman based upon your feckless wager."

"Barnaby Grosvenor will ruin me, Yvonne, and enjoy the doing of it."

"You have been ruined before, Reynaud." She shook her head at the tedium of it all and lifted the tea pot. Arthur shook his head, the earl ignored her, so she refilled her own cup.

"But he is devious, Yvonne." The earl leaned closer to make his appeal to his sister—who appeared unmoved. "He has bought enough of my debts that he can take Fairhaven from me, unless Arthur weds his daughter." He sighed. "By the terms of the agreement, I am to declare Arthur my heir after the wedding."

Lady Beckham set the tea pot down hard at that.

"The last thing I wish to inherit are your debts, Uncle," Arthur said, even as his thoughts flew.

"But you *must*. You must wed her. I entreat you!"

But Arthur straightened, his resolve set. There was no honorable way out of this unacceptable obligation, so he would do what he had to do.

He would lie.

He did not like it, but the solution had worked in the past—and of all people, Lady Beckham could not find fault with the choice.

"I cannot wed the lady in question," he said crisply, his decision made. He examined the sweets with apparent leisure, as if indifferent to his uncle's fuming, and chose a savory sausage roll instead, one that was no more than a bite. It was probably delicious, though it might have been dust on his tongue. He indicated them to Lady Beckham with favor, but she shook her head slightly, watching him with interest all the while.

"But there is no cause for defiance…"

"It is not defiance, sir, but a pre-existing situation, one of which you evidently are unaware."

"I do not understand." The earl looked between his sister and his nephew, his rising alarm undisguised.

"If you had consulted with me before embarking on such a foolish wager, you would have known that I am already betrothed."

"What?!" the earl roared.

Lady Beckham straightened. She could destroy this scheme before it began but Arthur saw her smile ever so slightly and was relieved.

She was entertained, and that alone might save him.

"A man, as you know, cannot wed two women, at least not in this country." Arthur swept an invisible speck of dust from his sleeve. "And I cannot possibly sever a bond promised with such a respectable family, made in good faith and entered with the approval of all parties. It would be unseemly, Uncle, dishonorable and a disgrace." He placed a hand upon his own chest. "My own honor is at stake, after all." He smiled at the outraged earl. "I know you would not ask such a foul deed of me, even for your own convenience."

"But I had no notion you were affianced," the earl said, sinking back down to the settee. "Why was I not informed?"

"The alliance is but recently formed," Lady Beckham said, as if she knew all about it. Her gaze flew to Arthur.

"And who is the lady in question?" the earl demanded. "What is her name?"

The only one lady Arthur found to be of interest.

He would have to throw himself at her mercy, and could only hope she possessed some increment of compassion. He had no doubt she would offer him a challenge in gaining her agreement, and in a way, he looked forward to the encounter.

"Miss Patience Carruthers, of course." He offered his cup for more tea and his mother poured it with a triumphant flourish. "I am surprised you have not heard. All the *ton* is talking about it. There is no doubt about it. You will have to wed Miss Grosvenor yourself." The earl began to shout, his mother scolded her brother for his poor manners, and Arthur sipped his tea, wondering how in damnation he was going to manage to convince Miss Carruthers to accept his lie.

The fact was that he would do anything to avoid a lifetime with Felicia Grosvenor.

If he told Miss Carruthers as much, would she take pity on him? Arthur doubted that, but there might be something she desired, something he could give her, something he could provide to make this most convenient agreement. Bloody hell, he had every asset at his fingertips. She must desire *something*.

He might have need of divine intervention to see success in this matter.

Perhaps he should learn to pray.

Surely, such dire action was not necessary as yet. Arthur still had his charm, though the lady in question might be immune to it. Either way, he could not regret having a logical reason to seek out Miss Patience Carruthers again.

Indeed, he was already looking forward to the encounter.

How to best prepare? He knew little of her affections and dislikes. He did know Rhys Bettencourt, who had married her older sister some years before. Perhaps Bettencourt could be persuaded to take Arthur's cause.

It could not hurt to ask.

Arthur only hoped that the baron was in town. They

did belong to the same club. He would stop at White's and see what he could learn. He excused himself, left Lady Beckham and her brother arguing, and made his escape.

~

PATIENCE HAD NOT BEEN in close proximity to a lady in the family way before, and could not keep her gaze from straying to her sister's ripening belly. She found her sister's dimensions surprising, even hidden beneath the graceful folds of a new dress. The babe was not due until December, thus it was clear that Catherine would become considerably larger before the happy day. The sisters sat together in the library of Trevelaine House, a comfortable room with a considerable store of books. Patience approved of it mightily.

Even better, there was a fire on the hearth and three broad windows admitting the afternoon sunlight.

"If I possessed such a room, I might never leave it," Patience said, not hiding her admiration in the least.

Catherine smiled. "I seldom do. Thank you for this unexpected visit, Patience. It is a delight to have company. If it was Prudence, I would believe there was a reason for your appearance, but not so with you."

"But there is a reason, Catherine. I came to return your book."

"My book?"

Patience offered the copy of *Childe Harold* and watched Catherine's eyes widen in recognition of the volume.

"My book!" she said and reached to take it from Patience.

Patience pulled it back a little. "Is it your book? For if it is, Catherine, I should like to know why such a volume is in your possession at all."

"You looked within it," Catherine guessed, then grimaced.

"Mr. Beckham told me there was something wrong with the book. I opened it to prove him wrong."

"Oh," Catherine said.

"Oh," Patience echoed. Their gazes met and Catherine was the first to smile. Her sister looked positively wicked.

"It isn't actually my book," Catherine admitted.

"Perhaps it belongs to your husband?"

"No." Catherine looked across the room, just the way she always did when she was deciding how much of a tale to share. Patience waited, knowing that nothing would veer her sister from her course, whatever she decided it would be. Her curiosity would not be readily dismissed though. If Catherine refused to tell, she would have to find another way to learn the truth.

She was considering how that might be achieved when Catherine met her gaze again. "The book belongs to an acquaintance of mine. You need not know her name, but she has composed a volume of her own, called *The Ladies' Essential Guide to the Art of Seduction.*"

Patience repeated the title, incredulous that she had heard it correctly.

Catherine nodded. "It is filled with amorous advice and details of a most intimate nature. The author's intention is to see ladies better informed for the realities of the wedding night, for example, and for subsequent intimate encounters with their husbands. Her conviction is that men turn to other sources of satisfaction because wives tend to know so little of...expectations, and her book would address that deficit."

"A book?" Patience asked.

"A book," Catherine agreed. "Fully composed and edited. I was uncertain that Father would consider it for publication, given the content, but the author insisted that much more salacious volumes already exist for men. She brought this volume from her own collection to show me."

They looked at the book as one.

"Then it is hers."

"And hidden inside the case of another book to disguise it. I tell you, Patience, I am most relieved to be able to return it to her. It was only to be a loan."

"Then her book will be published?"

Catherine frowned. "I had hoped as much, but I fear not. Father is adamant that he will not consider it. In fact, he is a little vexed with me at this juncture, for even daring to make the suggestion."

"You did not have this volume to show him, though, to better make your case."

"But he knew of it already." Catherine rose to her feet and walked the length of the room. "It is so frustrating to realize, Patience, how much of the world is hidden from us, how many truths are secured behind locked doors so that we, mere women, cannot partake of this knowledge." She flung out a hand. "This lady's book helped me and Rhys, and I am not ashamed to admit it. I knew nothing of what to expect, until I read its pages."

"Our mother died too young to give us such advice."

"But she might not have done as much, even if she had lived. All matters of the marital bed are treated as great secrets, never to be surrendered to respectable women, even before their nuptial nights." Catherine's voice rose in vexation. "How could we be prepared? How are we to know what to do?" She exhaled mightily. "And so, I did not know, and so we could not speak of it. I had no notion how to begin. I should never have dared to approach Rhys as I did without such counsel, to initiate encounters that gave us both great satisfaction, and now we are so happy together. I could not have borne if our earlier situation had continued…"

"You were not happy with your husband?"

Catherine considered Patience, choosing her words. "Men have expectations of marriage, Patience, and particularly of the marital bed. They have more experience in such matters, as a rule, while we are left—" she flung out her hands "—blind in the darkness, yet needing to resolve the situation. Rhys had concerns for my welfare, which I was able to overcome." She took a deep breath and Patience realized she would not surrender more detail. "I am convinced that many, many marriages would be happier unions if ladies had access to this lady's advice."

Patience had only one question, one that should have been obvious to anyone of her acquaintance. "May I read it?"

"No! You are unwed."

"I might be able to argue your cause with Father."

"If I let you read it now, he is more likely to disown me. He heartily disapproves of this book, Patience, probably because he believes ladies should only learn such details from their husbands." She heaved a sigh. "But all husbands are not as eloquent as Father must have been."

Patience could only consider how much she wanted to read this volume, given that it was going to repair marriages far and wide if read, given that its contents were forbidden to her.

Against every expectation, here was another cause to take a husband.

She eyed her sister, who was rubbing her temple, vexed by the situation and clearly in no mood to do any matchmaking. She found her gaze roving the shelves of the library, as if she might spot the book in question, without even knowing what it looked like.

"May I borrow this one before you return it to your acquaintance?"

"Patience! How can you ask me such a thing?"

"You have read it."

"Not all of it. Some of the details are most salacious."

"Oh!" Patience eyed the book with even greater interest.

"I already have to give the author bad news. I must at least return her book along with her manuscript."

"And who is the author?" she asked, suddenly struck by the gap in her sister's accounting. "Who is she to possess such knowledge in abundance and advice to share?"

"Her name is Mrs. Oliver and she is a widow several times over. She has the most remarkable manner." Catherine frowned, and Patience had the sudden impression that her sister's next words would not be entirely truthful. How unfair she was! Catherine was always honest. "The book has been lauded by another lady of experience beyond my own, but her name is not to be mentioned."

How like Catherine to keep such a promise. Patience smiled at her. "But if the content is so reliable as that, then its publication could not help but be a highly profitable venture..."

"I believe so, but Father refuses and so does Uncle Richard. I spoke to them both but they were resolute. As much as I wish to see the book published, I cannot even think of taking it to another publisher."

"You would be giving them the profits."

"Exactly. It would feel disloyal."

Patience considered the conundrum for only a moment. "Could you not begin a publishing firm of your own? You know how to structure the business, and I would assist you..."

"And I am in no condition to undertake such a venture," Catherine said, cupping her hand around her rounding belly.

"Is all well?" Patience asked, even though she knew she was not supposed to do as much.

Catherine nodded and smiled. "Do not start to fret like Rhys! All is well, but babies demand attention. I am tired and must ensure I do not exert myself overmuch." Her smile broadened. "And once there is one child in the house, there might well be another. I wager my attention is claimed for the next decade."

"Then Mrs. Oliver..."

"Has no interest in becoming a publisher herself, or in financing the production and distribution of the book. The other two ladies who are aware of the work similarly cannot provide the means for its publication. It annoys me to no end that such a volume will not find its way into the world and the hands of women in need of its advice, but I see no other eventualities."

"We must find a husband for me then," Patience said with heat. "One with sufficient resources that he can become a publisher and I can ensure the volume's success."

Catherine laughed aloud. "Oh, I have fed your enthusiasm," she teased. "For you to consider matrimony is a marvel, but then no one would be surprised that you would do as much for a book." They laughed together, as if it was a great jest, but Patience wondered whether there was any possibility of such a success.

It was unfortunate that she had not had a debut season, much less that she knew so few eligible men. She knew fewer rich bachelors. Even if they had allowed women into the gambling hells, it would have served little as she was notoriously unlucky at all games of chance.

She had time to think she should take that as a warning, when she heard Baron Trevelaine himself being greeted by his butler. Another man's voice could be heard as well and the sisters exchanged a glance before the door to the library was flung open.

Catherine's husband took one look at them seated together before the fire and laughed with genuine pleasure. Patience found herself smiling at his manner, for she had always liked him. "How fitting is this?" he asked heartily. "I am asked to contrive an introduction to your sister, Catherine, and come home to seek your advice, only to find the lady in question is here. Hello, Patience." He came forward to greet her. "What a pleasure to find you here." He seized her hands, his enthusiasm making her smile, then turned to gesture to his companion. "I believe you are already acquainted with Mr. Arthur Beckham?"

Patience stared as the man in question doffed his hat and bowed to her. His eyes were dancing with merriment when he straightened and his presence made her heart leap. The man had a scheme, for Patience could smell it, though she had no notion what it might be. Had there ever been a man who could look so wicked and so refined at the same time?

"Miss Carruthers," he said, bending over her hand in his turn. He looked up, his gaze locking with hers with a surety that made her heart jump. "I cannot tell you how delighted I am to see you again." This he murmured, his voice low and dark, his eyes filled with a promise that made her cheeks heat.

Truly?

Why? Patience watched his satisfied smile dawn as he surveyed her rising blush and could only wonder. What did Arthur Beckham want with her?

CHAPTER 3

It was clear to Arthur Beckham that Fortune smiled upon him and his quest. He was not a man to ignore such favor. Indeed, he was inclined to act upon it, with enthusiasm. A run of luck never lasted so opportunity must be seized.

Not only was Bettencourt in town, but he had been leaving White's at the very moment Arthur arrived there. The two had re-entered the club and retired to a private room at Arthur's request, where he confided his need to speak with the sister of his companion's wife.

Of course, Bettencourt wished to know why, and the story had tumbled out inelegantly, halfway making Arthur think he shared some common traits with the earl.

Bettencourt, for his part, had been highly amused by Arthur's predicament. His laughter had made other members of the club turn to peek into the room.

"Ah, you could do worse," Bettencourt said finally, finishing his brandy and rising to his feet with purpose. "Come along and see if you can persuade Catherine to take your side. She knows her sisters far better than I."

Thus possessed of an ally, Arthur left the club with

Bettencourt, daring to hope for success. Lo and behold, the lady herself was visiting her sister. He could not deny a sense that the stars aligned in favor of his scheme, though the assessment in Miss Carruthers' steady gaze could have destroyed the confidence of a man less convinced of his own inevitable success.

Good to his word, Bettencourt declared that his wife looked tired, and asked Arthur to escort Miss Carruthers home. The baroness might have protested the impropriety of this, but a hot glance from her husband silenced whatever she might have said. Miss Carruthers herself did not object, another encouraging sign, and Arthur shortly found himself opposite the lady he sought, in his own carriage.

Truth be told, he was surprised she had been amenable to the plan of him escorting her home. Was she unaware that she should have a chaperone? He could not imagine that she did not know, and wondered at her choice.

Perhaps she underestimated her own appeal.

There might be a great deal he did not know about Miss Patience Carruthers, which was not the most reassuring realization he might have had in that moment.

Arthur cleared his throat, uncertain where to begin. "Your sister looks well," he said.

The lady opposite him spoke crisply. "I gather you would speak to me upon a private matter, and not about my sister's good health," she said. "I recommend you commence, Mr. Beckham. Carruthers House is not that close but at this time of day, a carriage may make rapid progress."

Indeed, they had already left Portman Square behind and were travelling quickly along Oxford Street, in the opposite direction than he had journeyed just moments before. Carruthers House, he had already ascertained, was in Golden Square, not quite as far as Carruthers & Carruthers on Piccadilly, but not in Scotland either.

"I find myself, Miss Carruthers, in a predicament, one that you may be able to resolve."

Her brows rose. "Me? I thought you came to speak to me about the book."

The book? It took him a moment to realize which book she meant, then he was struck by how very long ago their last conversation seemed to have been. "What would I say to you about the book?"

She lifted one shoulder. "You might have comments about its accuracy, or disagree with some of its recommendations and referrals." She was watching him with those silvery eyes, her gaze so direct that he sensed little could be hidden from her.

"And what would I know of such descriptions?"

This time, she cleared her throat, a delicate sound. "You are an eligible young gentleman, Mr. Beckham, and one with somewhat of a reputation as a man who enjoys life's pleasures."

Arthur grinned. "You suspect I have visited these ladies."

"Such a revelation would not astonish me." She looked suitably prim and Arthur wanted nothing more than to tempt her smile.

"Well, it should, Miss Carruthers. I have never paid for the company of a lady before, much less for her affections."

She tilted her head to study him. "Then you are an innocent in such matters? I confess myself surprised, sir."

Arthur laughed heartily at that and her gaze flicked away from him. "Hardly that." Was she blushing? He could not quite tell in the dimmer light inside the carriage, which was a shame.

She eyed him while striving to do otherwise, her curiosity impossible to ignore.

"Let me make myself clear then. Such favors have been granted to me without the exchange of financial compensation, Miss Carruthers."

"Truly? I had no notion that society was so… familiar."

"It can be familiar indeed, I assure you. It seems vulgar to me, as well as unnecessary, to visit a whore when a widow will so often be just as willing a partner. Such a union can offer other advantages as well."

She nodded, though she seemingly could not meet his gaze. "Perhaps a widow's companionship might be less likely to result in an infection or other discomfort."

Arthur was astounded by this comment and did not know what to say. Indeed, this conversation was most uncommon, and he had not even commenced upon the topic he wished to speak about.

She smiled, just a little, reminding him of one of his cats. "I have read medical volumes, Mr. Beckham. It is clearly indicated that men who hire the favors of certain ladies are apt to experience subsequent illness, particularly in the example of syphilis. I, myself, would wish to avoid any circumstance that might add that ailment to my experiences for it is a most cruel progression of symptoms." She blinked once. "Indeed, you raise a salient point, for if I ever am to wed, I must find a way to ascertain that my intended will not bring me unwelcome gifts."

Arthur blinked.

"I can assure you, Miss Carruthers, that I share your view," he said finally, thinking she might wish some reassurance on that subject before their conversation was completed. "Though that is not the only reason to avoid the favors of courtesans and Cyprians."

"You do not like that it is a trade for them?"

"No," Arthur admitted. "I do not. First of all, the company of such females can be an expensive indulgence."

She almost smiled. "Are you frugal or poor, Mr. Beckham?"

"Prudent, most assuredly," he said with a smile. "In addition, I think that intimacy should be pursued when there is fondness or affection, even a measure of admiration between the parties. I find that more amenable than a transaction, not unlike the purchase of a cabbage."

She bit back a smile at that. "A cabbage, sir?"

"A book, then. Any commodity bought and sold without much emotional consideration."

"A book, I assure you, sir, should be a carefully considered acquisition."

He bowed his head, ceding to the correction. "A cabbage, then."

She studied him, seeming to see far more than he might like to reveal. Those grey eyes seemed to be filled with shifting lights, perhaps hiding a trove of secrets of her own. He was tempted in that moment to offer an exchange of secrets with her. He would take a wager as to who might have more. "Do you intend to recommend the merit of love, sir?"

"I think it a fine thing, to be sure, and a wondrous experience. It is not a firm basis for any decision, however, for it is a fleeting pleasure."

"Ah. I appreciate your endorsement and shall recall it in future instances when such a recommendation might be appropriate. Is this truly what you wished to discuss?"

"No." Arthur frowned, aware that he had wasted a goodly measure of time. There was something dashedly easy about discoursing with Miss Carruthers. "Are you acquainted, by chance, with Miss Felicia Grosvenor?"

The warmth faded from his companion's eyes and she sat a little straighter in apparent disapproval. "I would not say that we are acquainted, but I know who she is."

"And do you know much of her?"

"I know all I need to know." Miss Carruthers' eyes flashed in a most alluring way.

What qualities would result in the loss of Miss Carruthers' good view? Arthur wanted very much to know. "Do tell," he invited, not truly surprised that she embarked immediately upon reciting a list.

"She reads three-volume novels, by and large, and a great many of them, though sadly, she does not prefer the better ones. She is inclined to favor the melodramatic and even, I must say, the silly stories over those with more skillful character development and plotting."

"One cannot account for taste," Arthur said, impressed by her ferocity.

"And worse, she has returned books with *stains* upon the pages." This clearly was an unforgivable offense. "I assume the marks are from chocolate or some other confection that includes an oil of some kind, for they cannot be removed from the paper."

"How careless."

"It is outrageous and slothful." Miss Carruthers took a breath, her voice dropping in indignation. "And corners have been folded on the pages of books she has returned."

"How heinous."

She glared at him. "There is nothing amusing in the abuse of books, sir. It is one thing to show such disregard for one's own volumes, but those from a lending library are shared as a kind of sacred trust. They should be treated with more care."

Her passionate defense of books was both fierce and enthralling, that Arthur could only wonder how he had imagined she was dispassionate. Her eyes shone with conviction and she was entirely more animated than she had been previously.

She was as glorious as a warrior queen and he could only stare at her in admiration.

When he did not reply, she caught her breath and raised a gloved hand to her lips. "Oh, I fear I have been too forthright. Is there an understanding between yourself and Miss Grosvenor?"

"No, thank the heavens," Arthur said heartily. "I can only assure you, Miss Carruthers, that you would find the lady's character lacking in more ways than these if you were better acquainted."

"I shall never be better acquainted with her, Mr. Beckham. She is the daughter of a very wealthy man and will undoubtedly wed into the aristocracy."

Arthur was intrigued by her implication. "Do you not think you might?"

Miss Carruthers laughed, such a delightful sound that Arthur wished to amuse her again. "Not I, sir."

"But your sister wed a baron."

"Because the Duke of Haynesdale arranged the match. I still do not know what prompted his kindness to our family, but it has evidently been exhausted by that deed."

She did not seem troubled by this. She accepted it as a fact, a stroke of good fortune for her sister, and neither resented it nor expected similar advantage herself. Arthur had to admire her serenity and her apparent happiness for her sibling. That spoke well of her nature, in his view.

Her eyes twinkled a little as she studied him. "Was Miss Grosvenor truly the topic upon which you wished to consult me? I fear I cannot give anyone who abuses books a good reference."

"Not precisely. I must confess a tale, Miss Carruthers, that does not show me in good light, then cast myself at your mercy."

She only lifted a fair brow, her gaze steady upon him as she waited.

"My uncle, the Earl of Fairhaven, is a habitual gambler, and one not inclined to be lucky."

"It is a malaise shared by many, to my understanding."

"Indeed. And so, lacking for resource and likely in his cups, he made an uncommon wager with the father of Miss Grosvenor last night."

"Indeed?"

"He declared that I should wed that man's daughter if he lost."

"Oh!" He watched as she realized his implication. "Surely he did not lose?" she whispered.

Arthur nodded grimly. "Surely he did."

"And you do not desire this match?"

"No. If I had desired it, I would have offered for the lady's hand myself."

Miss Carruthers nodded agreement. "What a lamentable circumstance for you, with your uncle's honor at stake. Other than offering my sympathy, I do not understand how I might be able to assist."

"I lied, Miss Carruthers," Arthur admitted. "Faced with the prospect of wedding the lady in question against my will, I told my uncle that such an event was impossible, since I was already betrothed." He lifted his gaze to hers and saw a wary understanding appear there.

"Not to me?"

"To you."

Her cheeks were stained a fetching pink at that. "But why?" She shook her head, as if struggling to make sense of his choice. "No one would believe that you would choose me."

"Whyever not? You are pretty, you are sensible, you are educated…"

"I should have preferred to have heard those attributes in a different order, sir," she said with a small and mischievous smile.

Arthur continued, undeterred, though he could not avert his gaze from that smile. "You are from a respectable family. I wager we should never be bored with each other's company, for you read. Undoubtedly, you can discuss politics or whatever other topic I might wish to explore in conversation."

"These are thin reasons to make a lifetime bond, sir, and thinner ones to choose my name above all others."

"I had just spoken with you. You were in my thoughts, as was my admiration of you."

"Mr. Beckham," she chided softly, making her skepticism clear. "I will not countenance a falsehood in this matter."

But it was true. It was all true and, as he sat opposite her, Arthur was even more convinced that Miss Carruthers would make him a suitable wife. "You are right. You are honest," he added. "That is no small detail. There would be trust between us." He could not explain the wave of relief that coursed through him with the words. How long had it been since he had been able to completely trust anyone?

Over twenty years, since he had embarked upon a massive deception, though not of his own initiative. In that moment, Arthur realized the full weight of the burden he carried, and only because there was a prospect of putting it down.

Miss Carruthers, however, gave him a quelling look. "Even though the match would be based upon a falsehood you told to avoid a marriage you did not find appealing?"

"It was not truly a deception…" Arthur began, though he knew it was.

Miss Carruthers challenged him outright. "I cannot imagine how it might be more of one. You asserted that we were affianced when in fact, we are not." She raised a hand to invite his agreement. "That, sir, is a lie, a falsehood and a deception."

"But it was not malicious."

"It might be viewed to be so, if you did not expect anyone to believe it."

"Why would anyone doubt it?"

"Because I am old. Because my father is in trade. Because I have only a very small dowry, particularly in comparison to someone like Miss Grosvenor, and because, despite your flattery, I am not pretty. In addition, you fabricate attributes for my character, which you cannot possibly know to be true or false. There is no possible reason for you to court me, Mr. Beckham. It would not be *rational*."

Hearing her reasons listed so logically and clearly only made Arthur want to argue with her. "But I like you," he said simply. "And surely that is a better basis for matrimony and a better prospect for success in such an endeavor than money or advantage."

She considered this. "It is highly unusual, Mr. Beckham."

"I do not see that as a detriment. Hordes of people pursue bad choices all the time, simply on the recommendations of others."

She studied him again, her expression intent.

At least she had not refused.

"Who else knows of this fabrication?" she asked finally.

"If you think I have stained your name with a rumor…"

"Who?"

"My uncle, of course, and my mother." Arthur frowned. "But Lady Beckham had no social commitments today and I doubt she would share the story until it was confirmed by me. She understood that I was not entirely honest."

"Then you habitually fabricate stories. That is no good endorsement, sir."

"I am a terrible liar, Miss Carruthers. She saw through me immediately and I do not doubt that you would do the same."

"And your uncle?"

"There is no telling who he might have told by now," Arthur had to cede. "It has been some hours."

"Perhaps even Mr. Grosvenor?"

"Perhaps."

"Who would have undoubtedly told his wife and daughter?"

Arthur felt suddenly uneasy. "Perhaps."

"And what of the servants in your household? Our butler makes a point of knowing all that transpires beneath the roof of Carruthers House."

"But Stevens would not tell anyone…"

"Save the housekeeper and the cook." She smiled. "The upstairs maid and the head footman." She glanced up then considered him. "Do you think your driver knew before you handed me into the carriage? What of the footman riding at the back?"

Arthur was astounded. He had never considered how such tidings might travel, let alone how quickly. He had never considered that if Miss Carruthers did not agree, her reputation might be stained. "I do apologize, Miss Carruthers. I had no intention of placing a taint upon your name."

"You thought only of your own escape. I understand." She remarkably did not look inclined to judge him harshly. "If anything, Mr. Beckham, such a tale might improve my eligibility."

Arthur could not countenance the possibility of her wedding anyone else, not if he could convince her to accept him. "That will not be relevant if you wed me." He leaned closer. "I will do anything, Miss Carruthers, to win your agreement."

Her gaze locked with his, so bright and clear that he was certain she read his very thoughts.

"Anything?" she echoed as the carriage turned into Golden Square.

"Anything," Arthur repeated with vehemence. He knew she would not demand a feat that scandalous or outrageous of him. She was temperate in her desires and dignified in her comportment.

She would likely want books.

She could have entire libraries if she accepted him.

"You may name your prize, Miss Carruthers."

The carriage halted, though neither of them moved. "You must greatly dislike her," his companion said finally.

"I do," Arthur agreed, before he realized the obvious import of his words. He hurried on, lest she be insulted. "But I think, in this case, that impulse has steered me true. I am a great believer in the right possibilities presenting themselves at the right moment. Now that the notion has occurred to me, I intend to court you, Miss Carruthers, even if you decline me this time."

"You must have other expectations from marriage than simply avoiding Miss Grosvenor."

"A son, I suppose," he ceded. "Any man might expect a son from his marriage."

"And you offer *anything* in return," she repeated softly, so softly that Arthur felt a moment's uncertainty.

How bad could it be?

"Tell me," he urged as the footman opened the door. Miss Carruthers smiled, lowering her gaze so her thoughts were hidden from him. In this moment, she was a mystery and an enigma, a woman whose secrets could not be guessed. Arthur was intrigued. He alighted, then handed her down, escorting her toward the door of her father's home.

She seemed to be lost in thought, but looked up suddenly to meet his gaze. "Do you have any knowledge of business, sir?"

What a curious question. "Some. Why?"

She halted and turned to face him. "Because what I would like most in all the world is to start a publishing company. Clearly, I cannot do as much on my own, for such ventures are established by men. But as marriage is a partnership, such a firm might be established by a married couple."

Whatever Arthur might have expected of her, it was not this. "But your father is a publisher."

"And Carruthers & Carruthers will be inherited by my male cousins." Her eyes shone with a conviction he found most attractive. "I would build a business that could not be taken from me in the event of your demise, one that might provide a legacy for my children, one that might make a difference to others with its choice of offerings."

Arthur left the question of his demise for the moment. "I do not understand."

"I would cater to the tastes of ladies," she said as if she had thought all of this through before his appearance at Bettencourt's home. Arthur had the unexpected sense that she had been waiting for him to make her dream possible. "And they would frequent my lending library, and buy my books." She smiled, triumphant and more alluring than she evidently guessed.

It was not madness. Arthur thought of novels, naturally, for Lady Beckham was an avid reader and could not apparently consume her fill of them. Poetry, even. Ladies had great fondness for volumes of poetry. Lady Beckham was not the only lady of affluence in London. He knew enough of trade to recognize that one had to offer a product that was in demand, so he nodded agreement.

"If that is your term, Miss Carruthers, I would be delighted to consider our bargain made."

She dropped her voice to a whisper, those eyes opening wide as she leaned closer. "Do you have sufficient funds for such a venture, sir?"

"If not, I will find them." He raised her gloved hand to his lips, watching satisfaction dawn in her eyes. "I vow it to you, Miss Carruthers." She truly had the most beautiful eyes and when she flushed just a little, as she did now, Arthur wanted to argue against her conviction that she was not pretty.

He thought she was lovely.

In truth, Arthur could not imagine a more satisfactory outcome to his uncle's wager.

He kissed her hand, lingering over the gesture until she caught her breath.

"Have you any other expectations of matrimony, Miss Carruthers? Love everlasting, perhaps?" He shook his head, recalling her claims. "No, that would not be your request."

"And it is not," she said crisply, her expression becoming discomfited. "But there is one detail I would know, Mr. Beckham."

Her cheeks were crimson and her gaze flicked from his to his driver then to the butler at her father's door. Her face became impossibly more red and Arthur could not look away.

"I am at your service, Miss Carruthers."

She eased closer, lowering her voice and her lashes. "I should like to know if I have a bewitching spot."

Arthur blinked. "I beg your pardon?"

"It was in the book, the one you returned, the *wrong* book." Her expression was fierce when she looked up at him. "It said of a specific lady: *'neither has the too frequent use of the most bewitching spot rendered it the least callous to the joys of love...'*" She inhaled, perhaps unaware that Arthur was astonished to silence. "I would like to know."

"I find it very likely that you do," he managed to say. "And I would be delighted to be of assistance in locating it upon our wedding night."

She smiled with real pleasure, her eyes lighting as if he had hung the stars and the moon. "I thank you, Mr. Beckham. Then I accept."

Arthur had a wicked thought. "I do not suppose that you would care to verify the content of this volume you wish to publish, the better to ensure that we do not provide false or misleading information to any clients."

"But it is a book of amorous advice, by my understanding."

He smiled. "And we will be wed."

Her smile became mysterious. "Indeed, Mr. Beckham, I think that might be a prudent choice. I would like to be an example of a lady whose husband did not find such amusement elsewhere."

He kissed her hand, holding her gaze, doubting he would ever find another woman of any interest at all. "Shall I call upon your father tomorrow, Miss Carruthers?" he murmured so softly that only she would hear.

She nodded quick agreement, then glanced toward his driver and footman, who appeared to be inattentive but most certainly were not. She squeezed his hand briefly before pulling her own away and her eyes danced. Better yet, she flushed slightly and he caught his breath at the sight. "Yes, Mr. Beckham. I would be most gratified if you do."

"Then I will, Miss Carruthers." He smiled as he watched her run up the steps. The butler swept open the door, sparing Arthur a disapproving glance that prompted the recipient of that glare to beam and bow.

Doubtless Miss Carruthers was right and he already knew their plans. The prospect made Arthur want to laugh aloud.

His goal had been achieved so easily as that. A publishing firm. She could have asked for the moon, a diamond coronet, a house in Berkley Square, a library as large as a palace, anything at all, but no, nothing so predictable would suffice to win the favor of Miss Patience Carruthers.

He found himself distracted by the notion of hunting her bewitching spot, and of satisfying her curiosity about matters amorous. He would have to ensure that he did not disappoint on that venture.

"Home, Morris," Arthur said as he stepped into the carriage again. He took a long look at the family home of the lady he would marry, considered that this was unlikely to be the last time she surprised him so completely, and grinned as he rapped his cane on the roof of the carriage.

This match might prove to be entertaining, indeed. Already he felt a welcome sense of purpose, one that had been lacking in his life, and anticipated a merry challenge to meet the lady's demand. Arthur laughed aloud, knowing all ran in his favor.

While the run of luck endured, he had to make it count.

~

Was it a jest?

Patience did not even consider the possibility until Mr. Beckham was gone. She was well aware that he had teased her earlier, and he did seem the kind of gentleman to enjoy a joke. Surely, he was not so cruel as to make one at her expense, though? Surely, she had done nothing to earn such disdain?

She did not think so, but the notion made her uneasy all the same.

Pretty. He had called her pretty. Was that an honest assessment or a compliment intended to earn her favor?

What had Miss Grosvenor done to earn his dislike? He had not even been aware of that lady's abuse of books.

There was an entire wealth of knowledge that Patience realized she did not possess. She had no notion of the costs of establishing a publishing firm, not just the funds required, but the equipment and skilled individuals that would have to be retained. She had no notion of where such an establishment might be located or should be located, much less the cost of such a facility.

Worse again, she had no understanding of Mr. Beckham's worth. Women chattered all the time in the bookstore about inheritances and incomes, but Patience had never listened. On this day, she regretted her disinterest.

Could Mr. Beckham afford to keep his promise? Did he even know whether he could afford it? Many an aristocrat was a fool about money. His own uncle was proof of that. Just because he was reputed to spend lavishly and to shop without regard to expense did not mean Mr. Beckham could afford his lifestyle. He might owe his income and even his inheritance to a moneylender.

Had she just made an impulsive and whimsical choice? There was little that might have been more out of character—but then, she had never been confronted with Mr. Beckham and his twinkling eyes, his alluring smile and his determination to have her agreement at any price.

Her heart fluttered in recollection of his earnest appeal.

Patience believed that his vow had been made in good faith, but believing something was possible was not the same as knowing it to be possible, much less seeing it done. Marriage was forever, or as close to it as might be seen in this world. She needed to be certain before the agreement was made.

But how? Patience could not be so vulgar as to ask him.

Her father might not be disposed to tell her.

She could ask Catherine, but she had just left Trevelaine House and Mr. Beckham had said he would call upon her father the next morning. It was entirely possible that Baron Trevelaine believed Mr. Beckham's finances to be sound, given that he had facilitated the opportunity for that man to propose. But he could not know her condition for the match, and he might not even know the expense of that.

Her younger sister, Prudence, was the most accomplished gossip in the family. Doubtless she could provide some insight into Mr. Beckham's situation, if Patience managed to sound not overly curious. How could she ask for such detail without sharing the news of her agreement to wed Mr. Beckham?

How could she share the news without her father's approval of the match?

Discretion was imperative, until her father decided. As much as Patience hated that truth, she would have to wait.

Too late, she realized she had given her agreement without acquiring all the pertinent details first. Such haste was greatly unlike her, but Mr. Arthur Beckham had a way of muddling her thoughts.

Surely that was not a bad portent for their match? Patience did not know, but the collection of questions gave her much to ponder.

~

LADY BECKHAM WAS WAITING for Arthur when he returned to the house.

He had no warning of her expectation and had just put down his hat in the hall when she called him from the drawing room. It was late for her to yet be downstairs and he spared a glance at the hall clock. Generally, at this hour, she would have retired to dress for dinner.

But no. She was seated like a queen in the drawing room, hands folded in her lap, her manner so composed that Arthur felt a prickle of dread.

"Good evening, Mother. I had thought you would be dressing for dinner," he said, bowing as he entered the room.

"Close the door, Arthur," she said crisply, a slight emphasis on his name.

There was his warning.

Arthur did as instructed and returned to stand before her.

This would be the reckoning about Miss Carruthers. He had halfway expected it.

"Her father is in trade," Lady Beckham said quietly, using the timbre of voice she favored when she did not wish the servants to hear a syllable.

He nodded for that was indisputable.

"You could have chosen someone else," she said, her

tone a little waspish. "You could have made a choice that would not humiliate me."

But Arthur was done with playing by Lady Beckham's rules.

Doubtless his confession would surprise her, but it was time.

"Twenty years," he said so quietly that his words were no more than a breath. He held her gaze, knowing his resolve was evident. She might interpret it as defiance, but Arthur did not care. "Surely, you are due one disappointment."

She caught her breath. "You should not have said it. It was an impulse, no more than that, a tantrum, and you could rescind it. Choose someone else, *anyone* else, I entreat you."

"I will wed Miss Patience Carruthers and no other."

Lady Beckham considered him, and he wondered if she could see the depth of his resolve. She inhaled sharply and drummed her fingers on her own skirts. "You must guess the price of such impetuousness."

He shrugged. "It is yours to decree. The happiness of a man you call your son, or the approval of the *ton*." He did not doubt that his manner made his view of that choice clear. Once she had ignored the view of others, but in her later years, she was much more concerned with their approval.

Her gaze snapped before she looked away. "I suppose a man cannot evade his destiny and your heritage had to show, sooner or later."

Arthur straightened. He knew Lady Beckham was a snob, but she had not cast his lineage at him before. That she did as much now only increased his resolve—no matter the price. "I could have followed the earl's dictate and inherited the title."

She shuddered visibly and her eyes narrowed. "By

wedding *that* girl. He would never surrender it willingly and you know it well."

"Once you wished for a son to hold that earldom."

"Once, my brother was young and sickly, and I believed I owed my father an heir."

Arthur understood that resolve had faded. Reynaud had grown to manhood and despite his flaws, she saw him and his potential children as more deserving of the title than the boy she had adopted as her own.

It was a relief, in a way, to have the truth declared. Arthur had never desired the title, and in truth, he bored of the endless leisure and luxury of his position. He wanted a goal, an objective, a quest even—and Miss Carruthers offered him one. She might have been destined to put her hand in his.

The lady's lips pressed together as she met his gaze again. "I could cast you out."

He had expected this threat for years, though she had never before made it. "You could," he agreed calmly. "And we could tell all the world of our longstanding deception. I rather think you would be judged more harshly than me. I was just a penniless orphan, a mere boy, and you were an aristocrat with every advantage."

The lady caught her breath. "My brother cannot understand why you would decline a rich bride in favor of a young lady whose father is not only in trade but whose dowry must be smaller." Her lips tightened as she surveyed Arthur. "I told him it was love, that you followed in my footsteps."

Arthur did not correct her. He was not in love, but he imagined one day he might love Miss Carruthers ardently. For the moment, it was sufficient that she was his choice, not one made for him or forced upon him. "I trust the earl is content with your explanation."

"He is not. Nor am I." Lady Beckham inhaled deeply

and shook her head. "You will bring her to tea and if I do not approve, then you will not wed her."

Arthur leaned closer, his resolve strengthening with every word Lady Beckham uttered. "Independent of your view of Miss Carruthers, I will wed her," he vowed.

"But…"

"Our arrangement has been amusing and certainly an adventure, Lady Beckham, but I will not regret if it all ends tomorrow."

She stared at him in silence for a moment before recovering herself. "You cannot mean that. You would be destitute. You would lose all the advantages you have come to rely upon. You would be *nothing*. Again!"

Arthur did not reply.

Lady Beckham took a breath, scowling into the corner of the room. It was clear she considered the alternatives. "The truth would be a scandal," she whispered, naming her own fear. "After all these years." She fixed him with a look. "I will ensure that the children have nothing."

He shrugged. "I have had nothing and survived it."

"You forget yourself…"

"No, not I. This choice, Lady Beckham, is entirely yours." Arthur bowed over her hand, then spun to depart. His step was lighter than it had been in a long time, for he felt he had cast off a burden. He would be free again, perhaps more penniless than Miss Carruthers anticipated, but his choices would be his own again.

And that was more than worth any price he might have to pay.

He would not dine with Lady Beckham on this evening, not when she was vexed with him, but he would go out. Such indulgences might soon be beyond his means, after all.

And if the cards showed him favor, if this sense of opportunity continued, he might begin to amass some funds for his shared future with Miss Carruthers. Could they create a successful firm together? In his current mood, Arthur believed it could be so, but he knew that he had to make the most of every moment to contribute to the prospect of success.

He had a quest and he could not wait to begin.

CHAPTER 4

"Is it true?" Prudence appeared in the doorway of their shared chamber in her nightshirt. Her hair hung in golden waves to her hips, curling even though it was still damp.

"What did you hear?" Patience asked, guessing that her sister had heard a great deal.

Prudence shook her head, closing the door and flinging herself across the room. "Miss Grosvenor came to the shop, looking for you, and when she did not find you, she told everyone that Arthur Beckham had chosen you over her. Is it true?"

Patience nodded and Prudence squealed with delight.

"Good. I do not wish ill upon anyone but she is the kind of person who does not deserve to have everything she desires." She fell back on the bed. "Especially a man like Arthur Beckham." She sighed rapturously and Patience smiled.

"Perhaps you should wed him."

"He did not choose me, but oh, Patience, he is so handsome and daring." Prudence gave her a poke. "However will you tame such a man?"

Patience did not know.

65

Prudence sat up, fairly bouncing in her curiosity. "Do you know *anything* about him?"

"Very little," Patience was compelled to admit.

"Save that he is rich." Her younger sister fixed Patience with a look. "I never thought that would be your sole consideration."

"It is not."

"Then why accept him?"

"Because…" Patience had no good reply for that and she immediately saw that her sister knew it.

"Because his wealth means that you will be able to buy as many books as you like, and read as much as you like, so long as you give him a son or two. Oh, Patience, you are predictable."

"I might have fallen in love with him," she had to protest.

Prudence laughed and laughed at the very notion. "You will never be guided by your heart, Patience. Always sensible. Always logical." She rolled her eyes, then granted Patience a pitying look—albeit one filled with anticipation. "I am going to have to help you so very, very much."

"Are you?" Patience could only be amused.

Prudence surveyed Patience. "Your hair. You must change your hair."

"My hair is fine!"

"Your hair is acceptable, but you must choose a style that is less severe." Prudence tilted her head to consider her sister. "Some curls would not destroy your concentration overmuch. And you will need a dress for the wedding."

"I will wear my blue gown."

Prudence was visibly outraged. "You will not! This is your wedding, Patience, not just another day in town. You will only have one such day and you must look your best." She nodded with authority. "We will go tomorrow to the dressmaker. I will convince Papa."

"Wait a day, until Mr. Beckham asks his approval."

"You will need shoes and gloves, as well, and we will order a posy of flowers, too." This list compiled, Prudence smiled at Patience. "Do you truly know so little of him and his family?"

"I know some details," Patience said, which certainly sounded as if she knew more than she did. "Perhaps you might tell me what you know."

Prudence grinned to gain the invitation she clearly desired, then moved quickly to sit beside Patience, lowering her voice. "He is wicked to his marrow, by all accounts."

"I cannot believe it."

"Then you *are* smitten. They do say that opposites attract, and there could not be a man alive more different from you."

"How so?" Patience had the sense she should be insulted. Mr. Beckham was intelligent, to be sure. While he possessed an easy charm that she did not, and was handsome beyond all, he had called her pretty. His wealth was apparently boundless while hers was more moderate, but that was not opposite.

"You are cautious while he is not."

"I am not certain of that…"

"It is said he will do anything to win a wager. He races horses on Rotten Row, and has accepted no fewer than five challenges to duel." Prudence nodded with authority. "And he won four of them. They say he has a scar on his shoulder from the fifth, though he never speaks of it." She took a breath, visibly trying to contain her excitement and failing. "Of course, he is always dressed to perfection and more handsome than any seven lords put together, and he is richer than rich. He is rumored to be fortunate beyond all at the gaming tables and that only a fool will take a wager against him. He is wild, by all accounts, carousing out all night and sleeping until late afternoon, venturing into thieves' dens and gaming hells with equal fearlessness. They say he seized all the birds at a cockfight and set them free, earning the ire of all in attendance. I heard the bills for his wine and brandy would be sufficient to see three great houses supplied." Prudence took a fortifying breath. "And yet, he remains rich. I think he might be perfect, but you, I suspect, may find many deficiencies in his list of attributes."

"How rich?"

Prudence laughed. "Trust you to have need of a number. He has some twenty thousand pounds per year in income and stands to inherit over a hundred thousand pounds after his mother's demise."

Patience was shocked. "So much?"

Prudence was enjoying herself so much that Patience was glad to have more questions. "Yes, but he has no title!" Patience did not care, but she was interested. "His mother, a most formidable lady as I understand, was the only daughter of the Earl of Fairhaven and much favored by her father. He even allowed her to wed a widower considerably her senior. It was said to be a great love match and was the talk of the *ton* when it occurred. They had two children, Arthur in the first year of their marriage, and some years later a daughter."

"Amelia," Patience supplied.

Prudence nodded. "The siblings are said to be close, despite the disparity in their ages." She took a breath. "It was Viscount Meadstone who bought the house in Berkley Square where they reside, though he ensured that Lady Beckham owned it outright herself."

"Then she is a widow?"

Prudence nodded sagely. "He died eleven years ago,

passing in his sleep. They say she locked herself away for a year to mourn the loss of her beloved."

"What of his title?"

"He was wed before, as I said, and his son by that match has inherited it all. His wife died in the delivery of their daughter."

"But the son could pass…"

"No, no, no, Patience. The current viscount has two sons, and his sister has another. There must be a veritable plague for Mr. Beckham to become Viscount Meadstone." Prudence caught her breath. "And his uncle, the Earl of Fairhaven, is almost the same age as Mr. Beckham. Doubtless he will wed and have a bevy of sons of his own. If you desire a title, sister dear, Mr. Beckham should not be your choice—unless you are more of a gambler than I know."

So, Mr. Beckham had an aristocratic lineage, but no title of his own. Patience had to admit that she could find no fault with his situation. A nobleman might have been too concerned with his reputation to support her venture, but Mr. Beckham had been untroubled. It seemed he would have sufficient affluence to establish the publishing firm as well.

If he did not waste it on fripperies.

"Since coming of age, your Mr. Beckham has run wild, and some say he means to rid himself of his inheritance, one way or the other. Others say his mother indulges him overmuch, while yet others suggest that he has need of a wife to keep him in hand. He is thirty, after all. Perhaps that is why his mother approves of the match."

"Does she?"

"It does not seem that she opposes it. Perhaps because you are known for both frugality and practicality."

That did sound dull in comparison to Mr. Beckham.

Patience knew he would not have offered for her hand if he had not been confronted by the prospect of a match to Miss Grosvenor and a tiny part of her wished it might have been otherwise.

That was simply pride speaking. She knew that love had no place in a sensible match.

All the same, she remembered his vow that he would court her, even if she refused him, and her heart leapt as it seemed inclined to do whenever she thought of or saw Mr. Beckham.

Prudence kicked her feet, seemingly thinking. "Oh yes, there is a house in Devon, near Axminster, a legacy to Lady Beckham from her father, the earl, which she also owns in her own right. The earl's country house is on an adjacent property and said to be less grand. I believe the situation might vex him."

"What of the current earl?" Patience was curious about the man who had dared to bet her betrothed's hand in marriage.

Prudence wrinkled her nose. "The worst manner of wastrel."

"You said Mr. Beckham was a wastrel," Patience reminded her sister.

"But he can pay for his indulgences. And he is young and handsome."

Patience rolled her eyes.

Prudence continued. "Though there are some who find the earl attractive."

"Not you?"

"He has a look of dissipation about him, to my thinking. Otherwise, he might have been attractive, but never as handsome as Mr. Beckham."

Patience doubted there were many men so handsome.

"The earl is utterly without resource, for what he has not sold, he had mortgaged. I cannot have any respect for a man who fails to manage his own wealth, especially one who has wasted it so foolishly. The earl is lucky to have a sister who holds him in affection, though that may not last much longer."

"Indeed?"

"Lady Beckham is said to be heartily annoyed with her brother for this last wager, almost as irked as the Grosvenor family is with your Mr. Beckham over his escape." She nodded. "I think I like him just for that."

"Felicia Grosvenor leaves stains in books she borrows," Patience reminded her sister.

Prudence winced and nodded. "*And* she folds down the corners of the pages."

Both sisters shook their heads in unison at these most base of all crimes.

"I suppose you do not love him," Prudence said, scrutinizing her sister.

Patience had nothing to hide. "I do not know him well enough for that."

"But do you like him?"

Patience considered their recent conversations and found herself smiling. "I do. I fear he is concerned only with his own advantage, but many men are thus." Prudence nodded wisely in agreement. "And he has a certain charm."

"He lied to his uncle."

"But he was honest with me. And truly, in his place, would you not do anything to avoid such a match?"

Prudence laughed. "If only for the sake of my books."

"Precisely!"

Then the younger sister sobered, and her gaze turned searching. "Will you be happy, Patience?"

"I have no notion, but I shall strive to be. Does any bride know for certain before her wedding day?"

Prudence nodded in consideration of that. "But what if you never love him?"

"That does not mean I cannot be happy in his household, or that I won't bear children that I love, or that there must be no merit in my life as his wife."

"But what if you meet your one love after you are married?"

"If that happens, Prudence, I will worry about the situation then. For now, all is arranged and I will put my hand in his with every hope for a happy future."

Her sister considered her. "You are not wedding him just because he is rich and handsome, are you?"

Patience shook her head. "On the contrary, I think we will suit each other well."

"Then I hope you are right," Prudence said and gave her a hug. "And I hope you watch for a handsome and wealthy rogue for me." She dropped her voice again. "I must say that everyone believed you would be the one to care for Papa in his dotage, perhaps even Papa himself. Now the task falls to me, which no one could have anticipated or is likely to welcome."

"You could make a good match…"

"Love, Patience. Only love will do." Prudence sighed. "Without love, I would be more content to mend Papa's slippers and remain unwed forever."

Her sister, Patience could only conclude, placed an unreasonably high value upon such tender feelings.

But then, she had never been fond of mending slippers.

◊

ARTHUR BECKHAM FOUND HIMSELF UNEASY.

This, too, was a novelty and he told himself to savor it.

He failed.

He sat before the one potential obstacle to his plans, and in truth, Arthur could not have blamed the man before him for refusing his own request. Would he have willingly promised a beloved and sensible daughter to a notorious rake, no matter that man's supposed wealth?

Would the truth—that the rake was an imposter—weigh the scales in that man's favor? Arthur doubted that Mr. Edward Carruthers would think highly of such a deception. To spend most of one's life pretending to be another man was not a choice readily excused.

Who would wed a beloved daughter to a man on the brink of losing his position and wealth? Arthur could not imagine any father would do as much, but in a way, that only increased his newfound impatience with his life and its illusions.

A part of him could not help but wonder what would result from the revelation of the truth.

Another part of him, the larger portion, was indebted to Miss Carruthers' objective and how it granted him a plan. He had spent the night gambling and winning, building a fund for the venture while he could, yet granting every appearance of continuing to be a wastrel and ne'er do well.

The odds were long, but he thought they might make the venture work.

He sat in Mr. Edward Carruthers' office at Carruthers & Carruthers. The office had windows, which meant the printing shop was visible as was the bookshop itself. It also meant that Arthur was visible to everyone within the establishment but that didn't trouble him.

The gentleman had requested Arthur's indulgence while he completed a notation, one that seemed to take an uncommon measure of time. Arthur took the chance to study the father of his intended. Edward Carruthers was perhaps fifty-five years of age, though he possessed a liveliness reminiscent of a younger man. He was purposeful and apparently ambitious, having built the publishing business to pre-eminence in some twenty years alongside his brother. They were not without competitors, to be sure. Mr. Carruthers' hair was dark, though it had turned to silver at his temples, and his gaze was incisive when he glanced at Arthur.

Arthur saw where Miss Carruthers inherited the hue of her eyes, though in his view, the lady's were considerably more attractive.

He suspected the pair were each as perceptive as the other and hoped the father did not see more than would be ideal in this interview.

Mr. Carruthers put aside his quill, adjusted his spectacles and granted Arthur a polite smile. "I do apologize, Mr. Beckham. That one last detail had to be put in order lest I forget it. Now, how may I be of assistance to you on this day?"

"I have come, sir, to offer for your daughter's hand in marriage."

The older man frowned. "Prudence?"

"Miss Patience Carruthers, sir."

His companion looked to be astonished, though he strove to disguise his reaction. "And you are, as I understand it, Mr. Arthur Beckham?"

"I am, sir."

"Does my daughter know of your inclination?"

"I spoke to her of it yesterday, sir, and she was amenable." Carruthers' expression began to darken and Arthur anticipated his question, replying before he could ask. "I had the good fortune to meet her at Trevelaine House, when I was in the company of the baron."

Carruthers considered Arthur for a long moment. "I must say, Mr. Beckham, that I am surprised by your attentions. Your reputation is such that it has reached even my ears and I should have expected you to choose a bride from amongst the debutantes of the *ton*, as undoubtedly, your family also anticipates."

"My mother has expressed her delight with the prospect of my marriage, though of course, the question of your approval remains."

"Has she?" the other man murmured, then leaned back in his chair, his gaze locked upon Arthur. His perusal was so intent that Arthur almost felt compelled to confess all of the details leading to the arrangement, but held his tongue with an effort. "Delight in the act of marriage or your choice of bride?"

Arthur felt the back of his neck heat. "The former, sir, although I am certain that she will be enchanted by your daughter when they meet."

The older man surveyed Arthur for long moments, then folded his hands together. "I am well aware, Mr. Beckham, of the assets my daughter might bring to a match, but I must wonder whether they are of similar appeal to you. Do you honestly desire a clever wife? A practical and efficient one? Do you truly wish for the companionship of a lady who will not decline to share her views on any subject whatsoever? She will tell you when you err, of that I am certain."

Arthur smiled. "I welcome the opportunity of wedding such a lady, sir. Indeed, I hope for forthright speech and honesty in my marriage."

"Do you? And what of your uncle? Does he not have higher aspirations for your match?"

"He might, but I am disinterested in his advice when it comes to marriage."

"Indeed?"

"Indeed." Arthur spoke with resolve. "I was taught to manage my own affairs, sir, and to ensure that my uncle, a notorious wastrel and spendthrift, had no command over me or my finances."

"I see. I heard a rumor that he had won you a bride in a gaming den, not two nights ago."

Arthur realized that his intended's father possessed the ability to disguise how much he knew of a given matter. "He believes he did, sir, but I do not find the commitment binding. I also do not find the lady suitable."

Carruthers nodded. "Had you made this understanding with my daughter before learning of this?"

Again, Arthur suspected that the man before him already knew the truth. "I had not, as perhaps you have surmised. I presented the tale of our arrangement, purely out of my admiration for your daughter, and was subsequently much relieved to learn that Miss Carruthers welcomed the possibility."

"Welcomed?" Carruthers raised a brow. "*My* daughter?"

Arthur grinned. "She chastised me for the telling of a falsehood, sir, reprimanded me for potentially damaging her reputation, informed me that many people would have known of this tale by the time she heard of it, itemized the possibilities—and utterly captivated me in so doing."

Carruthers smiled. "I would have thought you were already captivated, in order to present her with such a possibility."

"I was only enchanted before that," Arthur confessed. "Now she holds me utterly in her thrall." Though the praise sounded fulsome, he knew it was close to the truth.

Carruthers chuckled, clearly content with that situation.

Arthur continued, while odds seemed to be in his favor. "I believe, sir, that opposites can attract, and that your daughter and I will make a good match."

"She must have had her price."

"I would not betray her confidence by revealing it, sir, but we have also agreed that we must have children. I intend to ensure that ours is a happy marriage."

"She will not countenance any dalliance with another woman."

"I have no intention of putting her to such a test. Marriage, sir, is a sacred bond."

Carruthers fixed him with a searching look and Arthur did not dare avert his gaze. He did not so much as blink until the older man nodded. "Patience reads avidly. If you do not share her enthusiasm for books, sir, I cannot foresee a future for the two of you, regardless of any such amenable agreement. You will bore each other to the point of despair within a month."

"Then I would appreciate your recommendation of suitable volumes, that I might embark upon the quest of holding my lady wife's attention."

Carruthers held Arthur's gaze for a long moment, then shook his head and chuckled. "Ah, Patience," he said beneath his breath, and not without satisfaction. "You may have met your equal, my dear."

"Sir?"

"I should warn you, Mr. Beckham, that my middle daughter has a will of iron. Once she sets herself upon a course, she will not be swayed."

"I am a great admirer of constancy, sir."

The older man met Arthur's gaze again, even as he nodded. "I would ask for an understanding of your financial situation, sir, and please understand that I will seek the counsel of the Duke of Haynesdale in this matter. He is more familiar with the reputations of the affluent than I might ever be. I know only that your mother is a reliable client here." He dipped his quill again. "Perhaps you might give me your address, that I could write to you once my researches are complete and my decision made."

"Of course," Arthur said, providing the address in question. "I would obtain a special license that the festivities might not be delayed, sir. My mother, I expect, will wish to host the wedding breakfast."

Carruthers glanced up, his gaze fixing upon Arthur for another long moment, then nodded once before returning to his notes. "I will keep that detail in mind, sir."

PATIENCE WAS LATE ARRIVING at the shop, for Prudence had taken forever to dress and the sisters were to ride together. She was out of breath when she burst through the doors, only to find that Mr. Beckham had already departed. The shop was filled with whispers about his presence and speculation upon his business with her father. She bade herself not show any disappointment.

Her father stepped out of his office then and fixed her with a look that could only mean one thing. She was summoned to give an accounting. She took a fortifying breath, knowing that no fiction would satisfy her father, and strode to his office with apparent confidence.

She was well aware of Prudence and the other women watching her go.

Her father nodded and she closed the door behind herself, remaining standing before his desk. He was too serious for Patience's peace of mind.

"What did he offer you?" he asked softly.

"I beg your pardon?"

He removed his glasses. "It strikes me, my dear, that as much as I appreciate your many assets, a man like Mr. Arthur Beckham would be unlikely to perceive them at all. He is a man much taken with foolish beauties, with feckless activities like racing and gambling, and with the indulgence of his own pleasures. While he might be momentarily intrigued by a young lady who chastised him, simply for the novelty, I cannot imagine that a match between two such would be a success."

Patience might have argued but her father raised a finger, indicating that he would continue. "Neither can I believe that you, a woman of splendid good sense, would be beguiled by such a man or perceive there to be any advantage in agreeing to be his bride. Therefore, it follows that there is an element missing from this equation, one that I do not as yet know." He sat down, templing his hands before himself, and waited for the surrender of that detail.

The truth would not aid Patience in the least.

But perhaps part of the truth would suffice.

She took the seat opposite her father. "I began to think recently, Father, of what my life would be in your absence," she began, which was not entirely false. "It seemed to me that as long as you are hale and I live in your house, that all is well. To be sure, that is why I have not thought about marriage in the past. But in your absence, Papa, my home would be with Catherine, if she can welcome me, or with Uncle Richard, so long as he lives." Patience frowned. "I cannot expect the baron to offer me shelter if he becomes a widower, nor is it reasonable to expect my cousins to gladly welcome me."

"You imagine many misfortunes, my dear."

"And I would hope that none of them ever come to be, but I would be prepared for the worst." She met her father's gaze and found understanding there, as well as compassion. "I wish to choose, Papa, to ensure my own future, and no sooner had I decided as much than Mr. Beckham presented his suit."

"Do you not find him a foolish wastrel?"

"I think he likes to let people believe he is one. I am not convinced that is his true inclination."

"You would be financially secure, as his wife and even as his widow."

"Yes. That is the greater concern, Papa."

He held her gaze for a long moment, as if sensing that there was more to the story. "And what will you do as his wife? Will you join him at revels and become as dissipated as he?"

Her father's disapproval of that possibility was clear.

Patience shook her head. "No, Papa. I will be as ever I was. I will read and I will live respectably, and maybe, my husband will be tempted to join me."

Edward Carruthers smiled slowly, then nodded approval. Patience sank into the seat opposite him as he donned his glasses again and drew a sheet of paper toward himself. He dipped his quill. "I thank you for that reassurance, Patience. You should know that Mr. Beckham has asked me for a list of books that he might read, the better that you might have common ground."

"Oh!" Patience thought this a very promising sign.

Her father, of course, had already compiled the list and handed it to her. She was so busy reading it, taking note of favorite titles and unexpected inclusions, that she almost missed her father's next words.

"All that remains is to seek the advice of the Duke of Haynesdale, and I will write to him immediately."

Patience frowned as she watched her father's quill sweep across the page. "But what interest might his grace have in this matter, Papa?"

"He knows more of such people than I, given his own rank. His opinion is always a balanced one, and I can rely upon him to keep our best interests at heart."

"But he is no relation."

"No." Her father smiled. "But there is a bond between our families nonetheless, an old one that I have often found myself glad of."

"Will you tell me?" Patience asked, guessing that her father needed only an invitation to do so.

He checked his watch, then nodded agreement and set the quill aside. "Once, many years ago, the duke's father came into his inheritance. I knew little of him beyond his excellent reputation before he appeared in the shop. We had only just begun the business, Robert and I, and we were far from profitability. There were presses to pay for, and paper and skilled men, the shop itself, and the books we chose to publish. In those days, neither of us took a wage, but we saw promise in the venture and had hopes for the future. Then the Duke of Haynesdale, the father of the current duke, halted his coach outside the door, and entered the shop himself."

"What a coup," Patience said and her father chuckled.

"It was remarkable. I don't believe the duke realized how many people noted his arrival and his presence. He was bent upon his errand, which was to consult with either myself or Robert. He had inherited, along with other assets, a remarkable collection of books and though he did not wish to part with any of them, he was in need of ready money. His father had bound much of the estate into land, which was an excellent investment but one that was not providing the returns that it should or could. The duke intended to adopt many innovations in agricultural methods, and to im-prove the accommodations of his tenants. In the end, the profits would be much higher, but in the short term, he was short of funds. He confided this to me later: on that day, he merely asked if I might buy several of his books."

Patience watched her father take an appreciative breath. "He said he had many fine volumes. A Gutenberg Bible, which I could neither afford nor readily sell. I visited Haynesdale House at his invitation, and we chose a dozen volumes between us. I then suggested to him that we might make an exchange, that if he could mention Carruthers & Carruthers to his friends—for I had noticed the increase in business after the appearance of his coach—then I would not have to sell the books. I could keep them for him, for the resurgence of his finances. He was much relieved, for he had not wished to part with any of them, and insisted that we set a time period upon the agreement out of fairness to me."

"Quite a gentleman."

"He was. Always fair in his dealings, even with the most lowly of tradesman. A man of honor, to be sure. He was good to his word and I to mine, and in the end, Carruthers & Carruthers prospered as much as the duke's holdings. He returned for each book, coming at regular intervals, and I would not charge him any interest, given his influence on our trade. Indeed, such was the improvement of our growth as a business that I felt obliged to simply give him back the last volume, for his endorsement had more than compensated me for the loan."

"What a wonderful story."

"And better yet, after that, we were friends. I could ask him about the reputation for any man in town, and he brought books to me from friends who were obliged to sell. Our collections were built from those volumes, offered first to me and Robert. With the passing of the old duke, his son continued the tradition. He buys from me, he endorses me, and he even took it upon himself to arrange Catherine's match. He was always fond of her and when I confessed myself bewildered by the entire question of matrimony for my daughters in your mother's absence, he took the task upon himself."

"I did not know."

"No. When he first came to the house, you were in the nursery as yet. Catherine must remember his visits, for she was in awe of him in his finery. He made your mother laugh, even when she was so unwell, and for that, he has my undying gratitude."

"So, you will ask him about Mr. Beckham."

"I know only the man's reputation, which does him no good service as a prospective match for you," Patience's father said. "His grace will know more of his nature, and will better assess the match. I hope his view aligns with your own, Patience, but if it does not, I will decline the suit."

"Thank you, Papa, for taking such care of us."

He smiled and reached across the desk for her hand. "A daughter should not be surrendered with indifference, Patience. I would not have a one of you unhappy in your match. I know already that Mr. Beckham possesses a good income and a small fortune. His grace will know of his debts and any other pertinent details that may not be widely known. Lady Beckham wishes to host the wedding breakfast, which is a good sign, to my view, that she welcomes the match as heartily as he indicates. That is no small thing."

Patience smiled.

Her father beamed at her. "Now, leave me that I might write to the duke."

CHAPTER 5

$\mathcal{A}$rthur could not fathom why he had been invited to the private box of the Duke of Haynesdale at the theatre that evening. He hadn't been planning on attending himself: the play was Molière's *Le Bourgeois gentilhomme* and he was escorting Amelia and her governess to the performance the following evening. On this night, he had been intent upon visiting a certain hell where the stakes were higher. While his luck was good, he would make the most of it.

Still, a duke was not to be denied.

He entered the box at intermission, only to find it vacant—except for a lady sipping a beverage. Her dark hair was elegantly dressed and studded with diamond pins that sparkled in the lights of the theatre. Her dress was of deepest sapphire, lavishly embroidered with silver. She wore long gloves and glittering bracelets on each wrist, as well as a necklace awash in diamonds. A tear-drop faceted sapphire of considerable size hung from the necklace and when she turned to survey him, Arthur saw that she wore earrings to match.

"You might be a goddess of the heavens, Miss Ballantyne, so adorned with stars," he said, bowing to the famous courtesan.

Her lips curved in a smile and she set aside her glass. "Mr. Beckham. I had heard that you were returned from Venice. How was the weather?"

"Perfect in every way, although I find myself with two new cats."

She laughed lightly. "I can imagine that they might have been desolated by the prospect of your departure."

"On the contrary, I was the one who could not leave them behind, although there were moments on our return journey that I doubted the wisdom of my impulse."

She looked to be truly amused. "Cats, in my experience, suffer worse from the discomforts of travel than most people."

"These do, indeed."

"How fortunate then that you have arrived and they can push such memories aside."

"Our cook has proven to be adept at finding them morsels of fish. I believe they would follow her anywhere."

They laughed together and Arthur was offered a glass of orgeat lemonade. As this was not a favorite choice of his, he declined, but Miss Ballantyne raised a brow. "You would prefer a brandy or a glass of Madeira, I suppose?" She clicked her tongue. "Best to abandon such indulgences until after your wedding night, unless it is your intention to disappoint."

Arthur blinked at this blunt advice. He knew that brandy could dampen his ardor, so to speak, but had not considered a greater effect. The famed courtesan held his gaze as if in challenge and he had to cede that she would know.

"I did not realize my suit was common knowledge," he said, accepting a glass of orgeat lemonade. He braced himself against the first taste even as he saluted Miss Ballantyne. "You are well informed."

"It is a habit that is difficult to abandon," she ceded and they sipped.

He did not mind the almond flavor and was pleased to find that Miss Ballantyne's concoction was less sweet than the one he recalled.

"I confess myself surprised at the news you intended to wed," she said.

"By my mother's accounting, I should have done as much already," he admitted, seeing no reason to disguise the truth. "But yes, I have formed an alliance and will wed shortly."

She looked into the depths of her glass, choosing her words with a care that Arthur could not explain. "And you are in search of his grace on this evening for a reason?"

"I was summoned by him."

"Summoned? That is a strong choice of word, Mr. Beckham. Surely the duke was more gracious than that."

"He has a talent, Miss Ballantyne, for sheathing an iron fist in a velvet glove. I had no doubt that my attendance was mandatory, nor was I so foolish as to be late."

She smiled again, but her gaze was thoughtful. "Do you know why he sought your presence here tonight?"

"No. I wonder, though, if it has to do with my pending engagement."

Her dark brows rose and she watched him closely.

"The lady's father did say he would consult with the duke on the matter."

Miss Ballantyne's confusion was clear. "But why?"

"I cannot say. Perhaps they are good friends. Perhaps he respects his grace's counsel." Arthur shrugged.

"How curious. I did not realize that Mr. Grosvenor and his grace were acquainted."

Suddenly, her reactions made sense. "Oh, you mistake my intention, Miss Ballantyne. It is not Miss

Grosvenor I would marry, but Miss Patience Carruthers."

Did he imagine that his companion was startled? Arthur would have denied it but Miss Ballantyne's expression became inscrutable and her attention fixed upon the glass she held. "What a curious match," she said softly, then raised her gaze to his. Her expression reminded him of one of those Venetian cats newly arrived in his chambers.

"I do not find Miss Carruthers that unlikely of a spouse," he said heartily. "She is clever and pretty, not so young as some other eligible ladies, to be sure, but I would have a wife closer to my own age."

His companion smiled. "I meant Miss Carruthers' choice of you as a spouse," she said, her eyes dancing at the surprise Arthur failed to hide.

"Me?"

Miss Ballantyne refilled her glass. "You are handsome, to be sure, young and no doubt virile, and I understand that you have wealth, as well, but the Carruthers sisters are daughters of a publisher. They have been raised to know their own minds, to think and discuss and read widely. Indeed, they are most uncommon young ladies, and thus I would expect their marital choices to be somewhat uncommon."

"But the eldest is wed to Baron Trevelaine."

His companion saluted him with her glass. "A match made by his grace, and thus a conventional one. Also a happy one, I believe." She sipped. "But the second daughter, Miss Patience, is said to be the cleverest of them all and practical beyond compare. I might believe that she had chosen you for your income, but beyond that –" she tilted her head to consider him, then shook her head minutely "– I cannot see why you would appeal to her. You have a charm, Mr. Beckham, but such a lady would require more substance than I would expect you to offer."

Arthur did not know what to say. He fancied he had been insulted, though he was not entirely certain what detail he would cite if he took umbrage.

Worse, it had never occurred to him that he might be deemed deficient in any way, particularly for the office of marriage. Debutantes and widows and ambitious mothers pursued him constantly, and his own mother was always making introductions to young ladies she deemed suitable. He was always hunted, it seemed, which surely implied that he was desirable prey.

Rather than lacking in substance.

The question of course was whether he truly was so superficial or whether it was only his disguise as Arthur Beckham that would not be of interest to his intended bride.

Miss Ballantyne set her glass aside. "I see that I have caused offense, though that was not my intention, Mr. Beckham. I simply do not see you as a philosopher or a man of ideas, though there may be more to you than anticipated." She leaned a little closer and dropped her voice. "Or is there, perhaps, more to this match than meets the eye?"

In a way, Arthur was relieved that she had guessed the truth. "The lady has a quest, which I have sworn to assist. We deemed it best to formalize our partnership with marriage as it will be a lengthy venture."

"Now I am intrigued," the courtesan murmured, and Arthur wondered whether he might have found a patroness for Miss Carruthers' project. More financial contributions than his own could only help—and given the topic of the volume in question, Miss Ballantyne might be a powerful ally.

He moved closer and lowered his voice. "There is a book, you see, or the manuscript of a book. It is not yet published, and Mr. Carruthers declines to publish it, despite the endorsement of his eldest daughter. The baroness confided in her sister, who is determined to publish the book." He straightened. "We intend to establish a publishing firm to do precisely that."

"For one book." Miss Ballantyne considered him. "It must be a work of tremendous interest to your intended."

"It is. She says it will change the lives of women everywhere."

Had something flashed in the courtesan's eyes? "Indeed?" she murmured, dropping her gaze as if to hide that reaction. "Do you know more of this volume?"

"Only that it is a work of intimate advice for women, intended to aid married women in maintaining the amorous attention of their spouses."

This time, he could not mistake it. Miss Ballantyne caught her breath. "And Mr. Carruthers has declined to publish such a work?"

"Evidently, he thinks the content inappropriate."

Miss Ballantyne took a deep breath of indignation, and Arthur could only imagine the matter was close to her heart. Would she prefer that women had the information to beguile their own husbands? Or would that interfere too much with her own trade? He could not guess.

"How laudable that you would undertake such an endeavor," she said.

"Miss Carruthers is very certain of its importance."

"I find I must agree with her."

"Then perhaps you might—"

Before Arthur could make a request for her patronage, Miss Ballantyne sat forward, her manner intent.

"You must not tell the duke of this venture," she said, her voice low and hot, her gaze boring into his own.

"But…"

"No. He will consider such an agreement unacceptable as a basis for your match. An arranged marriage is one thing, and a love match another, but I am convinced that you will never persuade the duke of the merit of this negotiation." She smiled. "I, however, find myself reassured of your prospects for a happy union."

"Oh!"

"Tell him that you are smitten," Miss Ballantyne said with urgency. "Tell him that Cupid's arrow has found its mark and you wish only to spend your life with Miss Carruthers. Convince him of your ardor and all will be well."

Arthur might have argued but there was the thump of a cane from outside the box, and the duke himself appeared. His expression was grim and his eyes narrowed slightly as he surveyed the two of them. He seemed more imposing than Arthur recalled, but perhaps that was because the future hung in the balance, based on his grace's conclusion.

"You look to be making mischief, Miss Ballantyne," the duke said in a low grumble then entered the box. He nodded at Arthur. "Beckham."

"I simply make a scheme to locate more orgeat lemonade, your grace," she said with a smile. "Alas, the heat has caused it to evaporate and there is none left for you."

"How disappointing," the duke said in a tone that made his lack of disappointment abundantly clear. He smiled a little, his eyes gleaming. "But your will must be done, Miss Ballantyne." He bent over her hand and kissed the back of it, then called for a servant to fetch more of the beverage, along with a brandy for himself.

He sat, putting aside his cane as he eased into the seat beside the courtesan, then turned an incisive gaze upon Arthur. "And so, you would wed Edward Carruthers' daughter, Patience," he said without preamble. "Why?" The last word snapped like a whip, a query demanding an immediate response, the duke's manner indicating that very few answers would suffice.

Arthur decided in that moment to take all of the courtesan's advice.

Who knew a man better than his lover, after all?

THE PREVIOUS DAY and evening had passed slowly for Patience, with no tidings, no hints from her father and no glimpses of Mr. Beckham. The arrangement might not have been, given the relentless routine of her day— or perhaps it would not be, depending upon the duke's reply.

Nothing was said at dinner, which Patience found most discouraging, though her father did grant her a wink when he retired to his library.

It was agonizing to wait so long.

It was impossible to sleep.

She rose and dressed early, leaving Prudence sleeping soundly, and made her way downstairs quietly. She entered the breakfast room, certain she would be alone, only to find her father in his place.

"It appears you have made a conquest," he said by way of greeting, his jovial conviction startling her.

He was reading his mail, glasses perched on the end of his nose, eggs getting cold as per usual. The man could forget the world completely when there was anything to read—which meant Patience had come by that trait honestly.

"Have I?" she asked, taking a seat and nodding at Wentworth. He dispatched a maid to get her usual breakfast of a poached egg and toast. "Anyone I know?"

Her father laughed, his good mood more than evident on this morning. "Why, Mr. Arthur Beckham, of course. You did not tell me that there were tender feelings involved. That would have made all the difference in my response. Surely you knew as much."

Patience looked down at her egg. What did tender feelings have to do with her agreement with Mr. Beckham? Rather than reveal that she was puzzled, she smiled. "I gather you have heard from the Duke of Haynesdale?"

"Indeed, indeed." Her father shook the missive in question at her, then set it aside to consider his breakfast. His nature was so amiable that he was never concerned to eat cool eggs. When he tucked into the meal with vigor, she wondered again if he even noticed. "He writes this very morning that he had the opportunity to speak with Mr. Beckham at the theatre last evening, where the man in question was fulsome in expressing his ardor." Her father's brows rose. "Not that I am surprised, of course. You are well deserving of a man's devotion, my dear." He chewed his toast, sparing her a glance of some concern. "Do not misunderstand me, Patience. If I am startled, it is that a man of his rumored inclinations was able to discern your merit. All in all, I am delighted. A perceptive man for my clever daughter. How can such a marriage go awry?"

It could go awry if it was formed upon a deception —and truly, this made two falsehoods in succession. Patience wondered whether Mr. Beckham possessed any affection for the truth that could rival his rumored adoration of herself.

"I must write to the duke immediately and express my gratitude to him. Truly, one could have no better ally and friend, than a man who puts all aside to ease one's concerns. He is of the very ilk of his father." Her father finished his meal and excused himself, gathering up his correspondence to hasten to his library. "I will go to the shop within the half hour, if you are inclined to join me there today, Patience."

"Yes, Papa. That was my plan." Though she had little interest in gossip and rumor, it might be time for Patience to change that inclination. She had to learn more of Mr. Beckham than she had thus far—marriage was forever, and she did not wish to err in her choice of spouse. Had Mr. Beckham simply told her what she wished to hear, with no plan to fulfil his pledge? Patience felt a momentary chill. She could end up wed to a wastrel for no good cause.

No, she had to learn more about him, and with all haste.

She would ask Prudence to assist her in the quest.

MISS FELICIA GROSVENOR WAS DISPLEASED, and when Felicia was displeased, everyone in her vicinity shared in that discontent. Two days before, there had been a definite prospect of her pending marriage to Mr. Arthur Beckham. Yesterday, all the gossip about Mr. Beckham included tales of an alliance, not with her but with Miss Patience Carruthers. Felicia had not even been certain who that was at breakfast, much less why Mr. Beckham should offer for her hand.

Learning that her supposed rival was the middle daughter of a publisher and bookseller—albeit the best publisher and bookseller in Felicia's view—had done precisely nothing to mitigate her disappointment.

This Miss Carruthers was not even rumored to be a beauty.

She was not possessed of a wealthy income, a rich dowry or due for a fat inheritance.

Felicia's dressmaker had never heard of her, neither had her milliner or her bootmaker. It was clear this Miss Carruthers did not frequent the best shops and had no taste at all. She was not even present at her father's bookshop when Felicia visited, intending to view her. Felicia had retired, hoping that the rumor was a lie.

Perhaps Mr. Beckham chose to tease her. He was known to be frivolous and often said to mock others. It was an encouraging possibility in this case, but if so, such a tendency in the man would have to be ended with all haste.

But, on this morning, she heard from her own mother that Mr. Beckham's alliance with Miss Carruthers was official and would be announced shortly in the papers. How dare this chit steal the man meant to be Felicia's own?

One thing was for certain—their wedding had to be stopped and soon. Her mother insisted that Mr. Beckham was seeking a special license. There would not be much time.

Felicia snarled at her lady's maid. She kicked her mother's yapping little lapdog on her way down the hall. She told the footman that he had not opened the door quickly enough, complained to her father that he had failed her again, and stood before the house with a sour expression as she awaited the coach and four.

"The brass is not polished," she informed her father. "And the horses' manes are not braided the same way."

"You were in such a rush, my dear," that man protested, but earned a glacial stare from his daughter that silenced him utterly.

"You should never have allowed the earl to rescind his wager, Papa."

"The pledge was not truly his to make, my dear. You

must understand as much. It was a question of honor, and truly, if your Mr. Beckham possessed an increment of honor himself…"

"He is not my Mr. Beckham," she said through her teeth, the words no less hostile for all their low volume. "That is the *point*."

"He should have risen to the occasion of defending his uncle's honor. After all, he might see a fine inheritance and early by so doing. That he did not, my dear, suggests that he is not worthy of you."

"But I have chosen him," Felicia said as the door was opened for her. "And I will wed him, or I will ruin him, one way or the other."

"But my dear," her father protested as he climbed into the coach himself. "You must see reason…"

Two footmen exchanged a glance and the driver's brows rose in silent commentary. They all knew that the daughter of the house cared nothing for reason. Her desire was the only thing of import to her, and often to her father as a result.

Not a one of the three men would have traded places with Arthur Beckham that morning, not for any price.

∼

PRUDENCE WARNED Patience that as soon as the news was known, people would come to look at her. Curiosity would bring them to the bookseller to view Mr. Beckham's unexpected choice of bride. Patience was glad of the warning, but had not believed it, not truly. Even if she had, she would not have expected so very many people to be curious about her.

There was a positive crush of customers outside the shop when the doors were unlocked, more than had been waiting when the third volume of the most recently published popular novel had been published. Patience might have thought it a coincidence, but the vast majority of people were women and they were disinterested in books. Several peered at her, one asked outright about her dowry—another laughed and said Mr. Beckham had no need of it. Patience was looked up and down, and her cheeks burned at half-overheard comments about her clothing. Others speculated upon her choice of assisting in her father's business and whether that would continue after her wedding vows were exchanged. There was even whispered consideration of how long it might take her to conceive of a son.

"Does anyone here wish a book?" she demanded in vexation. There was a twitter of murmured responses, all in the negative, then a familiar male voice called from the very doors.

"Me!" Mr. Beckham cried. There was a gasp, then the crowd parted like the Red Sea to let him pass. Patience had never seen the like of it, but her betrothed was unsurprised.

He strode directly to her where she stood behind the counter, looking as confident and impeccably attired as ever. He wore a navy jacket on this day and buff trousers, his black boots polished to a mirrorlike gleam. His waistcoat was striped silk and his cravat was ornamented with a large sapphire. There was a pink rose in his buttonhole and a celebratory smile upon his lips, and Patience found her heart taking a skip when he doffed his hat and bowed before her. "Miss Carruthers," he said in a low purr. "I am delighted to have found you so early today."

"I was unlikely to be elsewhere, sir." She noted when she studied him closely that he looked a little tired, though he strove to hide it. "While I might have expected you to still be in a gaming hell."

"I was for much of the night," he ceded easily.

Prudence knew her disapproval showed. "How much did you lose? Or is it impertinent to ask?"

"It would be impertinent in any other than my betrothed." He leaned closer and whispered. "I won," he confided, eyes shining at his triumph.

"Oh!"

"When the cards favor me, I do not insult them by turning away early. It was the others who called a halt at dawn." He stifled a yawn, which she thought might have been contrived.

She was itching to ask how much he had won and she realized he knew it. For that alone, she would bite her tongue. "Then I am surprised you are not taking your leisure this morning, perhaps sleeping."

"When I could savor your company? No, no, Miss Carruthers." He fixed her with a look that was all mischief. "I did call at Golden Square."

"Already?"

"Already. The entire day awaits us, for we must celebrate the occasion of our betrothal. There are plans, my lady, to be made and details to be determined." His eyes widened as if he made a jest and she could not tell how serious he was. Was he drunk? Still drunk from the revels of the night before?

He leaned closer. "I never imbibe when I gamble," he whispered and she was startled that he read her thoughts so clearly.

Patience eyed him, well aware that everyone in the shop listened avidly. She could not suppress her sense that he teased her. "I thought you wished for a book."

"I do." His eyes were sparkling so that they seemed to be brimming with stars. His enjoyment was a sign of their opposing natures. Clearly, Mr. Beckham savored being the focus of attention, while Patience preferred to work quietly and unobserved. She supposed she would have to become accustomed to his flamboyant ways.

"Your father has given me a list," he confessed, displaying the document in question. Patience glimpsed only a few of the titles there in her father's bold hand. "On this day, choose me a book, Miss Carruthers," he invited, his words carrying to the most distant corners of the shop. "Perhaps a volume of love poems, that I might read aloud to you as we ride in the park."

Ladies on all sides sighed.

Patience felt her eyes narrow as she considered the man before her. "I should not ride alone in the park with you, sir, not without a chaperone."

His eyes glinted and she thought he would note that she had already done as much. She flushed, watched his eyes twinkle, then glared at him.

"Even though we are betrothed?" he asked, instead of reminding her of her earlier concession.

"I am uncertain of the propriety of it." How curious that when she strove to be firm with this man, Patience found herself sounding dull.

Mr. Beckham held up a gloved finger, but she could not avert her gaze from those sparkling eyes. His merriment was ridiculously infectious. Did he always jest thus? Was he ever serious?

She frowned a little more sternly to hide her susceptibility to him.

"I anticipated that you might protest as much," he said, then turned to beckon toward the door. A young girl in a fine blue-green coat stepped forward and Patience could not fail to note the expense of the garment. Was it silk? It was lovely, to be sure. The girl's chestnut hair was artfully curled beneath her fashionable bonnet, and a peacock feather was tucked into the ribbon roses on her bonnet. Her eyes were a clear blue, and though their coloring was similar, Patience did not discern a strong resemblance with Mr. Beckham. This was not so curious as she did not resemble Catherine overmuch, but when the three sisters were together, the family connection was often noted. This girl might have been ten or eleven summers of age.

Patience guessed her identity before he spoke.

"May I introduce my sister, Miss Amelia Beckham? Amelia, this is my betrothed, Miss Patience Carruthers."

Patience curtsied as did Miss Beckham, and they murmured polite greetings as the occupants of the shop stood witness to this introduction. The whispers grew in volume.

"Amelia has a desire to see the Serpentine in the sunshine today," Mr. Beckham said. "As you might recall, Miss Carruthers, we are recently returned from Venice, so all of London's pleasures beckon anew."

"We returned with Arthur's new cats," the girl said with a roll of her eyes. She smiled a little, though, and looked toward her brother with a kind of amused tolerance that prompted Patience's own smile.

"Cats?"

"Two of them," Mr. Beckham supplied. "Fierce beasts that were in residence at our accommodations in the Serenissima. No one seemed to have a care for them. Though they are quite independent, convinced apparently that they have need of no human care, I could not bear to leave them behind."

"They are devoted to him," Miss Beckham whispered and Patience looked between them with surprise. "Perhaps it is because he saves fish for them."

"Does he?" Patience could readily imagine her betrothed ignoring any rules of the household or expectations of social conduct, but she would not have expected him to be indulgent of stray cats.

"They have no names," Miss Beckham confessed.

"You claim as much only because you called them all

variety of names when they howled all the way home," her brother added.

"I had no notion it was quite so far from Venice to London." Her tone was one of dismay but her eyes sparkled, much like those of Mr. Beckham.

Patience found herself biting back a smile.

"They do have names!" her brother protested. "The black one is Tar and the grey one, Feathers." He winked at his sister. "And they did not complain as much as you did."

"Arthur!" Miss Beckham protested and he chuckled, uncontrite.

"Those are terrible names for cats," Patience said without thinking and he turned his merry grin upon her.

"I had no notion there were rules."

"Protocol, perhaps," Patience said. "Tradition and expectation. Cats do have a certain dignity that must be acknowledged in their names. The ancient Egyptians held cats in such regard that they had cemeteries for cats and mummified their remains. There are those who suggest that cats were venerated in their society, and certainly they were respected beyond other animals…"

Mr. Beckham eyed her so intently that she fell silent and flushed. "Fascinating. Might I prevail upon you, Miss Carruthers, to see the situation remedied?"

"I shall have to meet them first."

He laughed at that. "You will!"

"But first you owe me an explanation, Mr. Beckham."

"Do I?" His eyes gleamed as he leaned closer. "Do you dare to tell me here before so many witnesses, or shall we discuss whatever crime I have committed in the privacy of the carriage?"

Patience flicked a glance at their observers. "Not here."

His gaze locked with hers and she watched his eyes darken. His voice dropped and her heart leapt as it seemed trained to do in his presence. "A wise choice, but then, you are reputed to be a most clever young lady."

Patience found herself blushing, a situation that was not improved by Mr. Beckham's evident satisfaction in her response to his teasing. He watched her, eyes gleaming, with a contented smile and she could only stare back at him as she felt her cheeks heat even more.

Miss Beckham then appealed to Patience. "Then you will come? I should so like to become acquainted with you, but do not wish to interfere with your plans for the day. Arthur is inclined to see his own objectives alone."

"I am the heart and soul of consideration, as you, dear sister, know more than any other."

Miss Beckham chortled. Mr. Beckham grinned, then he offered his hand to Patience.

She wished to accompany them more than she had desired any outing in a while. She looked over her shoulder and caught her father's eye. He was watching the exchange from the threshold of his office and smiled when their gazes met. He nodded and made a shooing motion with his hand.

"I shall despise you forever if you ignore me now," Prudence threatened beneath her breath, suddenly appearing beside Patience. Her bright smile made her expectation clear and Patience was pleased to introduce her.

She then left them chatting while she fetched her bonnet, gloves, coat and bag.

Riding in the park in the morning. Taking responsibility for naming a pair of cats. Goodness. Next, she would be leaving cards and making calls. The very unlikelihood of such a change in her priorities made Patience smile.

No, it was the prospect of Mr. Beckham's companionship that made her smile. She hoped he did not know it, but looked back to find him watching her and guessed that he did.

CHAPTER 6

$\mathcal{A}$rthur Beckham was rapidly becoming convinced that proposing to Miss Patience Carruthers had been the cleverest choice he had made in considerable time. First, there had been that scandalous book, and then her recognition of it. Had he ever seen a young lady blush so becomingly? Yet even when she was obviously agitated, she remained adamant that the book must be returned. And she had the most curious habit of beginning a lecture when he teased her, as if she thought he was in need of education. She was unlike any young lady of his acquaintance.

Who else would have insisted upon a joint venture as the condition of her agreement? Any other lady would have tripped in her haste to accept his offer, but not Miss Carruthers. And those silvery eyes, so serious, so intently fixed upon him. He might have sworn she could read the secrets of his soul.

No wonder he was compelled to coax her smile. Though it might have been a ploy to distract her from her perusal, the reward was beyond measure. Her smile dawned slowly, honestly, gradually capturing her lips and then her eyes, as if each feature had to be persuaded to merriment.

He wanted to make her laugh aloud, just to prove it could be done.

In addition, he had been summoned to explain his choice by no less a personage than the Duke of Haynesdale and had been given advice for that encounter by the infamous courtesan, Miss Esmeralda Ballantyne. And their agreement had been made less than two days before.

His life promised to be one sequence of unanticipated adventures with Miss Carruthers by his side. Arthur could not wait to discover what surprise awaited him next.

He would have a surprise for Miss Carruthers by their wedding day, one that was guaranteed to win her approval. All he had to do was keep his quest a secret until the day they exchanged their vows.

That wound be nothing, compared to a ruse of twenty-two years.

The lady's most recent blush was one that set his blood afire. Did she have any notion how alluring she was as the pink stole over her cheeks? Was she aware of how her lips parted, fairly inviting a kiss—and Arthur had a notion of just how he would kiss Miss Carruthers —or how her eyes shone, as brilliant as the shimmer of sunlight on a still sea? The prospect of exploring a volume of intimate advice with her was a most distracting notion.

It was a fine autumn day for a ride and he found himself particularly satisfied to have his betrothed seated on his left. Though she was careful to neither jostle against him nor even touch him, Arthur was keenly aware of her slender presence beside him. She smelled faintly of lily-of-the-valley and fresh linen. Her long coat was a deep blue that only made her eyes look more remarkable, and he could only admire her when he handed her into the carriage.

He knew Amelia was intrigued by Miss Carruthers and hoped they would find common ground. While his sister seemed to enjoy her lessons as he never had, he knew their mother wished she might have more companionship. Perhaps Miss Carruthers would not mind adding another sister to her collection.

For her part, Amelia frequently drew curious gazes. She was a markedly pretty girl and an heiress so he did not doubt that there would be interest in her hand when she had her season. Arthur was not in the habit of appearing with a female companion other than his sister, so he enjoyed the many inquisitive studies of his betrothed.

He felt fortunate indeed, a mood that suited him well.

"Does everyone always stare thus at you?" Miss Carruthers asked in an undertone when they were underway and Arthur laughed.

"I believe, Miss Carruthers, that they are staring at you."

"Goodness. I had no notion I should wear my best for the day."

"You look delightful," he said firmly. "Never doubt that whatever you choose to wear is perfect, regardless of notice from those who have nothing better to do than gawp and gossip."

"That is a lovely endorsement, Mr. Beckham, but I wonder if I can believe it."

"Surely you do not accuse me of stating anything less than the truth?"

"Surely I do, for I was informed just this morning that you were in love with me." She turned and gave him such a cool glance that Arthur was startled to momentary silence. "That was not my understanding of the basis of our arrangement."

"You do not approve of marriages made for love?" Amelia asked, reminding Arthur of her presence.

"Whether I do or not is immaterial," Miss Carruthers said crisply. "The issue is that I had no notion that Mr. Beckham's heart was so engaged until my father informed me of that situation this morning. 'You have made a conquest' he said to me, as if that explained everything." She granted Arthur a stern look.

"Then you are in agreement," Amelia said happily. "For Arthur does not believe in love, and has sworn that he will never wed for such tender emotion and fleeting impulse."

"How strange then that I should be told otherwise, and not a fine basis for a beginning, to be sure." Miss Carruthers' tone was icy. She waited, her steady gaze fixed upon him, and Arthur felt she would coax a confession from his lips.

He had done what was necessary to achieve the end they both desired, but he sensed she would not favor that explanation. What a remarkable lady he had chosen.

Perhaps she was the sole woman who would find fault with his choices. Arthur wished for her good opinion more than anything he had desired in a long time, which meant he had to pace his confessions. He guided the carriage through the throng of riders and conveyances while he thought, well aware that Miss Carruthers watched and waited, like a sphinx at a crossroads demanding the answer to a riddle before he could pass.

Despite his conundrum, he could only admire that she was both persistent and clever.

"That was well done," she acknowledged softly, and

perhaps with an increment of surprise, when they were free of the throng.

"At least I have not failed on all fronts already," he said lightly, hoping for her smile. She lifted a brow, giving him a look of consideration, and he smiled at her. A welcome flush touched her cheeks and he dared to hope for the best.

"Arthur is an excellent driver," Amelia said with approval.

"I suppose these tidings came from the Duke of Haynesdale," he guessed, returning to the subject at hand, and Miss Carruthers nodded.

"I understood the confession was yours."

Arthur nodded. "I was advised to do as much to earn his approval of the match."

"You lied."

He winced despite himself at the harshness of that word. "Are you certain of that?" he asked and felt her turn to study him. He dared not meet that steady gaze, but kept his attention fixed upon the horses. "Perhaps I confided the truth in him before surrendering it you."

"You cannot be smitten with me!" The very possibility seemed to fluster her. "Not so soon as this."

"And you cannot know the truth in my heart."

"Oh, Arthur," Amelia said, shaking her head. "You cannot tease Miss Carruthers over a detail of such import." She gave him a poke in the arm.

"I fear you mock me, Mr. Beckham."

Given her cool manner, Arthur pursued his point. "And I fear you fail to grant credit where it is due, Miss Carruthers. How many men have been smitten at a mere glance of the lady who will hold their hearts captive forever? Novels, poems and songs are filled with similar tales, implying that the situation is a common one."

"But not outside of stories, surely."

He risked a glance her way. "Can you be certain? Truly, Miss Carruthers, you are a young lady unlike any I have known. Surprise might surely gain a man's attention, and intrigue might lead to admiration, even love."

"So quickly as that?" she asked, ever skeptical.

"Who are we to fault Cupid's efficiency?"

She smiled, just a little. "I think you tease me, Mr. Beckham, and strive to cover your falsehood with flattery."

"I think, Miss Carruthers, that you have a woefully low opinion of your betrothed."

She smiled outright at that. "Not so low as that, sir."

He met her gaze, glad to find her eyes sparkling a little. "I am glad to hear it. Can I be faulted for wishing to win your smile?"

"Of course not, Mr. Beckham." She sobered and concern lit those eyes. "But I do have a great affection for the truth, sir. I would have honesty between us, even if it means you must tell me truths I might prefer to evade."

There was the rub.

Where to begin? His entire existence was a careful fabrication of falsehoods. Even though he yearned to dissemble it, to surrender his secrets and grant Miss Carruthers the honesty she desired, Arthur knew he had to proceed with caution.

They had gained the park and he pulled the horses to a halt that he could grant his lady his full attention. "How very bold of you. I knew from the outset that you were a most intrepid lady." He wondered how much truth she truly desired, for he had bushels of it to offer.

She shook her head. "Not so bold as that, sir. Truth has a way of making itself known, particularly truths that are unwelcome. I would rather know than be subsequently surprised, perhaps in an unwelcome situation."

"There is good sense in that," he agreed, studying her. "And I suspect, an increment of experience."

She flushed crimson and dropped her gaze. "It is of no importance."

Arthur put a fingertip beneath her chin, compelling her to meet his gaze. He found shadows in her eyes and was surprised by his ardent need to defend her cause, and see the damage repaired. "You may trust in me, Miss Carruthers."

A tentative smile lifted the corner of her mouth. "As surely as I may trust in your undying love?"

"Did his grace say that?" Arthur feigned outrage and was rewarded by the blossoming of her smile. Then he sobered. "I tell you this in all honesty, Miss Carruthers. You surprise me. You confound me. You fascinate me. And though I exaggerated the tale of my feelings last night, I did it to gain the duke's approval of our match and the furthering of our mutual objectives. I was advised by one who knows him well that if I told him the truth of our agreement, he would advise most strenuously against our match, and that was a situation I wished to avoid. Can you blame me?"

"No," she confessed softly.

He let his gaze drop to her lips. "I also feel there is something of a portent in my claim. Though I may not be smitten as yet, I could very well be and soon."

"Oh, Arthur," Amelia said, this time with a rapturous sigh.

"You are incorrigible," Miss Carruthers said beneath her breath and Arthur smiled at the glint in her eyes.

"Guilty as charged," he admitted and when she laughed at him, he felt triumphant. "But I tell you this, Miss Carruthers. I too desire honesty between us and agree with you of its merit as a foundation to a marriage."

"Then you pledge to never tell me a falsehood?"

Arthur managed to hide his grimace. That horse was long out of the barn. "I cannot make such a sweeping pledge." The lady's disapproval was evident. "But I vow that whatever I do, it will be for the benefit of our union, just as last night with the duke, and not with any intent of doing you injury."

She studied him, her expression solemn. "That is rather less than I asked."

"And yet it is the most possible at this time."

"Will you tell me the truth when I ask for it?"

"Yes." He touched his jacket over his heart. "You have my oath upon that, and my promise that all truths will be surrendered to you in time."

"You have many secrets then, Mr. Beckham?"

"More than you might imagine." He spoke as if making a jest, but Miss Carruthers' survey did not waver. He knew he was being judged and could only hope for the best result. When she smiled and shook her head slightly, he dared to be relieved.

"You are a most unusual man, sir," she said quietly and Arthur grinned as he urged the horses to continue.

"Dare I hope the fascination is mutual?"

"You know it is," she said beneath her breath, as if admitting a detail she would have preferred to keep to herself.

Arthur laughed aloud. "That is a triumph, my lady, and one that must be celebrated. You have seen the Serpentine in the sunlight," he said to Amelia. "Dare I suggest a visit to the Exeter Exchange?"

"Arthur!" Amelia crowed with delight, while Miss Carruthers caught her breath. He had no doubt that her concern was for the possible cost as the shops and merchants in the exchange were reputed to be expensive.

That was why he would shop for her there. Let the Beckham fortunes see his new wife with a new wardrobe in case the purse strings were to be drawn taught in future.

"Fear not, Miss Carruthers," Arthur said, his own affection for his notion growing with every step. "Amelia and I are most discerning of customers, and I will pay the bill."

~

SHOPPING!

Truth be told, Patience had never shopped with the enthusiasm of this pair. She and her sisters had always been careful with funds, handing dresses down one to the next, adding bands of embroidery themselves, and strategically choosing when to add items to their wardrobes. They could spend half a day selecting a pair of gloves upon which they agreed and which could be shared between them.

It was immediately clear to her that the Beckham siblings had not learned the same restraint. En route, Miss Beckham demanded details of her wardrobe, undoubtedly with an eye to her future commitments, and Patience had to think of which shared items she would leave behind and which she might take. It was resolved that she possessed four day dresses, two more plain than the other, a velvet Spencer that could be worn with all of them and a long coat of good wool. She possessed no dress suitable for formal parties and balls though she expected to choose one for her wedding, and she was forced to cede that the riding habit fit Prudence better than her. At least she rode. She was glad of that when Mr. Beckham granted her an appreciative nod.

How much was her life going to change? Prudence would have loved the prospect of stepping into the life of an aristocrat, but Patience was less enthusiastic. She had always hoped that money would grant choice and opportunity, not restriction. She had no desire to call upon ladies and discuss trivialities, to compare the merit of one dress over another, or to be always attending parties. There was work to be done that could make a difference and that was what she hungered to do.

Mr. Beckham regarded her with a sparkling eye as the dressmaker cast lengths of silk over her shoulder. "I fear my betrothed is a most uncommon lady, one who does not enjoy the task of choosing a new dress or two."

Patience could not take offense for he regarded her with what could only be approval.

"It seems frivolous to expend much attention upon such fleeting details," she confessed and the dressmaker's eyes narrowed.

"No doubt you would prefer the companionship of a good book," he said easily and she could not entirely hide her approval of that notion. He laughed, untroubled. "Then let me hasten the endeavor to its conclusion," he said, setting aside his walking stick with purpose.

"Oh good," his sister said with undisguised delight and Patience wondered what she was about to witness.

What she saw was practiced good taste in action. Mr. Beckham was decisive and quick, each selection unerringly perfect. He chose the cloth and the cut, conferring with the dressmaker about the length of the sleeves. He picked the ribbon for the sash, the embroidered tulle for the overskirt—the blue matched the ribbon perfectly—the satin for her slippers and the perfect hue of gloves, neither white nor cream, to finish the ensemble. A deep blue, but not one as dark as the ribbon, was his choice for the evening coat, its trim in the same cream, its delicate buttons in gold. He added gold ribbon flowers to the slippers and requested snippets of all for his sister to ensure the hat matched.

He bent his attention to the riding habit with the same focus upon detail. Patience much admired the deep dove grey velvet he selected, the pewter buttons and silvery blouse. These gloves were black leather, the hat of black felt with a silver tumble of a veil, and he informed her that she must have black boots from the bootmaker. Patience could only nod in awe as his sister swept through the array of delicate fabrics, choosing petticoats and stockings with as unerring a hand as her brother, adding a glorious shawl when Patience confessed that hers was better left to her sister, another pair of gloves and two purses.

"Goodness, Mr. Beckham, you are generous," she whispered and he bent to kiss the back of her hand.

"Every gem must be given the setting it deserves," he murmured and her heart fluttered when he looked up at her, his gaze dark with something she could not name.

Then the door of the shop opened, a group of ladies spilling into the space. Patience was aware of their arrival but could not look away from Mr. Beckham. She heard Miss Beckham catch her breath, then a swish of silken skirts announced the arrival of another.

"You cannot make a silk purse of a sow's ear, Mr. Beckham, regardless of the weight of your purse." The lady's voice was light, as if she made a jest, but it was clearly one at Patience's expense. She saw Mr. Beckham's lips tighten, then he straightened and turned, his smooth gesture leaving Patience's hand neatly tucked inside his elbow.

They stood together as a couple as she faced her competition and she felt the steel in him as he inclined his head to the lady. "Miss Grosvenor. What an unexpected pleasure." His tone indicated otherwise in a most gratifying way.

"Mr. Beckham," that lady replied, hunger in her eyes as she studied him and ignored Patience.

Miss Grosvenor was not an unattractive young lady. Her figure was good, a little more curvaceous than Patience's slender curves, but more fashionable for that. Her dark hair was set in a volley of curls; her lips were ripe and rosy; her green eyes sparkled and altogether she was a fetching sight, attired in the latest mode to the last detail. Perhaps she was a little too embellished. Perhaps there was a sharp gleam in her eyes and a petulant curve to her lips, but few would have found fault with her appearance.

One could not see at a glance that a person was in the habit of defacing books, of course.

"I am certain you are acquainted with my sister," Mr. Beckham said smoothly to Miss Grosvenor, who was glaring at Patience, and the two curtsied to each other. "But not perhaps to my betrothed, Miss Patience Carruthers."

"Charmed, I am sure," Miss Grosvenor said, her tone indicating she was anything but.

"You should be," Mr. Beckham said softly, and her gaze flew to him as Patience watched. He turned to smile at Patience, his expression softening for the first time since the other lady had arrived. "Never have I encountered a lady of such grace and wit as Miss Carruthers. Much of society could take a lesson from her manners, if not her other charms." He smiled down at her, looking so much like a man smitten that Patience found herself blushing—and that only made his smile broaden. "Come," he murmured to her. "We will be late."

"Of course," she said, letting him lead her from the shop as Miss Grosvenor fumed behind them. Patience felt the other woman's regard upon them as Mr. Beckham granted a coin to the urchin who held the door for them, as he handed his sister into the carriage, as he turned and fitted his hands around her waist, lifting her to the carriage but not with undue speed. "Mr. Beckham," she whispered, scandalized that he should touch her thus in public and fearing her heart would burst.

"Every champion deserves a reward from his lady, does he not?" he murmured, that mischievous glint in his eyes.

"What reward would you desire? I have no token to tie upon your jousting lance."

His grin flashed. "One kiss, Miss Carruthers, no more and no less."

"Before everyone?"

"Before one person, to be certain." His tone was grim and she knew he was angered by Miss Grosvenor's remark.

She smiled and leaned toward him. "You are irresistible, Mr. Beckham," she teased then kissed his cheek. His grip tightened on her waist and she caught her breath, savoring his proximity. "But wicked, to be sure."

"I can be so much more wicked than you imagine, Miss Carruthers," he said, turning his head so that his mouth brushed across her own, a fleeting but thrilling caress. "You have but to encourage me." She caught her breath and felt his heat against her own. "How else am I to find and honor your most bewitching spot?" he asked.

Their gazes met, so very close, and Patience felt a yearning beyond any previous sensation. Mr. Beckham lifted a brow, his gaze falling to her mouth, and Patience did not dare to breathe.

This time, he kissed her upon the mouth, slowly and

sweetly, and she hoped she was not the only one who had forgotten about their audience.

"Incorrigible," she whispered as her heart raced and he laughed, then lifted her the rest of the way to the carriage.

"While you, my lady, are irresistible." Without a backward glance, he swung into the vehicle, taking his place between Patience and his sister and gathering the reins with purpose. The boy who had held the horses was tossed a coin before they were off.

Irresistible.

Patience bit her lip, wishing she might truly be the kind of woman who might haunt the dreams of a man like Mr. Beckham. She was keenly aware of the brief taste of him and how his touch lingered, leaving a heat against her skin. His thigh was close to hers, his arm brushing against her own, the sound of his voice as he spoke to his sister making her happy beyond all. As much as she preferred to be tranquil, it was exciting to be with Mr. Beckham and she enjoyed that a good deal more than she might have expected.

And a kiss, virtually in the street! Two, in point of fact. Patience felt like a wanton.

Especially as what she wanted most of all was another longer embrace.

~

THEY HALTED at the milliner and Amelia darted into the shop with her handful of samples, bent upon her mission. Arthur took his time handing down Miss Carruthers, wanting a chance to speak with her alone.

"You are quiet," Arthur said when she remained silent. Had he shocked her? Had he offended her? What he had wished to do more than anything else was ensure that Miss Grosvenor knew there was no hope of any scheme succeeding that was contrived to see they two wed.

Ever.

That she had spoken thus of Miss Carruthers was unacceptable. If she had been a man, there would have been pistols at dawn.

"Only because you startled me, Mr. Beckham," she confessed with a sidelong glance that was almost coy.

Arthur dared to be encouraged. "Are you vexed with me?"

She flushed a little and her eyes sparkled. Her gaze danced toward Amelia, already in the shop, then back to him. She lowered her voice as she leaned closer and he wanted nothing more than to gather her close and kiss her properly. "Only that it was so short a salute," she whispered, to his astonishment.

He feigned shock and she laughed. "Miss Carruthers," he said and she laughed even more, a sound that eliminated his concerns. He offered his arm and she slid her hand into the crook of his elbow. "Perhaps you should call me Arthur."

The suggestion pleased her, he could see that immediately in the flutter of her lashes and her quick upward glance. She smiled again. "Then you must call me Patience."

"Patience," he murmured, savoring the sound of it.

"Arthur," she echoed, glancing up at him. She shook a finger at him. "You must tell me the truth, sir. I expect all of your secrets surrendered in full before we are wed a year."

That was fair enough. Arthur thought she would know them all within a month. "I give you my pledge upon that, Patience. Upon my word, you can rely." He held her gaze for one last moment, then escorted her into the shop.

He leaned down as they crossed the threshold, his

voice so low that only she would hear his words. "I thought that a fine start, Patience," he murmured and she glanced upward, her expression surprisingly mischievous.

"As did I, sir," she admitted. "Given the book we are to publish."

The book. Arthur had almost forgotten the details of the book. "Have you read it?"

"Not yet, but I will."

He leaned closer again as she pretended to consider three different ribbons with the flowers Amelia had chosen already. "I hope you have not forgotten the plan of confirming all its details," he said, hoping for a blush and gaining one that almost set him aflame.

"Incorrigible and outrageous," she whispered, those eyes dancing.

He feigned solemnity. "I would not risk the reputation of a new firm by publishing a volume that had not been thoroughly reviewed by its owners."

She appeared to be fighting a smile, and losing the battle. "I fear that I find myself shocked by your audacity, sir, and impressed by your determination to attend to detail." She looked up, meeting his gaze steadily. "I accept your challenge."

"Was it a challenge? I meant it as an invitation."

"Either way, I agree to embark upon it."

How soon could they be wed?

He strove to hide his impatience as Amelia embarked upon the hunt for the perfect hat. He knew she could spend a week in a milliner's shop. Finally, having compelled Patience to try four different hats, Amelia pronounced one superior to all others—a matter that could not be disputed. The shape of it was perfect for his intended and Arthur would not have troubled her with the others. Another boy caught the copper Arthur tossed to him and they were shortly upon their way. He should stop at a bookseller to begin her father's reading list.

"There are so many details to decide upon for the wedding," Amelia said with enthusiasm. "I cannot wait to learn more of your plans, even to assist if I may. Which church and what date will it be, and what will be served for the wedding breakfast, and—"

"Mother has claimed the wedding breakfast as her gift to us," Arthur interjected firmly, seeing that the planning of this happy event could readily spin into months of deliberations. "The church will be that frequented by the Carruthers." He granted Patience a glance and saw something that might have been relief in her eyes.

"St. Martin of the Fields," she provided and he nodded.

"And the date will be at the discretion of Patience," he concluded.

"The banns will have to be called…"

Arthur shook his head. "No. I will obtain a special license, so the date can be as soon as you like. My mother requests to meet you tomorrow afternoon at four, so I would suggest a week from Saturday."

"Oh! So quick as that!"

"I see no cause to delay," he said, granting her an intent look. "Do you?" He could not read her expression, which troubled him.

"I thought the details might take longer to arrange."

Arthur was not entirely content with her hesitation. "Would you cancel our agreement before it is more widely known?" he offered, knowing that was the last possibility he desired. He would, however, be gracious to a lady.

Especially this one.

Miss Carruthers flushed crimson. "Of course not," she said, a little hastily. "I was simply surprised. I was thinking, of course, that the banns would be called and it would be closer to a month before we pledged to each other." She took a breath, seemingly to compose herself, and Arthur was not entirely convinced that she still wished to wed him.

He was surprised by the magnitude of his concern.

They rode in silence for a moment, Arthur's thoughts spinning as he strove to identify his error.

"Were you aware that the Romans believed that only the month of June was auspicious for weddings?" Miss Carruthers said abruptly, her words falling quickly from her lips. "Its association with Juno, the goddess of marriage, women and childbirth, made it the most suitable time for the exchange of marital vows. Ceding to Juno's authority over that month also offered a better prospect of earning her favor, thus ensuring both fertility and prosperity in the match." She took a shaking breath.

"June is rather a long time away," Amelia said after an interval of silence.

"Yes! Yes, it is, and that was not my suggestion. A week from Saturday it will be," she said, as if girding her loins for an ordeal.

Arthur slanted a glance at her to find her watching him. She smiled pertly, but the expression was forced. He halted the carriage before her father's house and moved quickly to help her down. Their gazes clung when her hand was in his, hers searching his, then she smiled again. "I apologize for my surprise, sir," she said softly and he dared to be reassured.

"Less than a fortnight, and then you will be together for the rest of your lives!" Amelia said with delight.

Arthur bent to kiss the hand of his betrothed. "To-morrow afternoon then? At three?"

He would not have blamed her for striving to avoid an interview with Lady Beckham but she straightened and nodded. "At three, sir," she said with welcome re-solve, then stepped past him. Arthur stood, watching her until she vanished into the house, wondering what truly was amiss.

And, of course, how he could find out.

CHAPTER 7

$\mathcal{H}$e was lovely.

Truly, Patience had never met Mr. Beckham's equal. His manners were impeccable. He was handsome, charming and comported himself well. His habit of giving coppers to impoverished children was more than endearing, and his taste was exquisite. He was kind and he was generous; he was an amusing companion and that kiss would keep her awake all the night long. He was courteous to her, yet assertive. She felt safe and confident in his presence. His younger sister clearly adored him, so Patience had not been misled as to the truth of his nature.

She had never been inclined to believe in the merit of love, but she had to cede that she could find herself in love with Mr. Beckham. Her sole doubt was whether she had seen the fullness of his nature, or whether he deliberately showed her only a part.

His reputation, after all, held that he was undeniably frivolous. She was inclined to trust him and to believe that the man who had both teased and defended her was the true man, but what if he had hidden part of his nature, the part he would expect her to find less appealing? It was not so ridiculous a possibility, given how little time they had actually spent together.

Could she trust him? Was his promise to aid in the publication of the book—the entire basis of their agreement to her view—a sincere one? Patience could not say. She could not imagine that such a man - a fashionable dandy, a gambler and a wastrel - would cast himself into the business of publishing with even her father's fervor. Had he deceived her?

Was the prospect of Miss Grosvenor so fearsome as that? Patience admitted that she did not like the other woman, and marriage was a lifetime bond, but a man was less constrained by his marriage than a woman might be. He could wed Miss Grosvenor and never see her again. They could live in separate houses. Marrying her to evade that match seemed extreme.

She supposed he simply did not like to have his choices dictated to him, and she could sympathize with that.

She considered the possibilities all of the night, then through the following morning. She dressed with care, fearing that Lady Beckham might have requested this interview because she intended to withhold her approval, and was in a state of great agitation by the time Mr. Beckham called for her. The burgundy dress was one of her favorites, and it looked well with her dark grey spencer. Prudence did her hair and they eyed the result in the mirror together.

"You might slay dragons in that dress," Prudence said.

"For the blood would not show."

They laughed together.

"She will adore you," Prudence said, with a confidence Patience did not feel.

"Perhaps only because she shares our view of Miss Grosvenor."

"He has chosen you and she dotes upon him. Everyone says as much."

Patience straightened and smiled. "You are right, of course."

"But do not lecture them upon trivia," Prudence advised in a whisper and Patience looked up with surprise. "It is what you do when you are uncertain. You choose a topic and explain it in minute detail. It is rather tedious to the unwary, if endearing to those who know you best."

"Endearing?"

"You are so inclined to hide your thoughts and it is a hint, at least, of what you feel."

Did she do that? Patience recalled her comments about June weddings the day before and grimaced. Mr. Beckham and his sister had been disconcerted. She nodded agreement at Prudence's counsel and left the room.

She descended the stairs to find Mr. Beckham in the foyer, his hat in one hand and his walking stick in the other. He looked marvelous, of course, in yet another perfectly tailored jacket she had not seen before, gleaming boots, and a perfectly tied cravat. He smiled at her appearance, a slow smile of appreciation that lit his eyes and launched a glow within Patience.

"I have a confession to make," she said, after they had exchanged greetings and were descending the steps to his waiting carriage. She waited while he gave the inevitable penny to the boy who had held the reins for him, anticipating his action, then let him hand her into the carriage.

"A confession, Miss Carruthers. I cannot wait to hear what you feel deserves such a feat."

She smiled, as she knew she was supposed to. "My sister reminded me that I am inclined to recite reams of

trivia when agitated. I spoke of June weddings yesterday, which is an example of that trait."

He nodded once. "And what troubled you, if I may
enquire?"

"I find myself doubting the strength of your conviction to keep our terms," she admitted and he glanced
quickly at her.

"Why? I granted my word to you." He was not insulted, to her relief, merely curious. Truly, it was simplicity itself to converse with the man. If she was not
careful, he would know all of her secrets without even
trying to discern them. She would simply offer them up.

"But it seems beyond your nature to embark on
such an endeavor. Yesterday, I saw how adept you are at
living in the style that you do."

"Do you not believe that a person can willfully
change his or her perspective?"

"What I doubt is that you have the will to do as
much. Why would a man born to leisure choose to
labor?"

He smiled. "You assume I was born to leisure." He
was watching the horses and the road, and she could
not discern his thoughts at all.

Her annoyance at that showed in her reply. "What
else would I conclude, sir? You are the grandson of an
earl. You have a generous income and can expect a considerable inheritance, by all accounts." She pressed on,
determined to know. "Is Miss Grosvenor so heinous a
potential bride as that?"

"Yes!" he said with surprising vigor, then laughed at
Patience's evident shock. He leaned toward her. "She
was, indeed, to drive me to invoke the name of another.
But it was not a mere whim to choose you of all the
ladies I have met in recent years." His gaze locked upon
her, his eyes darkening as he looked at her. The corner

of his mouth lifted in a most alluring smile, one that reminded Patience of his thrilling kiss. When his voice dropped lower in confidence, she felt the most curious and pleasurable sensation. "She might have been the impetus, Miss Carruthers, but now I cannot imagine taking another lady to my side. You are remarkable and I am honored that you have accepted me."

Patience could have drowned in his eyes. She certainly could not easily avert her gaze. She flushed that he would speak so plainly to her, and saw his smile broaden as he watched her cheeks turn pink.

"More perfect than a sunrise," he murmured and the heat rose yet more in her cheeks. He raised a gloved fingertip, touching her cheek with a reverence that made her catch her breath.

"How many sunrises have you witnessed, Mr. Beckham?" she managed to ask.

He laughed at that. "Far more than are respectable, Miss Carruthers." He leaned closer to murmur wickedly to her. "Do you think marriage will tame my errant ways?"

When he looked into her eyes with such intensity, as if he truly cared what she might say—as if he might heed whatever she said—Patience could not take a breath, let alone reply. She stared back, spellbound as he lowered his gaze to her lips.

Then another driver shouted and Mr. Beckham returned his attention to the horses.

Patience looked at the crowded street, her heart leaping, and uttered the first words that came to mind. "Did you know that London is home to over one million individuals and may soon be the largest city in the world? That city, currently, is Peking. London is already the largest port in the world." She heard Mr. Beckham chuckle beside her and fell silent. "I am doing it," she whispered in horror.

"And it is delightful. But why in this moment? Am I so fearsome as that?"

Patience chose to be bold. "On the contrary, sir. You unsettle me in a way I do not understand."

"How?"

"By your touch, your comments, your teasing." She did not speak of his kiss. "I am not accustomed to the attentions of gentlemen."

"And I am glad of it, otherwise you might have been already wed with three children or more, and I should have been compelled to make an unfortunate match."

"You would have chosen another."

"But there is no other I would prefer," he said, his hand landing upon hers for a glorious moment. "Do you regret your response?"

Patience could not lie. "No!"

He laughed, clearly content with this reply. "Then I must issue fair warning, Patience, that I will continue to tease and to touch you, ideally for all the days of the rest of our lives."

"You make this sound like a love match," Patience said before she could catch herself. He drew the horses to a halt before a fine house and turned to look at her.

"Would that be so foul a fate?" he murmured and she could only shake her head.

He bent closer and kissed her cheek. Patience took a deep breath of the welcome scent of him and found herself meeting his curious gaze. Again, his finger rose to her cheek, his stroke one of unexpected affection. His expression, for once, was serious. "Do not fear Lady Beckham or her conclusions," he advised quietly. "I cannot envision my life without you, whether she approves or not."

"But you would not risk her displeasure?"

His expression became so resolute that she doubted all of her conclusions about his nature. "I most certainly would," he said with conviction. "Never doubt it, Patience. Never."

Patience opened her mouth and closed it again, unable to evade his conviction or the thrill it sent through her. She might not believe in love or its merits as a basis for matrimony, but there was much to be said for a suitor who would not be turned aside.

And better yet, Arthur's steadfast manner offered all the fortification she needed to face his mother.

WHY THIS GIRL?

Lady Beckham knew that any port could serve in a storm, and certainly she understood her son's desire to avoid a match with Miss Felicia Grosvenor, but why had he named this young woman as his fictitious fiancée?

Miss Patience Carruthers was not unattractive, nor was she plain, but neither did she make the most of the assets that had been granted to her. Her dress was pretty but she did not wear it with a confidence that marked it to be her own. It must be a garment that had passed between sisters and was deemed to be the best. Yes, she would have ordered the hem to be let down slightly for Miss Carruthers, but perhaps there was neither time nor sufficient fabric. There was nothing wrong with frugality, though in this case, it was a reminder to Lady Beckham that the Carruthers family made their way in trade.

Lady Beckham preferred to believe that she was not a snob, but that she was keenly attuned to the opinions of others. She did not mind challenging expectation with good cause, she reminded herself as she surveyed Arthur's choice, but in this case, she could not discern one.

She would have forgiven Arthur anything if he had been in love with Miss Carruthers—and she with him, of course, though Lady Beckham could not imagine any sensible woman failing to appreciate the many merits of her son.

Miss Carruthers appeared to be sensible, at least.

She was not shy, evidently, for her gaze steadily held Lady Beckham's own. She was not so young as might be ideal, though she looked sufficiently healthy to bear children.

Sadly, one could not be sure of such a detail in advance.

"But why?" she said, giving voice to her question.

"I beg your pardon, Lady Beckham."

"Why? I know why Arthur wished to avoid the fulfillment of his uncle's inappropriate wager. I am not entirely certain of his reasons for naming you as his betrothed, but what I truly wish to know is why you agreed. I doubt that you love him, yet."

Her guest smiled. "I find him most charming company."

"That is not the same thing," Lady Beckham said sharply.

"I would always hope for affection to deepen and grow in future. I understand that may happen in a marriage based upon rational agreement."

"But why did you agree?"

Miss Carruthers considered the question. She looked to her tea, then at the window. Her gaze swept over the drawing room again. Lady Beckham was certain the younger woman was aware of the cost of her surroundings and she showed a polite appreciation of it, but there was no avarice in her expression.

She was not marrying Arthur for his money, which was a relief.

"I like Mr. Beckham," she said finally, choosing one thing with which a mother could not find fault.

"I suppose you are attracted to his financial security."

The younger woman shook her head. "Not particularly. I have no ambition to be wealthy, Lady Beckham, although money certainly makes matters simpler."

"If you meant to make an arranged match, you could have done as much sooner."

Miss Carruthers smiled. "When I was in the bloom of my youth, you mean," she said, not taking umbrage. "But the fact is that I had no interest in matrimony until recently. I am content with my life and comfortable in my father's home."

"What changed?"

She frowned a little, turning her cup in its saucer. "I began to consider future possibilities. Though I would not wish for such a circumstance, my father may pass away before me and my mother is already gone. The business would become that of my uncle and my father's partner, and thence be inherited by my cousins, who are his sons."

"You could be left without comforts." Lady Beckham did admire the girl's practicality. She was not witless either.

"Indeed. It occurred to me that my older sister, Baroness Trevelaine, is the only one of us whose future is assured. Though she would be kind to myself and my younger sister, prospects are somewhat less certain than would be ideal. I had only just concluded that I should wed, if possible, to ensure my own future, when Mr. Beckham made his offer."

"I suppose you, like Arthur, believe that opportunity arrives when it is most welcome."

She shook her head. "I did not." She smiled a little, a mysterious expression which transformed her utterly.

She looked lovely and radiant, her eyes shining when she thought of Arthur. "But Mr. Beckham is rather persuasive," she confessed, then lowered her gaze and sipped her tea.

Arthur had chosen her and his reasons were unclear, but Lady Beckham saw in that moment that Miss Carruthers could come to adore Arthur. If ever a man had deserved an adoring wife, it was her son.

Lady Beckham put down her teacup. "I see, and I thank you for your candor, Miss Carruthers."

"I believe honesty to be the best policy, my lady."

"Indeed. Perhaps you would like to see the room that will be yours, and recommend any changes you would like. Some details can likely be resolved before the wedding."

"I'm certain it is lovely as it is, just like the rest of your home."

Lady Beckham had some work to do, it was clear. This young lady had to learn that she could be demanding as Arthur's wife—in fact, she should be demanding and not accept whatever she was granted.

Lady Beckham supposed she could work with what was offered, in this case.

She sensed that she would have to. Arthur showed an unwelcome stubbornness when it came to this girl and as much as she preferred to have her own way, she feared the price of demanding his surrender in this matter might prove too high.

LADY BECKHAM'S house was in Berkley Square, which was sufficiently daunting in itself. The house was one of the larger ones, and decorated with enthusiasm. Patience had to ensure that she did not gape at the paintings and draperies as she was led to the drawing room.

Lady Beckham was a large and loud woman, impeccably dressed, and with a precise method of speaking. Her hair was of a hue closer to that of her daughter, who more closely resembled her, but it appeared both children had her to thank for their blue eyes. Patience had the definite sense that her betrothed's mother liked to organize matters and also that Arthur had inherited —or been taught - her good taste. In truth, Patience was relieved for she doubted that any fête organized by herself would have every possible detail anticipated and every social convention observed. She was more likely to become distracted by a book, while Lady Beckham would derive great satisfaction, Patience guessed, in ensuring that all was perfection.

There was no cause to fear any lull in the conversation, for Lady Beckham did not require the contribution of anyone else to ensure a smooth patter of conversation. She speculated upon the anticipated weather for the day chosen for the wedding. She informed Patience of the refreshments she was ordering for the wedding breakfast. She reviewed the list of invited guests, which was so extensive that Patience could not think of anyone left uninvited, save perhaps the Prince of Wales himself.

She dared not mention as much lest Lady Beckham take it upon herself to add that name to the list.

She was informed that she would reside in this house with 'dear Arthur', notified as to which rooms had been assigned to be her own, and guided upstairs to view them after their tea was consumed. It was a cluster of three rooms on the southeast corner of the house, with a view over the square from the main bedchamber. The room's proportions were majestic, though Patience guessed it had not been used in a while. The pillared bed was enormous, the armoire and dressing table opposite were old-fashioned but very pretty. The fireplace was of such size to ensure a cozy room in any weather, though Patience did not let her gaze linger upon the door beside it, which had to lead to Mr. Beckham's chambers.

There were no paintings hung and Lady Beckham explained that the draperies and wallcoverings had been installed when her husband had bought the house. Though the room was attractive, she had preferred the one to the west as she favored a view of the traffic entering the square and this chamber had never been used.

It was evident to Patience that she was to be more of a guest, at least initially, than lady of the house herself. She wondered about that, though truly, she would not have wanted to dislodge Lady Beckham from her customary responsibilities—or to incur the resentment of her betrothed's mother so early in their association.

Would she and Arthur ever establish a household of their own? She supposed such independence was too much to ask when his mother was so determined to oversee all details, as that lady must be the source of his finances as well.

There were two smaller rooms to the north, one on the exterior wall with a small window and a desk, as well as its own smaller fireplace. It was a room of a size more familiar to her—though in her father's house, she and Prudence shared a bedchamber of such dimensions. The north wall was entirely bare and she ran a hand over it, envisioning a bookcase there, filled with her favorites.

The third room might have been a nursery or a maid's room, and was quite empty.

"Will you be bringing your lady's maid?" Lady Beckham asked, as if already aware Patience would not.

"My sister and I rely upon the same maid. I thought Price should stay for Prudence."

Lady Beckham looked her up and down. "I will see the matter resolved, if you prefer."

"I would be delighted to defer to your experience in such matters," Patience said, sensing that Lady Beckham would like nothing better than to do as much.

As they returned to the drawing room, she reminded herself that her future would be assured by this arrangement, with or without Mr. Beckham by her side, and that it did offer the best chance of seeing Catherine's book brought to publication.

How could she contrive to read it before her own wedding?

ARTHUR ATE three sandwiches waiting for the ladies to return from their tour of the rooms allocated to Patience. It was true that he had been dismissed, but he was not feeling particularly biddable.

He wanted to ensure that nothing damning was said to Miss Carruthers. He would not have put it past Lady Beckham to interfere however she could. Contriving that Miss Carruthers changed her mind about him might be the simplest way of putting a stop to the match.

Would Patience care if his inheritance was removed? Arthur did not know. He feared she would take a dim view of such circumstance, given their plan of publishing that book. She had already expressed concern about his finances.

He thought of his considerable earnings at the tables this week, and had a notion where they might be safely hidden.

"Arthur!" that lady declared upon her return. She feigned indignation as if making a jest over it, but he recognized that she was displeased to find him present.

"I made it plain that I wished to speak with your young lady alone."

He refilled the teacup that had to belong to Miss Carruthers and offered it to her, fairly daring Lady Beckham to cast him out. "And you have had the opportunity to do as much," he said smoothly. Miss Carruthers took the cup, glancing between them, doubtless aware of much that was unsaid. "Do you like the room?" he asked her with a smile.

"It is absolutely lovely," she replied politely.

"But..." he invited in a murmur.

Her eyes sparkled, the sight sending triumph through him. "You will not provoke me to criticism, sir."

"There is no bookcase," he guessed with a sad shake of his head

Patience laughed and he grinned, noting how his mother watched them. "You are too perceptive."

"Give me credit for noting a detail of such import," he teased and she took her seat, smiling up at him. "Undoubtedly you have a small collection of books already and intend to bring them."

"It is the closest to a dowry I possess," Patience admitted freely. She was watching him so keenly that she must have missed Lady Beckham's quick intake of breath.

He knew he did not imagine Patience's relief that he had joined them, and the conversation was light afterwards. He had felt protective in the past toward Amelia, but his desire to defend Patience was of another magnitude altogether. He appreciated how she blossomed when he put her at ease, and could only hope that Lady Beckham would be mollified.

Instead, she sat quietly and watched them, sipping her tea at intervals, her eyes dark. A storm brewed, for Arthur knew the signs, though it took him much longer than it should have done to realize that his adopted mother was jealous.

She feared losing command of him. It made perfect sense once he had the realization, for Lady Beckham was fond of organizing all details and commanding all of the players. His loyalty might be divided now, between mother and wife, indeed it should be—and perhaps should skew more favorably to his bride.

He wondered if he should reveal that he had never been fully under her thumb.

He suspected that a measure of her displeasure was that she could not fully anticipate Patience either. While Arthur found that situation charming and most welcome, he knew Lady Beckham would despise any hint of uncertainty.

Though he gave no outward indication, he took a warning from her manner. He would have to be prepared for his situation to go awry. He would visit the bank after taking Miss Carruthers home, and move his funds to another institution. He would think of some tale or another for the banker. And he would not deposit his recent winnings in either bank, the better to be prepared for disaster. No, those would be hidden in Patience's wedding gift, thus under her care.

And he would hope that the cards favored him, each and every night, the better that he could build a nest-egg for himself and his bride. What had been freely given could be readily taken away. He had been with nothing before and he did not fear a return to that situation.

He did fear the loss of his lady or her admiration.

He would keep his promise to Patience, and that would require money.

And so, this night, he would return to the tables again.

~

ALL IN ALL, Patience did not find much difference between being betrothed to a rakehell and the eldest unwed daughter of a prosperous bookseller. There was a veritable avalanche of calling cards when she returned home each day, but she resolved that she would not entertain the curious. She resolved to spend the days before the wedding in her father's shop, helping people to find books they would enjoy—although she did strive to learn more about the production of the books. She initiated a conversation with Old Joe, who had been operating a printing press in the shop for as long as she could remember. He was both less taciturn than his fellows and inclined to be more polite to ladies. Seemingly delighted by her curiosity, he showed Patience how the press inked the letters and printed the image on the paper, though watching the press in action at such close proximity did make her jump.

He sent her to Lewis, who picked the individual cast metal letters and composed each page for the press. She was impressed all over again by his dexterity and speed in assembly. She talked to her uncle about paper and ink, about supplies and inventory management. That was sufficient to make her head spin. She talked to her father about the binding of books, his particular passion, the security of different stitches and threads. He also spoke of the relative merit of various glues, leather suppliers and gilt inks. None of these men slowed their work as they spoke, for their tasks were familiar.

She watched in awe as Simmons smoothed the colored and prepared leather over the case of a book, gluing and clamping it to dry. He spent a day doing this, then the subsequent day finishing the dried books, adding gilt and lettering to the leather case. She watched as marbled end papers were tipped into almost completed volumes, and the edges of pages were colored, then admired each finished book.

It was fascinating, such a combination of skill and fine materials, and one that gave her a new respect for a fine volume.

She read also, perusing what medical volumes she could locate in her father's library to better learn the details of what she might expect upon her wedding night. How she wished for the book in Catherine's possession, but she would have to manage that first night without it.

There were two visits made to the shop by Miss Grosvenor that week, though she did not deign to address Patience either time. On both occasions, she made such a ruckus with her friends, gossiping and laughing, that her party was asked to hasten about their business. On both occasions, she spoke loudly of Mr. Beckham's exploits, as if to be certain Patience knew all the details.

Of Mr. Beckham himself, there was no sign. The man might have left London entirely for all Patience knew.

Miss Grosvenor, however, ensured that Patience knew Mr. Beckham was experiencing a remarkable streak of fortune at cards. He was seen several times to have danced all the night long. Mr. Beckham had been seen at this theatre and that one, at this party and that soirée, dining at this club and another. Miss Grosvenor intimated that he was visiting all of his former paramours—including even herself by her telling, a detail that made Patience doubt every word the other woman uttered. Mr. Beckham had made this clever remark or that amusing reply. Mr. Beckham had acquired a new waistcoat, two new pairs of boots, a walking stick of ebony, a quizzing glass, a collection of porcelain birds, a hunting dog and her puppies, three horses, a new carriage. Mr. Beckham had visited three courtesans in a single night, then two the following morning. The list was endless and Patience could not imagine that half of it was true.

Even the tales of Mr. Beckham's adventures were exhausting.

She wished she were able to better ignore the other young lady and her malice, but in truth, she missed Mr. Beckham. She began to fear that he was the kind of person who paid no heed to a matter once he deemed it to be resolved, which was troubling, indeed.

Was he reading the books recommended by her father? Was he savoring the final days of his freedom from nuptial bliss? Or was this how he planned to continue, now that her promise would help him evade Miss Grosvenor? She had no idea what to expect of him, save his appearance at the church—and even that, she doubted in the night.

On Wednesday, the results of their shopping expedition began to arrive, much to Prudence's delight. Each item was unpacked and remarked upon, and Prudence even tried on a number of the garments. "You must find me a Mr. Beckham," she said, admiring herself in the mirror, though Patience did not reply. "Indeed, Patience, I think it most uncharacteristic of you to fail to ensure that your generous husband-to-be had an equally handsome and appealing brother."

"You are welcome to strive to influence the choices of Lady Beckham," Patience replied then as her sister laughed. "And I wish you luck in that endeavor."

The arrival of Mr. Beckham's sister at the shop, the Friday before the wedding, was both a surprise and a delight. Prudence escorted another customer to the displayed books, leaving Patience alone with the new arrival. The girl was dressed impeccably, this time in chocolate brown and teal. To Prudence's regret, she was accompanied by an older woman of stern countenance and not her brother.

"Miss Beckham! How lovely to see you." Patience yearned to ask her visitor for details of Mr. Beckham but did not wish to appear overly curious. One of Miss Grosvenor's friends was perusing books, no doubt gathering tidings to share. Patience would give no sign of her many doubts.

"You should call me Amelia now," that girl said solemnly.

Patience smiled. "And you must call me Patience."

Amelia cast a glance at her governess who dutifully retreated a step and averted her gaze. The girl leaned closer and lowered her voice. "I did not have time to ask you all of my questions the other day, and I should like to do as much before you are married."

"Then ask me now."

"There is really only one question that matters. You simply must tell me your favorite book, and then I will know all that is of importance about you."

It was a measure of character that Patience could only respect.

"Have you a favorite?" she asked. "For I would like to know the same of you."

Amelia considered this. "There are many books I am not permitted to read." The governess earned a quick glance, one that made Patience determined to see that her husband's sister had access to all the books she might desire. "We have been reading the *Lais of Marie de France* and I am fond of *Bisclavret*."

"The werewolf," Patience said and Amelia smiled.

"I like him," she said with enthusiasm, then cast another glance at the apparently oblivious governess. "Although there are those who insist that a man so cursed as to become an animal should not be granted a happy ending."

"He was more honorable than his own wife, who was not so cursed."

"Indeed," Amelia said with heat, evidently glad to have found common ground. "Now you."

Patience considered the possibilities. "It is difficult to choose a favorite from all the volumes I have enjoyed, but there is one novel I would recommend to you most heartily." She led her companion to the appropriate shelf and removed one volume, placing it in the girl's hand.

"*Pride & Prejudice*," Amelia read, her gaze rising to Patience's own.

"A novel, published several years ago by T. Egerton, a publisher my father much admires for his editorial taste. The author's name is not known, but it is a fine novel, perhaps one of the finest of recent publication."

"I may have heard of it."

"It is a love story, the tale of a couple who seem utterly different from each other when they first meet but who find an abiding love together."

Amelia studied her. "And you are fond of such stories?"

"To be sure, my younger sister is more inclined to read romantic novels than I. She recommended this one and I liked it very well."

"Why? Because you believe in marrying for love?"

The governess drew near, disapproval in her eyes.

Patience had to be honest. "No. Because it is written well and it is clever. There is nothing salacious or immoral about it. The author is observant and has an ability to provide details about her characters that make them seem entirely real. I also like that the characters had to learn more of each other to truly fall in love." She paused, considering her own situation, then continued. "In addition, the heroine had four sisters, and none of them had much chance of wedding very well. They were comfortable and respectable, but not rich by any means, for the estate had been entailed away from her father. I could understand their circumstance well."

"Entailed away because he had five daughters but not a son," Amelia said.

"Exactly."

Amelia turned the first volume in her hands. "I wish often that I had a sister."

Patience smiled. "And so says the younger sister of the hero in this book. When the couple agree to wed, she then has a sister in the bride."

Amelia smiled just a little as her gaze lifted to Patience's own. "Then you will be my sister?"

"And you will be mine, and that is the most important detail between us. We need not be the same or agree on all matters."

"Save that Arthur is lovely," his loyal sister interjected and Patience laughed.

"He can be very charming, to be sure."

Amelia studied her. "You do believe in love, don't you, Patience?"

"While I can appreciate that love has its merit, I believe marriages should be based upon good sense rather than a fleeting attraction. Love that takes time to flower must be more vigorous than an immediate infatuation."

Visibly reassured, the younger girl gripped the book. "May I borrow this volume?"

"Of course. I hope you enjoy it."

"I shall read it first," the governess said crisply, liberating the book from the hand of her charge. "Then I too shall have your measure, Miss Carruthers."

Amelia and Patience exchanged a glance of complete understanding as the governess turned crisply away.

"I have all three volumes myself," Patience whispered. "You may borrow them from me if you keep them safe."

Amelia smiled at her, clearly delighted, then kissed her cheek. "I can see why Arthur chose you," she said, then at a call from her governess, spun away.

"You will not rout me," Prudence whispered from behind Patience. "I insist upon remaining your favorite sister."

Patience laughed. "We are three already. We can be four."

"True enough," Prudence agreed.

Patience watched Amelia leave the shop, deftly avoiding Miss Grosvenor and her friends. The girl had a composure far beyond her own. "I like her."

"You must if you mean to lend her your own books. You do not even surrender them to me."

"Because you keep them too long, then pretend they are your own and slip them onto your own book-shelves."

Prudence laughed, untroubled by her own avarice for books, and the sisters returned happily to their tasks. *The Lais of Marie de France*. Patience had not read them in a while and knew she did not have a copy of her own. She would take the copy from the lending library home with her, even if it was in French.

CHAPTER 8

Arthur slept late on the day of his wedding.

He thought to take only a short nap after another successful night at the tables, but instead, he slept deeply and Taylor had to bodily shake him awake.

It was raining buckets, which Taylor insisted was a sign of good fortune, though Arthur suspected it merely meant the entire party would be wet.

Being late agitated him beyond expectation and he spoiled four cravats before Taylor impatiently insisted upon doing it for him.

"I have more of a flair with a cravat than you," he complained as the valet deftly knotted this fifth one.

"Indeed, sir, the evidence of your prowess is all around us, flung upon the floor."

Arthur grinned at Taylor, who was almost his contemporary. "Is a man not allowed to be disconcerted on his wedding day?"

Taylor arched a brow, finishing the knot with a flourish. "I might consider, sir, that such concern could be a portent."

"Everything is not a portent," Arthur said with impatience.

"But when a man who is always calm and composed

has hands that shake in the morning, he either senses his own doom or has indulged overmuch."

"Attribute it to brandy, then, Taylor. I am utterly confident in this match." Despite his claim, Arthur dropped his cufflink. It scuttled under the bed and was unlikely to be retrieved in a timely fashion so he chose another pair.

This vexed him. He preferred the monogrammed silver ones with his sapphire pin.

Taylor gave his boots a last buff and fairly pushed him out the door. Everyone in the household seemed to be waiting upon him, though only one had comments to make upon his tardiness.

"Late, late, late," Lady Beckham said. "A bad sign for the future, to be sure."

"Tardiness is not a portent of doom!" Arthur protested. "I simply overslept."

Lady Beckham arched a brow and he knew that was not the best argument. "Even you know that a match to a tradesman's daughter is a poor choice, regardless of what you say of the matter…"

"But I like Miss Carruthers," Amelia protested, winning a smile from her brother.

"As do I," Arthur said with a surety that made Lady Beckham snort.

"That must explain why you spent the last week avoiding her as if she carried the plague," she said. "That must explain why you have been celebrating your final days as a bachelor as if you face your death this day." She fixed him with a look. "That must explain why you slept late as if dreading the planned event of this morning."

"I mean to become sober and sedate," Arthur insisted. If she knew the truth of his plan, he would be banished for certain. "One last hurrah hurts no one."

Lady Beckham chuckled. "Oh, I will enjoy that, to be

sure. You, sober and sedate." She laughed again. "Truly, Arthur, you do not have to wed the girl."

"But I wish to do as much."

"You do not even have to wed her to avoid the other one," she continued tartly, unshakable in her view. Arthur realized Amelia was watching him with some concern.

"Mother, I wish to wed Miss Carruthers," he said with authority, but the older woman simply shook her head.

"I give you credit for constancy, at least. Do not cry to me when you regret the bond you willingly made."

They rode to the church in silence, Arthur feigning fascination in the view outside the windows. He knew Lady Beckham was waiting for his capitulation, for he felt the weight of her gaze upon him.

But he was resolute. Perhaps that was what troubled Lady Beckham.

He realized that his palms were damp within his gloves and marveled at that. Like Taylor, he was accustomed to his own surety. He was not afraid to wed Miss Carruthers, for he liked her better than any young lady he had yet encountered.

Arthur realized with a start that what troubled him was his own concern. He had spent two decades not caring a whit for anything, taking advantage of all that was offered to him, savoring his good fortune and seeking more. He did not truly care if Lady Beckham cast him out, for he had experienced twenty years of unanticipated comfort, if not luxury. He kept his secrets and confided in no one, and gave every appearance of being a reckless and shallow fool.

But he liked Patience. He could not bear to think of losing her, even at this early juncture, and he feared that if and when Lady Beckham reached the limit of her tolerance, Patience might find him less interesting than once she had.

She was practical, after all.

Had the root of his allure been his fortune—or access to one—and not himself?

What a daunting notion!

But then, if there was one person in all of England who would so confound expectation, it was Miss Patience Carruthers.

The coach halted and a footman offered Lady Beckham a hand.

"Your jacket is stained," Amelia whispered once their mother had descended and Arthur checked his cuffs with concern. They were perfect, as he expected from Taylor, as was the front and the lapels—and Amelia laughed wickedly before she, too, stepped out of the coach.

"I made you check," she whispered and Arthur grinned, pretending to reach and ruffle her hair. She ducked from his hand, then darted back to his side. "You look wonderful," she said, kissed his cheek, then stepped out.

Arthur took a breath, adjusted the rose in his buttonhole, then seized his hat and stepped out of the coach. He nodded amiably to those gathered on the steps as he strode to the church, telling himself that he would win his bride's admiration, one way or the other.

Once inside, he discovered that his bride's family outnumbered his own, which was most curious. On his side of the church stood his mother, uncle and sister. On Patience's side, were two sisters and Baron Trevelaine, two young male cousins—undoubtedly those who would inherit the publishing business one day - an uncle and aunt, and the Duke of Haynesdale. Arthur was well aware of the Duke of Haynesdale's stern eye upon him, and recalled his own insistence that it was love that drove his choice. He nodded to the vicar who cleared his throat and pointedly checked his pocket watch, then turned with everyone as his bride entered the church with her father.

Arthur's breath caught. He knew Patience was pretty—his first compliment had not been an idle one—but on this day, she looked so lovely that a lump rose in his throat at her appearance. Her dress was silk and of the perfect shade of blue to make her eyes appear even more mysterious. She had done something different with her hair, for soft golden curls framed her face, making her appear more delicate and feminine than was her usual choice. She carried a nosegay of lily-of-the-valley, the scent filling the church, and wore a modest string of pearls.

He felt, looking upon her, that marriage was a far more sacred and special bond than he had considered before, and could not evade the sense that he stood on the cusp of something entirely new. It was humbling, and it was thrilling, and his heart thumped as she stepped to his side. He hoped she felt even slightly the same.

They began a new adventure together and he could not have imagined a more steadfast companion.

He smiled when she reached his side and Patience smiled back at him, her wondrous eyes lighting and her cheeks flushing as she looked up at him. It was a sight he would never tire of seeing and he offered his hand to her, feeling a tide of satisfaction when she put her hand in his.

Clearly, he was ready to make a change.

~

ONE GLIMPSE of Arthur standing before the parson and Patience's heart began to skip. She could not look away from him, his dark jacket making him look larger and broader, the waves of his hair as dark as midnight, his boots gleaming. When he turned, she was sure she could see the fierce blue of his eyes even at a distance and when he smiled, she blushed to her very toes. There was no one else in the chapel for her, no one save Arthur, though as she drew near, she could not help but notice that he looked tired. She would not heed the poisonous tales of Miss Grosvenor, not when she could lose herself in the intensity of his perusal.

He offered his hand and, heart in her throat, she placed hers upon his. She saw him catch his breath, she noted the quick glance he flicked her way, and she fairly felt his satisfaction. "Good morning, Miss Carruthers," he murmured, his voice sending a thrum through her. "Shall we wed?"

She smiled, not troubling to hide her delight. "Yes, Mr. Beckham, we shall."

His smile flashed, then they turned as one to the parson to join their lives together, for better or for worse.

PATIENCE CLOSED the door of her new room behind herself later that afternoon and took a breath. Though the day had been wondrous, she was unaccustomed to so much social activity. The solitude of her bedchamber was a welcome change, though the room was large enough to host a reception. Indeed, the space was so commodious that the silence seemed to echo. She stood for a moment and looked about herself, marvelling that this should be entirely her own.

Affluence was seductive, to be sure. She scarcely spotted a servant in this house, but every detail was attended in a timely manner. Perhaps there were other passages for the staff.

The wedding had been lovely, all the familiar words taking on a wealth of new meaning when she said them herself. Arthur had been solicitous, always at her side, his hand upon her elbow, his murmured commentary in her ear. She knew she did not imagine that he had ensured she was never left alone with his mother. His sister had been delighted and given her a hug, then had spent much of the wedding breakfast discussing fashion with Prudence. Lady Beckham had hosted a lovely breakfast at the house in Berkley Square and most guests had lingered, openly admiring the gracious home. Catherine and her husband had only attended the breakfast briefly as Catherine was tired. Catherine had pressed a letter into Patience's hand upon her departure, with a whispered "for tonight". It was addressed to Mr. and Mrs. Arthur Beckham.

Patience had stood in the doorway when Prudence and her father left, waving as the coach took them back to Carruthers House, feeling as if she had been left behind. She was well aware of Lady Beckham's disdain of her choice. It was Arthur whose hand landed on the back of her waist. He urged her back into the house, they made their farewells and he escorted her up the stairs.

Patience met her new maid there, a pretty girl named Gellis who had been in service in the Beckham household for some time. She had dark hair and dark eyes, as well as a lively smile, and Patience had liked her immediately. Arthur had left them alone and they had reviewed Patience's wardrobe in her new room. Gellis fussed with the fire and the lamps, then the girl had left.

It was late afternoon by the time Patience was alone.

Though the rain still drove against the windows, the room was warm and welcoming. The rugs were thick beneath her feet and a fire crackled on the hearth. The lamps glowed against the growing darkness, but the quiet only allowed all of Patience's doubts to gather and assail her.

There was no sign of Arthur and the door to his chamber was resolutely closed. Patience could not hear anyone else in the house—she might have been alone in an enormous palace—but when her gaze fell upon the boxes of her books, relief surged through her. Wentworth had seen to their delivery, of course, and she sighed once, telling herself that she should not miss home so soon as this.

There was nothing to say that the butler here was not as conscientious and efficient as Wentworth. She wondered if this house would ever feel like home, or if she would always feel like Lady Beckham's guest.

Was she as unwelcome a guest as she suspected?

Had she been mad to accept Arthur's offer? In this moment, she feared she had been. Though she had believed Arthur's promise when they made their agreement, his manner since had not been reassuring. Were the tales of his evening revels all true? If they were, how might such a man establish a reputable business? How might his promise be fulfilled? Every moment in this house, so much more lavish than the one she knew, added to her uncertainties. His mother did not like her. She was a guest in Lady Beckham's home, but there had been no mention of she and Arthur establishing their own household.

The heart of her concern was her fear that he had seen his goal achieved and hers would be forgotten. They were married, or at least had exchanged their vows, and he had not changed his habits a whit. To be sure, he was charming, but after their shopping excursion, he might have forgotten her very existence.

Had that only been to ensure that she gave a suitable appearance as his wife?

Doubt gnawed at Patience, growing as the minutes passed.

Her life had been her own, her choices hers to make within some restrictions, but now she had ceded authority to her husband and possibly his mother. What would be the expectation of her here? Would she be kept from working in her father's store? Would she be expected to become frivolous herself, a lady who only shopped and visited and left cards, or who rode in the park each morning? Patience could not bear the prospect.

And what of the night ahead? What would it be like? Would the consummation hurt? There was some intimation that it might. How much? Or would their union be as wondrous as hinted in many novels? Would she and Arthur find a magical accord like that acclaimed by poets, or would the consummation simply be a physical deed, completed without preamble or fuss?

She considered the note from Catherine but did not open it in Arthur's absence. It was addressed to both of them, after all. What was inside it? A page from the mysterious book? Patience hoped as much, with all her might.

And where was Arthur?

Patience paced the ample room. How she disliked any absence of information and detail! If only Catherine had surrendered the entire book of intimate advice! She felt in desperate need of instruction.

The boxes of her books had not been placed in the small adjacent chamber, but were beside the door to that room. Patience looked inside it to find that a new bookcase filled what had been the empty space. Her heart glowed that Arthur had remembered. Delighted, she went to examine it, running a hand over the beautifully finished wood, and admiring that there were glass-fronted doors to protect the books from dust.

"Does it meet your specifications?"

She spun to find the man in question watching her. Arthur leaned in the doorway, hands in the pockets of his breeches. His jacket had been discarded, the glint in his eyes making her feel warm. He might have been a cat for all his stealthy approach.

Patience's heart skipped a beat. "You surprised me."

"Was I not expected?"

"Of course! Are you responsible for this addition?"

"I thought you wished for one." He took a step closer and her uncertainties blossomed.

She spun to the bookcase again, avoiding Arthur's steady gaze as her heart leapt. "It is beautiful," she said, running a hand across it again. She saw that her hand trembled ever so slightly, and she told herself that she had no cause to fear him. "A fine piece of workmanship."

"It was not my plan to offer a deficient gift," he said, his tone teasing.

Patience caught her breath as he came to stand beside her and could have lost herself in the warm scent of him. The memory of his previous kisses brought heat to her cheeks. She granted him a sidelong glance, noting how imposing and utterly male he was.

Her husband.

Goodness.

"I hope the doors were a good addition," he said. The room seemed very small with Arthur so close beside her and curiously lacking in air. "They were my suggestion to the cabinetmaker."

"They are perfect." Patience caught her breath. "Books, as I am certain you know, are adversely affected by exposure to humidity or bright light, due to the lack of stability of the paper. A book protected from both light and dust will retain its original condition for a considerable period of time…" Her words faltered as she realized what she was doing. She risked another glance toward Arthur to find him smiling, just a little.

"Am I so fearful as that?" He leaned closer, his gaze locked upon her and his eyes dark. Once she met his gaze, she felt snared and could not look away.

Patience swallowed, aware that he watched her closely. "I merely meant to show my appreciation for the addition of the doors. Few would have considered them, given the expense," she managed to say.

Arthur turned to consider the bookcase himself, leaving her simultaneously relieved to have his attention diverted and missing his perusal.

The man confused her beyond all expectation! She watched him through her lashes, hating that she was essentially his possession now, and desperate for some reassurance that all would be well.

"And what is the merit of having funds if one does not acquire what one desires?" Arthur did not seem to expect a reply, which was fortuitous. His hand landed on the back of her waist, a possessive weight that sent a thrill through her—and struck her dumb. His thumb moved against her spine in a slow caress that Patience felt keenly even through all the layers of her clothing. She stared at the bookcase without seeing it and swallowed.

The man would think she was a fool.

Indeed, she felt like one. There was not a thought left in her head. Her entire being was focussed upon the slow motion of his thumb, of the waves of pleasure emanating from that spot, of the sense that time stopped and would remain thus until he chose otherwise. In a way, it was terrifying to feel herself so close to losing command of herself, to surrendering to sensation.

But that was the effect Arthur Beckham had upon

her. She supposed she should become accustomed to it, even learn to trust it. The notion was startling.

"Thank you," she managed to say. "It is a delightful surprise."

"Is it such a surprise that I would see my bride pleased?" Arthur said softly and she shook her head. "I never thought to silence you with a bookcase," he teased. "What should be the result if I gave you a library?"

She felt herself flush. "I am pleased, sir…"

"Arthur," he corrected gently.

"And perhaps overwhelmed by such generosity."

"Is that it?" he whispered, then urged her closer as if he guessed otherwise. "Might a kiss be in order on this day?" he asked and she heard a challenge in his tone.

"Yes. Of course!" A wife should kiss her husband. She should kiss Arthur. She wanted to kiss Arthur.

But Patience could not initiate the embrace. Once again, she felt an unwieldy mix of emotion, anticipation and uncertainty churning together so that she could do nothing but wait.

Arthur turned her to face him, his hands fitting around her waist. She held her breath as he bent down, then his mouth closed over her own with ease. His kiss was sweet and gentle, much like the first one he had bestowed upon her in the carriage, the one that had haunted her dreams in the nights since. He did not demand but seemed to cajole her to join him.

Patience chose to surrender to his invitation. She eased a little closer to him, well aware of his heat and stillness, then stretched to her toes to lean against him. Arthur made a little growl of satisfaction and angled his head to deepen his kiss.

Goodness. She found she could only close her eyes and enjoy, her hands clutching his shirt. She had never felt such warm and welcome pleasure. His kiss was enticing and seductive. She felt as if something warm unfolded within her, something that promised far more than even this. She dared to place her hands upon Arthur's shoulders and lean against him, tilting her own head that she might kiss him back. She opened her mouth to him and sighed at the perfect caress of his tongue, the way his broad palm slid up her back, the heat of his fingers at her nape.

Oh.

He broke their kiss and looked down at her with a satisfaction that pleased her mightily. "Good afternoon, Mrs. Beckham," he said with a smile, his eyes glowing, and she laughed despite herself.

"Good afternoon, Mr. Beckham." Their words reminded her of Catherine's missive but before she could speak, Arthur raised his hands to remove the pins from her hair with purpose.

"I have wanted to do this since we first met," he confessed, his eyes dark and his voice low. Patience did not know what to say. "The prospect of you in disarray has haunted my dreams," he said, further astonishing her. "Patience, the siren of my visions, hair unbound, a beguiling flush upon her cheeks. Temptation personified."

Was he teasing her? Patience had never thought to haunt the dreams of any man, but Arthur was so solemn that she was tempted to believe him. "Me?" she whispered and he chuckled.

"You. Lovely, clever Patience." He stole a kiss and murmured against her throat. "I yearn to see how far this blush extends," he confessed, his fingertip sliding along the neck of her bodice.

Oh! His touch lit a line of fire that melted her knees and ignited a heat in her belly that was new and wonderful. His hand slid lower, his palm cupping her breast through her dress and Patience could not take a breath. She looked up and he captured her mouth beneath his own again, the sweet urgency of his embrace leaving her dizzy.

He whispered her name when he broke his kiss, cleared his throat and returned his attention to the task of unfastening her hair. Her mouth was dry, her heart racing. He was close, so very close. She took the opportunity to study him, to note the thickness of his dark lashes, to wonder at his thoughts. In this moment, Patience was keenly aware of the differences between them. His caress made her feel treasured and protected, even while the brush of his fingertips aroused her, a combination so alluring that she could not summon a word to her lips. When his gaze flicked to meet hers and he winked quickly, her heart jumped. She lowered her gaze to the sapphire pinned to his cravat as his hands moved through her hair. She felt unbound, unfastened, revealed, and uncertain. She trembled, wanting something she could not name.

Was it possible to err in this endeavor?

The pins from her hair landed upon the desk behind her as Arthur discarded them. She felt her hair fall to her shoulders, then his fingers slid into its length with possessive ease.

"Like honey," he whispered with a surprising reverence. He lifted the weight of her hair aside, kissing her slowly beneath her ear. She felt the quick flick of his tongue, the graze of his teeth upon her earlobe, and was certain her heart would burst when it beat so fast.

She heard herself whisper his name, her voice trembling.

"Shall we commence the hunt?" he whispered in her ear, his fingertips sliding down her back. His other hand rose to her breast, his thumb sliding across the nipple so firmly that she gasped aloud. Patience felt both hot and shivery, filled with a desperation to know more.

"The hunt?" she echoed.

Arthur smiled. He bent and nuzzled her beneath her ear, sliding his teeth across her earlobe before kissing it. Patience caught her breath, then shivered at the murmur of his words so close in her ear. "For your bewitching spot, of course," he whispered, a thread of humor in his tone.

Patience might have laughed under normal circumstance, but this was too overwhelming. "I wager you know where to seek it," she whispered and felt the breath of his laughter.

"I do." He cupped her face in his hands, smiling as he backed her into the small desk. His hips were pressed against hers, his chest almost against her breasts, a proximity that sent fire through her veins. His leg eased between hers, a move that felt outrageously intimate even though they were both fully dressed. She caught her breath at the feel of his thigh between her own, so firm and powerful. His gaze was unswerving and so hot that her mouth went dry.

Patience could not take a full breath. She hated the sudden awareness that she was no more in command of herself or her situation than a leaf blown in the wind.

Could he desire her this much? She wanted to believe his response was honest, but feared it might not be. Perhaps he could burn for a great beauty, or a rich heiress, but not for plain Patience whose price was the publication of books with his fortune.

Once she surrendered to him and this deed, she might be consumed so completely that she might as well cease to exist. There would be only her husband's expectations and demands, her duty to deliver a son, and his wishes, whatever they might be. She feared that she stood on the cusp of losing herself forever and despite the temptation, Patience could not bear that truth.

She spun away from Arthur and retreated a few

steps, desperately needing to gather her thoughts. He watched her avidly, as if she were one of the fascinating beauties of the *ton*, and that only bolstered her sense that his fascination was feigned. No man had ever looked at her as if she held the key to every hoard of treasure known to mankind.

Certainly, no man of the ilk of Arthur Beckham had ever done as much.

"What is amiss?" he asked, leaning against the desk to watch her. His confidence, as ever, was disconcerting, and she found her words spilling forth.

"Catherine gave me a missive, addressed to the both of us," she said, knowing she sounded prim and practical but unable to help herself. "It seems a good moment to savor her good wishes for our match." The very practicality of her own suggestion helped her to regain her usual composure.

"Does it?" His tone was calm, but his eyes had narrowed slightly. "I should have thought such felicitations could wait a little while."

"Surely there is time." She knew she sounded breathless when she replied.

"Surely there is a more pressing demand."

"What might that be?" Her voice fairly squeaked.

"It is our wedding day, Patience." The way he said her name made her heart thrum in a most irrational way. "We will celebrate our union. *That* is our course for the immediate future." His lashes swept down as he surveyed her. When he met her gaze, his own filled with hunger, she nearly jumped. "It might take some time." He smiled a little, clearly anticipating that endeavor.

Patience caught her breath and averted her gaze. "I was thinking of the book," she lied. She thought of no such thing. She thought of Arthur's lips upon her earlobe and the resulting sense that she stood on the lip of an abyss, that she could tumble into sensation and be lost forever.

It was utterly unlike her, a temptation to madness, a sure sign that she lost command of herself already.

"The book?" he echoed. She realized he was very still and her heart fluttered.

"The one we will publish, of course. The book at the root of our entire arrangement!"

"Ah yes, the book."

"Catherine might have surrendered a part of it, to offer advice for this night."

Arthur chuckled, his expression was so wicked that Patience caught her breath. "I assure you that I have no need of advice upon matters of intimacy. I guarantee that I shall see you satisfied." He beckoned to her with one finger, his surety proving his experience to be more complete than her own. She felt she was invited by the devil himself to partake of some forbidden pleasure, and was more tempted than she had ever been before. "Come and find out, my lady."

Patience forced herself to be resolute. Such revels could wait, if indeed he meant to keep his pledge. She needed an assurance before she surrendered, a gesture of good faith, a proof of his commitment to their shared future.

Arthur waited, those eyes gleaming. "Tell me, Patience," he invited, his gaze so fixed upon her that he might read the very truth in her eyes. Patience felt her lips part. She knew she clutched a fistful of her dress. She could not look away from him.

And yet, she had to be sure.

"I must open the missive first."

He gestured for her to do as much, so watchful that she felt she entertained a powerful predator. A great cat lounged in her chamber, perhaps, prepared to pounce upon her and claim what he believed to be his due.

Her hands shook as she opened the missive. Catherine had written out what had to be part of the volume she had in her possession. Patience read it, then cleared her throat and straightened. "Here. You see? I should demand a secret of you," she said, then read the passage aloud before Arthur could respond.

PATIENCE COULD NOT REALIZE how very alluring she was. Arthur had never seen a lady so lovely. Her unbound hair cascaded over her shoulders and gleamed in the light of the fire. It was the hue of honey, filled with lights of gold, and so lustrous that he wanted to bury his hands in it. Her lips were ruddy and the neckline of her dress slightly askew, the sight of her neck and shoulder reminding him of the sweet taste of her skin. He had felt her shiver at his touch and easily recalled the feel of her nipple tightening to a bud beneath his hand. He had sensed her capitulation and yearned for it.

Her trepidation, however, could not be mistaken. He was certain the reading of the missive was a delay. What did she fear? Him? Pleasure? He did not know but he wanted to defend her more than he had desired anything.

He was so snared in his admiration that he did not immediately understand her words.

"Upon the matter of secrets..." Patience read. *"No deed creates a stronger bond between lovers than the confession of a secret. A secret is often, by its very nature, a matter of tremendous personal importance, so the sharing of it with any other being implies a profound trust. The secret once revealed also creates a bond between confessor and recipient, one that is not readily compromised. Thus, I can only encourage any lady reading this volume to consider the possi-*

bility of her beloved having a secret, and thence to contrive to learn it. This is not, it must be noted, in order to use this secret as a threat, for that would be a breach of the entire marvel of love, but instead to gain greater understanding of the hidden depths of the lover's nature. We each have details of ourselves, dreams and visions, history and secrets, that we surrender to few others, if any at all—to become the custodian of another's secret is the sweetest burden of all." She lowered the missive, her gaze rising to his. "I would have a secret of you, sir, before we proceed."

She might have been a sphinx demanding the answer to a riddle at a crossroads. Her gaze was steady, her eyes darker than was typical. She stood straight and did not blink, challenging him to offer what she desired.

"A secret?" Arthur echoed.

"You confessed earlier that you had many of them."

"Several, to be sure, but that is not many."

"Then offer me one, as a sign of good faith."

The very prospect filled Arthur with agitation. "I see no reason to burden you thus, Patience."

"Save that I have asked you to. You did promise to share your secrets with me, which is why we wed. I ask for only one on this night, before our match is consummated and our joined future sealed."

But the last thing Arthur wished to do was surrender a secret. He was not in the habit of confiding in anyone, and he knew that until their match was consummated, their shared future was not guaranteed. "In the morning," he countered, but Patience shook her head.

"No," she said with resolve. "It must be now, and it must be a secret shared with no one else. You must show me that you desire this match, and you must do it with a deed instead of a word, since words come so readily to you."

"You ask a great deal, Patience, and for what cause? Are you afraid to keep your pledge to me?" He kept his tone light but she did not smile.

"What I fear is that you think this marriage is a diversion and a game, another wager that may or may not yield the results you desire. We have an agreement that I fear you mean to break."

"Patience! We are agreed that we will publish books, or one book in particular."

"And yet I see no indication that you intend to adhere to that agreement." She lifted her chin, her eyes blazing in challenge, and clearly had no notion of how enticing she was. It was all Arthur could do to hold his ground instead of kissing her senseless.

She would despise him if he overwhelmed her objections by touch. He understood as much instinctively. Whatever his inclinations, he had to regain her alliance with logic.

"What indication should there be?" he asked. "We have only just exchanged our vows."

"I would have hoped you might have changed your habits."

"Why should I do as much?"

"Because your habits are wasteful." Patience spoke with resolve. "To drink and gamble and cast money at every indulgence is wasteful. You have so many resources, and instead of using them for some good purpose, you seek only your own pleasure. You think solely of your own comfort and entertainment, when there is so much that could be achieved."

Arthur knew he should tell her of the funds he had collected, but he could not. The confession stuck in his throat. He had never confided in anyone in his life for fear of betrayal. He knew he should trust Patience, but in his heart, he feared the result. Change could not be accomplished so quickly as that.

After all, it sounded as if his situation was perilous. What would she do?

It did not help that he was aroused and addled, that he wanted only to kiss her again and ensure her satisfaction, then gain his own.

Patience strode away from him when he did not reply, doubtless having no inkling of how tempting he found the sight of her nape, her loosened hair, the curve of her ankles. She could have been a siren sent to guarantee he lost this debate, for his thoughts were filled with the memory of her hair in his hands.

And desire for more.

Did he dare to surrender a secret? Which one? That he was not who he claimed to be? That his life was a deceit from one end to the other? That Lady Beckham might withdraw every penny from his reach that was derived from her income and holdings? Arthur found he did not—for without the funds to publish her book, Patience might find him an unsatisfactory spouse.

It was a poor moment to realize that he was falling in love with his clever wife.

It was a worse moment to realize he would do almost anything to keep her by his side.

A secret. How unfortunate that every one of his secrets had the potential to turn her against him forever. He was snared between bad choices.

Dame Fortune, it seemed, had abandoned him at the worst possible moment.

CHAPTER 9

"You ask for proof of my intention, Patience, but I might ask for your trust."

She flung out her hands. "But you cannot continue to live without a care for anything beyond your own entertainment! A man of enterprise needs to be sober and prudent. He cannot gamble. He cannot cavort all the night long when there is a business to be run in the morning!"

"I do not *cavort*," Arthur said tightly, but she dismissed this argument with a wave of one hand.

"You gamble, sir. You dance and you drink and you wager and you duel, and –" she made the most alluring sound of frustration, distracting Arthur from the argument at hand "– and I do not even *know* half the pastimes you undertake. I know only that you should abandon them all."

That he was found lacking when she had no notion of his plans, annoyed Arthur as little else could have done. He had long understood the risk in divulging a secret to others, and the fact that Patience judged him and found him guilty before she asked after an explanation did not encourage him to change. "You should have wed a bookkeeper," he said tightly.

"I thought you were a man of good sense. I thought you would strive to better understand the business you mean to enter."

Arthur's temper, though seldom roused, flared.

"Why?" he demanded of her, hearing his voice rise. "When I order the roofs to be rethatched on the tenants' houses on my mother's estate, I do not have to know how to thatch a roof myself. I do not have to judge the thatch or its thickness or compare the price of labor from this town to that. I decree that it shall be done and people who know how to ensure that a good job is done see the task completed, then I pay the cost on her behalf. Why should this venture be any different?"

Patience, to her credit, did not retreat but folded her arms across her chest, looking as stubborn as Arthur felt.

To his dismay, tears gathered in her beautiful eyes. He took a step toward her, but she abruptly turned away.

She took a breath. "I warn you, sir, that I cannot remain with a man whose word cannot be trusted."

There was a moment of complete silence. If ever Arthur had wished to lay the truth bare to another, this was that moment. He would have liked nothing better than to have surrendered the entirety of his truth to Patience, but he feared that the revelation would only make matters worse.

First, it would prove that he had deceived not only her, but all of London.

And second, it would prove that he did not have the funds for her venture.

"Do you mean to leave?" he asked in a whisper, hearing his own fear in his tone.

She tossed her hair and met his gaze, her own eyes

filled with tears so that he felt like a cur. "A secret, Arthur. Just one."

He stared at her, wanting honesty between them, wanting her to desire him for his own sake. But no one had ever desired Arthur for his own sake, and he could not believe that this sensible and pragmatic woman would either.

His characteristic charm abandoned him, just as he feared his new wife might do.

There was an irony, to be sure, in the fact that one woman in all of England found him lacking, and she was the sole one he desired. Worst of all, there was nothing he could say to change her view.

Save surrender a secret that would drive her away.

There was only silence between them, a silence that yawned with a thousand unwelcome prospects to Arthur, a silence interrupted by the patter of rain against the windows. He found it a chilling sound.

He turned and went to the window, purportedly looking into the street, wondering how he might gain her good view again. He feared there was no victory to be had in this chamber on this night.

If he left, he might make some progress on her goal and thus regain her favor. It was a slim chance, but the sole one he had.

"I will leave you then, to the unpacking of your books," Arthur said, his voice more terse than he would have preferred. "I will put my time to better use than engaging in an argument that cannot be won."

"Doubtless there is a game of cards awaiting your attendance," she said, her tone tart.

Little did she know that such a venture might aid their own.

"Perhaps I will find one." He turned and strode to the door to his own chamber, wondering if his own trust was misplaced. His winnings were hidden in her chamber, but he could not retrieve them now without making matters worse

"I have placed some of my own books on your shelf," he said on the threshold to his chamber, as if that might keep her from looking within them. "Perhaps that will not inconvenience you overmuch." He glanced back to find her lips set and her eyes full of tears. He might have returned to her side, but she abruptly turned her back to him.

"Good night, sir," she said tightly, dismissing him, her very manner sparking his ire anew.

Sir. He was *sir* again. The very sound of that word sent fury through his veins. Arthur marched through his chamber, seizing his hat and gloves, claiming his greatcoat. He shouted for the carriage to be brought around and slammed the door as he headed to the stairs. He was frustrated and angry as he seldom was, his mood black, and he knew that at least half of the blame was his alone.

Why had he not confided in Patience?

How did she not realize how much she asked of him?

He was striding toward the waiting carriage, seeking a destination, when a thought occurred to him. Had Patience deliberately provoked their disagreement? She had responded to his kiss in a most promising way, then had become fearful.

Why?

Arthur looked up at her window, sensing that she had seized upon a point of dissent—and that any item of disagreement would do. It was a sobering notion to have a wife afraid of one's touch.

He must proceed with care. The first task before him was to bring proof of his good intentions. How did one establish a publishing firm? He would ask his solicitor, a competent man of business, for advice. The hour was not so late as that and that man would yet be in his offices. Arthur gave the direction to Morris, then settled back, discontent with his own progress.

Perhaps he would discover a secret to surrender on the way, or choose from his collection.

Perhaps Dame Fortune could be tempted to smile upon him once more.

Arthur could only hope.

As soon as Arthur was gone, Patience feared she had not been fair. What had she done?

She heard his boots on the stairs, his haste to be gone more than clear, then the sound of the front door opening and closing.

The house was silent then, as if all within it held their breath and Patience realized she was holding her own. She released hers slowly, hating that she had been such a coward. Arthur had been gentle with her and patient, but she had let her fears claim command. She had challenged him and provoked him, and now she was alone.

It was her own fault.

To be sure, she was concerned about his wasteful habits, but if he did not even speak to her, she could not effect a change. If she was a demanding shrew, he might have cause to abandon their agreement. She eyed the page and read it again. What was her secret? If Arthur had asked her for such a confession, what would she have admitted?

That she feared he would tire of her once his conquest was gained.

That she found him intriguing beyond all other men.

That she feared she might come to love him.

Patience sighed at the resonance of truth. What then? She feared she was a means to an end for Arthur, that she had surrendered all and might end up with naught. On this night, her solitude was her own fault. In this moment, it seemed all was lost. The rain slanted against the windows with renewed vigor, as seemingly even the elements echoed her new husband's displeasure.

She had provoked him for no good cause, creating trouble for its own sake, and as she rested her forehead against the cold window pane, Patience knew why.

Fear.

In her heart, she believed Arthur would keep their agreement. She had been unreasonable, which was not like her, because of her fear. She had started a fight to avoid the obligation of her wedding night.

But how could anyone trust that tide of sensation, let alone abandon themselves to it? To abandon one's restraint and be carried away by desire was so seductive that it had to be dangerous. She feared to lose command of herself not only in that moment, but forever, to cede all to Arthur for all time. The very fact that such yearning rose in a torrent, as if to overwhelm any objections, meant it had to be untrustworthy.

Did it not?

She recalled Arthur's kiss and that heat filled her once again. His touch made her yearn to surrender everything to him, perhaps in exchange for nothing, and abandon her practicality for his satisfaction—however fleeting it might prove to be. How could one man, however handsome and charming he might be, have gained such power over her in such a short time?

How could he not have even tried to change his ways, just a little?

Patience watched the rain, and decided the issue

was not Arthur, *per se*. She was simply overcome by a new experience. By the descriptions in novels, this was not an uncommon occurrence. Others had lost themselves in a haze of pleasure before. Was it possible that she might become accustomed to it?

So many experiences were wondrous the first time and less so the second. Would Arthur's kiss ever become routine? Patience could not imagine as much.

All the same, she would welcome the opportunity to know for certain.

In fact, she felt a measure of dissatisfaction, as if something had been left unfinished. She did desire more of whatever Arthur offered, and she knew in her heart, that it was not simply knowledge she craved.

Yet she feared to err again. One detail was for certain, she had need of that book. If ever there had been a woman in need of intimate advice, it was Patience, for she had dissuaded the most notorious rake in London from consummating his nuptials.

She smoothed out the page that she had been granted and read it again, wishing for more of that volume's advice as well as her husband's sweet caress. On this night, she would be without both, but Patience would collect the book from Catherine in the morning.

ARTHUR FOUND his solicitor on the verge of locking up his office. Mr. Sommerset welcomed him inside with a gesture and Arthur was quick to state his business.

"I have only a query for you, Mr. Sommerset," he said. "I do not mean to delay you."

"It is no matter." That man smiled. "I am always prepared to be of service to the Beckham family. Please, sit down."

"My wife has raised a question and I find I do not know the answer."

"Oh, yes, you wed today, did you not? May I offer my congratulations, Mr. Beckham?"

Arthur smiled. "I thank you."

"And the lady's question?"

"Do you have any knowledge of printers and publishers, Mr. Sommerset?"

That man's brows rose. "Strange that you should ask, sir. Are you seeking an investment?"

"I am. My wife would like to learn more of the possibility of establishing a publishing firm catering to the tastes of ladies."

"Carruthers," Mr. Sommerset mused, clearly recalling Patience's name. "Of course. But would that not compete with the trade of her father and uncle?"

"She feels strongly about the appeal of several titles, but her father and uncle disagree. They have declined to publish the works in question, but I trust her judgement and would see the endeavor launched."

The solicitor smiled. "She is reputed to be a clever lady."

"And she is one indeed." Arthur smiled. "I sense that you have a solution to share."

Mr. Sommerset chuckled, then sobered. "You read my thoughts, as ever, Mr. Beckham. I am currently resolving the estate of Henry Parke."

"Of Fanshawe & Parke?" Arthur guessed, recognizing the name of one partner of that publishing firm.

"The very same. He has no son or relation interested in entering his trade. His partner, John Fanshawe, wishes very much to continue the business, but has need of additional funds if not an active partner. We have been discussing the prospect of selling half of the business, if a suitable buyer could be found."

"I should like very much to discuss this possibility

with Mr. Fanshawe." And with Patience. She would know the reputation of the firm.

Mr. Sommerset shook his head. "I must warn you that it would be a cash transaction, sir, for the assets of the company are heavily mortgaged. They had recently acquired new equipment and the investment is not yet paid. I would not dissuade you, but you should understand the magnitude of the expectation for a new partner." The solicitor named a sum that would take the majority of the funds Arthur had hidden in the box in Patience's room.

He did not reveal his surprise but nodded his interest.

"I should also warn you that Mr. Fanshawe has the notion of a silent partner," Mr. Sommerset continued. "I cannot ensure that he will be more welcoming of your wife's notion than that lady's father and uncle have been."

"I should like to have the opportunity to find out," Arthur said. "Perhaps it might be possible to arrange a meeting with Mr. Fanshawe in the near future."

"I can offer you better than that, Mr. Beckham. I am to dine with Mr. Fanshawe this very evening, and I am certain he would be delighted to learn of your interest. Do accompany me and be introduced, at the very least."

Arthur sensed the turn of the wheel and the return of his good fortune. Given the stakes, he could not possibly decline this opportunity.

AVOIDING the memory of Arthur's seductive touch, Patience opened the first box of her books. She smiled as if she greeted old friends and lifted out the first volume with real pleasure. The task of unpacking the books soothed her and she peeked within several of them, reading a few lines of familiar prose, and feeling her usual calm manner return.

Soon she realized that she was no longer alone. An enormous grey cat had somehow found its way into her room. It sat between her and the fire, its long fur a thousand shades of silver and grey, its gaze fixed upon her. As she watched, it flicked its tail, wrapping it elegantly around its own paws. Those green eyes glowed as it considered her and Patience smiled.

"Good afternoon," she said and curtsied, for the creature's manners were so regal that such a gesture seemed deserved. "Though I do not as yet know your name, you are welcome to stay."

The cat yawned mightily, displaying a collection of sharp teeth and a very pink tongue. Then it bounded onto the armchair before the fire, trod down the cushion with its paws and curled up to sleep with one last flick of its tail.

Patience watched, then returned to her beloved books. The space inside the bookcase was much bigger with the doors open than she had realized.

He was routinely thoughtful and instead of appreciating his generous nature, she had demanded more. She owed him an apology, to be sure.

As Arthur had warned, the bookcase was not entirely empty. She had not seen his books with the doors closed. There were a dozen or so books already on the bottom shelf. Curious about his tastes, she lifted them out. Plato's *Republic*, a book she suspected he had read at a tutor's behest. Ovid's *Metamorphoses*, a curious choice but one that reminded her of his sister's favorite work. Perhaps the siblings shared an interest in beings who could change shape—or in tales of romance.

The Rime of the Ancient Mariner. Waverley, The Canterbury Tales. She smiled, guessing these might have been her father's recommendations. There was a bookmark in the first, a sign that he had tried to follow her father's injunction and one that made her heart squeeze.

There was a volume of Greek plays by Euripides, along with Shakespeare's *Comedy of Errors* and *Twelfth Night*. She could not say who might have chosen those volumes. She looked at the Greek volume with interest. Her Greek was not as strong as it might have been, and this could offer good practice. Perhaps Arthur would advise her. She liked that idea very much.

Indeed, she could envision them together before the fire, each absorbed in his or her own choice, comparing impressions at intervals or sharing passages with each other. He would speak clearly when he read aloud and she smiled at the prospect of such an evening together.

Were they all plays about mistaken identities? Surely, she imagined that.

The Decameron in Italian. She knew that was a collection of tales told by wealthy friends who exiled themselves from Florence to avoid the plague. There was a work by Dante as well. It made sense that he read some Italian as they had been in Venice.

Faust: A Tragedy in a volume that included both German and English. Her father had spoken of Goethe's play, and about the character who made a bargain with a demon.

There was another book, one with a title that could not be easily read. A thick volume. Patience removed it, admired the tooled leather cover, then opened the volume in search of a title. To her surprise, it was not in fact a book, but a box constructed to look like a book.

And it was filled with banknotes.

They were neatly bundled and there was a tally on the top, the total sum making her eyes widen. Where had these funds come from? Why were they hidden? They had to belong to Arthur, but why would he have banknotes? She knew that the affluent relied upon credit and paid their bills later instead of immediately.

Perhaps they were his winnings from gambling. If so, he was luckier than she had imagined. She replaced the notes and the volume, nudging the other books more closely around it. Now that she knew the volume's contents, its hiding place no longer seemed ideal. Anyone might look at the books, realize the title of this one was difficult to read, and guess the truth.

She began to unpack her books, mixing them with Arthur's so that the book-that-was-not-a-book was less easily noticed. So much money!

Why had he left it in her room? Because she would have more books?

Because he trusted her? The possibility made her heart glow, then she frowned. She wished he returned home soon so she could apologize and they could reconcile.

She took note of the time and rang for Gellis, assuming the Beckhams dined at eight. The girl arrived promptly, her cheerful manner of earlier in the day somewhat diminished when Patience requested assistance in dressing for dinner.

"She did not send you word, then, ma'am?"

"Who might send me word of what, Gellis?"

"Her ladyship will not dine downstairs this night." The girl caught her breath. "She often has a tray in her rooms when there have been other events in the day."

Patience guessed that this was not entirely true by the girl's discomfiture. "And Amelia?"

"Dines in the nursery as yet, with her governess, ma'am."

"Then there will be no dinner laid?"

"There will be, ma'am, if you choose to dine downstairs, but if Mr. Beckham does not return, you would be dining alone."

Patience eyed the clock, disliking that prospect.

"When he means to dine at home, ma'am, he is always here by seven."

It was seven thirty.

She was to dine alone or have a tray in her room on her wedding night. Patience was not a demanding individual, but that seemed a little odd to her.

"You must not mind her, ma'am," Gellis said, clearly sharing her view. "Her ladyship does not like when Mr. Beckham dines at his club, though she never tells him as much. She changed her mind about dinner when he left." The maid smiled. "Shall I bring you a tray?"

"I suppose you had best do as much," Patience said, forcing a smile and Gellis left upon her errant. The situation was not the maid's fault and there was no cause to be unkind.

Patience refused to feel sorry for herself. She had her books and a fire on the hearth. There were plenty in this city with less advantage on any given night.

In that moment, when her spirits were low, Patience felt the weight of another gaze upon her. She knew without turning that it was not the sleeping cat, and glanced over her shoulder to find Arthur's younger sister peeking around the door to the corridor. How had the girl opened the door so silently? It was clear there were feats Patience had to learn in this house. She smiled a welcome and Amelia came into the room. Her hair was brushed out and in a long plait already, and she wore a plainer dress than she had worn at the wedding.

A black cat wound around Amelia's legs and slipped into the room at the same time. Its hair was as dark as midnight and shorter than that of the one that still slept by the fire, as well as glossy with good health. It had one white paw and its eyes were yellow when it turned to survey Patience.

It jumped onto the other chair before the fire and curled up to sleep, the mirror image of the first one.

"Now you've met both of Arthur's cats," Amelia said, coming to stand beside Patience. She angled her head to read the titles on the books, such a sure sign of an avid reader that Patience smiled.

She also found herself taking a step to be between Amelia and the bookcase, the better that she might not glimpse the book with a secret.

"Are they the pair brought home from Venice?" she asked, diverting the girl's attention.

Amelia nodded. "Tar and Feathers."

"Maybe we should translate their names to Italian, given that they came from Venice," Patience suggested and her companion's eyes lit at the very idea.

"*Catrame e Piume*," she mused.

Patience nodded. "Much better."

"I agree. We will call them that and confound Arthur." The younger girl smiled at the prospect, then eyed the bookcase. "I told Arthur you could not possibly have enough books to fill it, but it looks as if you might."

"There will be a little space left, I believe."

"You said I might borrow that second volume from you," the girl reminded her shyly. "I have finished the first but Carruthers & Carruthers will not be open until Monday."

If there was one thing Patience could understand, it was the need to finish a story once begun. She retrieved the volume and handed it to Amelia, who smiled and retreated, leaving Patience alone with the two dozing cats. She placed the last of her books upon the shelves, then impulsively chose the third volume of the novel she had just loaned to Amelia.

～

ARTHUR MIGHT HAVE THOUGHT his errand done for the night after his discussion with Mr. Fanshawe, which had concluded well for the moment. He felt there was promise in an association there, but the funds might provide the difficulty. He considered his choices and went to his club rather than returning home. He had already missed dinner, for Lady Beckham was utterly inflexible about her schedule and he knew she would not have waited the meal for him. He would dine at his club, then return to the house.

Once at the club, he was invited to a game. He declined, but learned that the Earl of Queenston had arrived in town and would be playing. That man lost more routinely than Arthur's uncle, so he sensed that once again, opportunity knocked.

And he was right.

The cards could not have been more in Arthur's favor. Indeed, he had only to think of what card he needed to win, and it came to his hand. He knew better than to ignore such a flight of luck. He played all evening and into the night, then into the following morning, his purse becoming fatter by the moment. Others left the table, their funds exhausted for the moment, until the last game was played, just before the dawn. He had just picked up his cards when he smelled a lady's sweet perfume in close proximity.

He did not so much as glance her way. He fixed his attention on the cards, on his opponent, on what had appeared and what had not. The lady did not speak, but watched the play in silence. Arthur took a calculated risk, won, and gathered his winnings before he saw that it was Miss Esmeralda Ballantyne who stood by his side. She wore a gown the color of claret wine, which seemed to make her eyes appear more vibrantly green.

"I do not mean to interrupt your pleasure, Mr.

Beckham," she said softly when he turned from the table to bow to her.

"And you do not, Miss Ballantyne. It was my intention to leave the table now."

"You depart triumphant, by appearances."

"I do." He smiled. "I find the acquaintance of my lady wife has brought me good fortune."

Her gaze became assessing. "And yet, I had understood that yesterday was your wedding day. How is it fortuitous to fail to share your bride's companionship on your nuptial night?"

Arthur felt the back of his neck heat and he was keenly aware of the courtesan's scrutiny. He should have been home and he knew it, but his absence would bring about the endeavor Patience desired. Was there a right answer?

Miss Ballantyne chuckled as if she understood his plight. She averted her gaze, surveying the other occupants of the club with a smile. "It is an honor to have the opportunity to introduce someone to intimate pleasures," she purred and Arthur felt his discomfiture grow.

"If you say as much. I would not know." Arthur strove to change the subject. "Would you care for a glass of wine, Miss Ballantyne?" he asked, indicating a servant who carried a tray.

"No, I thank you. I did not come for entertainment or sustenance."

"Why else does one come to a gaming hell, Miss Ballantyne?"

She smiled. "I seek a man who shares a common trait with you, Mr. Beckham. He also seems unaware of where he should be on this night." Her tone hardened a little at that confession but before Arthur could decide how to reply, he heard her quick intake of breath.

The Duke of Haynesdale appeared from another

room, leaning on his cane far less than Arthur recalled was his custom. Indeed, he looked as formidable as he had in years past, though something clearly had annoyed him. His dark brows were drawn together and he cast a glare across the room. He froze when his gaze fell upon Arthur and Miss Ballantyne, and Arthur feared there might be repercussions from this short conversation. Miss Ballantyne held the duke's gaze proudly, as if she would challenge him to speak his mind. Truly, lightning might have crackled between the pair, so avidly were they aware of each other, and whatever annoyance had been in the duke's expression melted away.

"If you will excuse me, Mr. Beckham. I have spotted the man in question." Miss Ballantyne did not wait for a reply but crossed the room, cutting a direct path to the duke who only stood and awaited her. She might have said something to his grace—Arthur could not be certain as her back was to him—but the duke smiled, then swept her up with one arm and lifted her against his chest, bending to claim her mouth with a possessive kiss.

There was a gasp, then someone gave a low whistle. By the time the pair broke apart, the other men were cheering and stamping, more than one applauding the effort.

Arthur was amused that the duke seemed to have recalled where the lady believed he should be, for he caught her elbow and urged her toward the door, a path the lady followed quite willingly.

And Miss Ballantyne was right. Arthur should be home. He had welcome tidings to share, after all, and an apology to make. This could be the secret he shared, that of the fund for their venture. He did not doubt Patience would welcome news of his progress. He gathered his winnings, took his departure, and made for home. It was still raining steadily, the water pooled on the streets, but he dared to be optimistic.

He nigh whistled as he entered the house, Stevens having been awakened by his vigorous knocking. He took the stairs three at a time and entered his chamber, casting aside his hat and gloves as he headed for the adjoining door.

When there was no reply to his gentle knock, Arthur opened it the merest crack and peeked. The fire in Patience's room had burned down to embers, though still it cast a golden glow over the room. The drapes had not been drawn and in the pale morning light, he could see that she was in bed.

He eased into the room on silent feet, listening. Patience breathed softly and deeply. He crept closer to the bed and his bride, noting the empty boxes and the laden shelves in the small room beyond. He smiled that they were just as he had envisioned them. The shelves were nearly full and his most precious volume was precisely where he had left it.

Patience looked soft and delicate in her sleep, more vulnerable than she appeared to be when awake. Her lashes were surprisingly dark against her cheeks, which were gently flushed. Her lips were parted and Arthur was tempted to ease into bed beside her.

He checked his impulse, not wanting to startle or frighten her.

He bent and kissed her cheek, wishing she would awaken and welcome him, for he was prepared to set matters to rights between them.

But though she smiled at the touch of his lips upon her cheek, she nestled a little deeper into the warmth of the bed, sighed and slept on.

Had they consummated their match already, Arthur might have awakened her with a bold caress. But if their match was to be a happy one, then his first visit to her bed should be a deliberate and merry one.

He quietly added his newly acquired funds to those hidden on her bookcase, noting with satisfaction that the contents of the book box had not been disturbed. Of course, Patience could be trusted.

He eyed her, knowing he should tell her everything, fearing he would lose any admiration she had of him if he did. He had lied, for most of his life, not at his own behest, but he imagined Patience would decree a lie to be a lie.

He had to earn more of her admiration first.

He would begin that very day.

He turned with regret toward his own cold bed in the adjacent room, and realized that his comrades had abandoned him as well. Tar and Feathers slept in Patience's room, each on one chair before the fire, neither looking inclined to move. Faithless creatures. He smiled to himself, noting a book abandoned on the footstool. Had Patience been reading it, a cat in her lap?

He picked it up, curious as to her choice. *Pride & Prejudice*. It was the third volume of a novel and not one he knew. He fanned through it, noting that this edition had been read repeatedly. A favorite, then, which meant he might learn more of his wife by reading it himself. He scratched the ears of the cats, smiling as they purred, then retreated quietly to his own chamber. In moments, Arthur was wearing only his nightshirt and tucked into bed, opening what soon proved to be the finale of a beguiling book.

More importantly, this novel provided Arthur with a map. The gentleman depicted in the tale had been rebuffed by the lady in some earlier chapter, it was clear, his proposal declined. A sister then had embarked upon a scandalous path, but this gentleman made it his concern to see all put to rights.

He made the lady's interest his own, and thus earned her admiration and her hand.

Arthur closed the book as the clock in the hall rang six and others in the house stirred. Here was his directive, the very definition of Patience's expectations, and better yet, he had already embarked upon this path. He pinched the wick, much reassured, and fell into a deep sleep, content that all would come aright and soon.

CHAPTER 10

The rain had stopped when Patience awakened. The fire had burned down to embers, though her room was still warm, and the cats looked to be at ease in the chairs before the fire.

She was alone.

There was no sign of Arthur.

Had he not returned home yet? She had heard nothing. Surely no ill had befallen him?

She slipped from the bed and listened at the adjoining door.

Silence.

She could knock and disturb him, or she could look. She steeled herself to be audacious, reminding herself that she had an apology to deliver, then turned the knob and opened the door soundlessly. She waited on the threshold for a moment, relieved when she heard the steady rhythm of his breathing.

Arthur was home! Patience sniffed but did not smell brandy, another encouraging sign.

Unlike her own room, her husband's chamber was in darkness. The drapes had been pulled and she could not discern any details of the room beyond. One cat whisked past her ankles and vanished into the darkness with the confidence of one who knew its surroundings well. She heard a weight land on something padded.

She crossed the room cautiously then opened one drape to admit a beam of sunlight so that she would not trip. When she turned, she caught her breath at the sight of Arthur sleeping nude, the black cat curled against his side and a book fallen to the floor beneath his hand.

Patience stared, her mouth dry. His room was larger and more splendid than her own, but she could not look away from Arthur himself.

Goodness. What a remarkable specimen he was. He must have cast off his nightshirt for it was on the floor in a heap, his tanned skin revealed to her view.

She took a step closer and looked, emboldened by fascination. She could not find a single flaw. Everything was as it should be—perhaps even more artfully shaped than any ideal. Those who illustrated medical volumes could have used Arthur as a model, perhaps even of the ideal man, or maybe an artist would see him as inspiration. He was powerfully built, his body all sinew and strength, and so gloriously male that something deep inside her quivered. There was a shadow of stubble on his jaw and a tangle of dark hair in the middle of his chest. His hair was ruffled and his eyes were closed, his strong fingers barely grasping a book.

Her book.

Patience yearned to touch him. The thought was startling and bold. But she wanted to run a hand over his skin, to learn how he felt. She wanted to lift aside the linens draped across his hip and thighs, and see all of him.

Even that.

She took a step closer, realizing only after she had done as much that she had blocked the sunlight. A beam of it fell across his face and he grimaced, rolled to his stomach to evade the light.

His move granted her a view of his bare back and buttocks. This, too, was worthy of scrutiny, particularly as the sheet had slipped lower, and she could find no cause for complaint. Arthur was as lean as a Greek statue and nearly as perfectly formed. She could see a scar upon his shoulder, perhaps the one she had been told about, and she averted her gaze, unable to even consider the peril of him at duel.

The sight of his discarded breeches and boots on the floor made her frown. He had returned home too late even to call for his valet. He could not have been doing any deed of merit at such hours and her heart sank that he would be a wastrel forevermore.

She started to turn away but he stirred sleepily.

"Patience," he murmured with a lazy satisfaction that would have weakened her knees, had he whispered thus in her ear. Instead, he mumbled into his pillow, frowned and seemed to struggle against his need to sleep.

He might be drunk upon some substance of less strong scent than brandy. In truth, Patience knew little of spirits.

But the discarded book hinted at sobriety. As one who routinely fell asleep reading, Patience found it difficult to harden her heart against him.

How could she chastise a man who lifted her own book from her hand as she slept and read it himself? In truth, she could find no fault with that.

In truth, she admired the choice.

And Arthur was quite alluring when rumpled and nude. The sight made all of Patience flutter.

"I would apologize to you, sir, for my doubts of last night," she said and he stirred.

"What is this?" Arthur mumbled then glanced over

his shoulder at her. "Patience?" He pushed a hand through his hair and peered at her, evidently confused by her presence in his chamber. "What time is it?" He collapsed onto the bed before she could reply, his lashes fluttering before his eyes closed once more. In a heartbeat, he was breathing deeply once more.

Had he visited another woman? The very prospect was devastating, but it made Patience realize that she dared not make the same mistake twice.

Whatever he had done the night before, it was time to repair matters between them.

Patience needed that book—immediately. She could only start anew with information.

THE LAST PERSON Catherine expected to welcome on a Sunday morning—the Sunday morning after her sister Patience's wedding—was Patience herself.

Her heart squeezed to see that her sister was looking a little saddened and a little stubborn, and guessed that all had not proceeded well the night before. Rhys had noted that he had seen Beckham at White's, worse, that he had seen the newly married man in discussion with Miss Esmeralda Ballantyne. Catherine urged Patience to join her in the library, where the fire was blazing, and called for tea. The sisters sat opposite each other and Catherine took Patience's cold hands in her own. She guessed that her sister was not entirely at ease in Beckham's fine house and had not wished to call for a carriage.

"Tell me you did not walk here," she said with a smile.

"I did." Patience took a quick breath. "The rain has stopped."

In that very moment, the rain began to patter against the window panes again. They both turned to look, then back at each other.

Patience lowered her gaze. "I would ask you for the book, Catherine. I *need* the book."

Catherine had no doubt which book her sister meant. But if she was still a maiden, that book's contents were not appropriate for her to see. "I gave you a passage from it."

"Which only encouraged me to prompt a disagreement. I must make matters right, Catherine, and you must help."

"The wedding was lovely," Catherine said instead of immediately agreeing

Patience nodded, her impatience clear.

"And the wedding night?"

Patience wrinkled her nose. "We argued and he left." She sipped her tea. "It was my fault but I do not know enough to be sure I can repair matters."

"You could ask Mr. Beckham."

"Please give me the book, Catherine, before it is too late."

"Has he abused you? Has he done you injury in any way?"

"No, he is most gentlemanly."

"And you like him?"

Patience blushed. "I do. I find him more intriguing than any other man I have met, but I cannot anticipate him, which is most vexing." She lifted a hand. "I cannot understand why he does what he does!"

"Perhaps that is interesting rather than vexing."

Patience looked up, consideration in her gaze.

Catherine, of all women, knew that a rocky beginning did not doom a match. Though their match was not consummated, Mrs. Oliver's book could be of assistance to her sister, just as it had been to herself. "I never told anyone but Rhys spent our wedding night at his club. He did not even come to my chamber to have an argument first."

"No!" Patience was visibly shocked. "But you are so happy together."

"It took a year for us to find our way," Catherine admitted, the memory making her more confident of her decision. "And it was the early pages of that book that assisted us." She rose and retrieved the manuscript of Mrs. Oliver's book. "It is curious, but I unexpectedly received some additional pages this morning about wedding nights." She handled the bundle to Patience, hoping she made the right choice. "They are on the top as I have not edited them as yet, much less decided where they should appear in the volume itself."

"It is a weighty opus."

"The author has much to say about relations between man and wife. Will you promise me to read it first in Mr. Beckham's company?"

Patience's cheeks burned anew. "Oh, I could not!"

"I cannot surrender it to you without you having an understanding of the material, and if you mean to publish it with Mr. Beckham's assistance, he needs to be aware of its contents."

Patience stared down at the bundle of papers, her indecision clear.

"It might help you to find your way," Catherine said softly. "Any prize worth the having requires some effort, Patience."

"I know." She finished her tea and picked up the book again. Catherine pointed her to the carpetbag that had held the manuscript and adjured her not to lose a single page. By the time she had made that promise, Patience looked to be both encouraged and filled with new purpose. She glanced at the window—and the sound of the falling rain—with some trepidation. "I suppose I must ask you for your coach lest the pages become wet. Perhaps I can return before Arthur awakens and he need never know I left at all."

But Catherine heard the jingle of trap and horses coming to a halt before the house. "I have a feeling he already knows of your departure."

Patience went to the window and looked out at the street. The change in her expression was all Catherine needed to be convinced she had chosen correctly. Her sister's lips parted and her eyes lit with anticipation, then she looked back at Catherine with a smile that might have been triumphant. "He is here," she whispered, as if her voice might be overheard though the closed windows.

"Then I am encouraged. And you will read it with him?"

"Oh, Catherine. I will, though I cannot imagine how I will suggest as much."

"Read it together. Invite his views. It will all be well." Catherine stood and kissed her sister's cheeks. "Good luck," she whispered. "Though I suspect you do not need luck when you have that book."

Patience laughed, then left with a quick step. Catherine returned to her chair by the fire, sinking into it and savoring a sip of hot tea.

"That book will turn you into a fairy godmother yet," Rhys teased from the doorway. Catherine's heart leapt when she turned to meet his warm gaze and she smiled as he crossed the room toward her.

"You should not complain, given how it aided us."

"Did I complain? Not a syllable." He kissed her hand, sitting on the footstool beside her, his gaze searching hers. "You still feel well?"

"I remain in robust health, sir, and vow that your fears will soon be proven false."

He kissed her hand, holding it against his cheek. "So I pray, my Catherine, so I pray."

She watched him, knowing he struggled against his earlier convictions that childbirth must be fatal to the mother, and she gripped his hand more tightly. In a matter of months, he would be assured of the truth, and her husband's deepest fear would be banished forever.

For Catherine did not intend to leave her beloved alone.

ARTHUR AWAKENED with the familiar sense that he had slept late. The light coming through the windows was so dim that it provided no insight as to the time. It was the hall clock, chiming eleven, that provided a hint. He rolled to his back and considered the canopy overhead, wincing at the embroidered insignia of Fairhaven as was his daily custom.

It was also his habit to take a reckoning before rising from bed to begin his day. On the upside, he had nine thousand pounds he had not possessed the morning before. That was no small asset.

On the downside, he had completely bungled his wedding day and night, at least from Patience's perspective. Would she listen to his explanation?

He had a vague recollection of Patience standing over the bed, the sunlight behind her. Had he dreamed that? If she had entered his chamber willingly, all might not be lost—even if she had done as much to chastise him. An angel of judgement did not spend time upon a soul already lost.

He rose with purpose and enthusiasm. Taylor must have anticipated Arthur with his usual accuracy, for the water that had been left by the valet was still steaming hot. He washed and shaved, then changed to a clean shirt.

He tapped gently on the adjoining door.

There was no reply.

He knocked a little more vigorously, but again, there was no reply.

Arthur opened the door and looked into the room. There was not a lamp or candle lit, and the drapes were pulled back. The bed was unmade. A breakfast tray was on the footstool where the book had been the night before, and apparently Tar had already charmed the lady in question, for there was an empty saucer on the chair cushion beside his clearly contented self. The black cat did love his morning sip of tea. Feathers was snoring gently, as was her custom, but the room was otherwise unoccupied.

He crossed the room and opened the door to the corridor, listening for voices below. There were none, which could mean that his wife was in the breakfast room alone. Would she eat twice in rapid succession? He had no idea. Amelia would eat as many breakfasts as were presented to her. His mother would remain in her room all day, after her exertions of the day before. He knew that as well.

But Patience was a mystery.

As yet.

He caught sight of a maid at the end of the corridor and hailed her when she might have vanished into the servant's stairs. "Gellis! Do you know where my wife might be found?"

The woman curtsied and kept her eyes downcast, a reaction that made Arthur realize he stood before her barefoot and wearing only a shirt. He grinned and she blushed. "She went out, sir, early this morning it was."

"Early? How early?"

"I should say it was nine or so, sir. She was already dressed when I brought her breakfast, but she had granted no direction as to how early she might desire it. Your mother calls for hers." She curtsied again. "Mr. Stevens has said she must have her tray earlier tomorrow, sir, but perhaps the lady might advise us as to her expectations."

"Of course, Gellis. I will ask her to do as much. I believe Carruthers House has a smaller staff and my wife may not have considered such details." He began to turn back to the room, thinking of potential destinations. Home to Carruthers House? He hoped that had not been Patience's choice. They had not yet been wed a day and it was early for her to abandon hope in him and the match.

"Sir, I wish only that she had not been obliged to wash in cold on her first day in the house," Gellis said behind him. "She must know where the bell is, sir."

Arthur thought the location of the bell was evident. What might be lacking was Patience's desire to trouble anyone in the house. She did strike him as being quite independent. He smiled for the maid. "I will ensure that she does, Gellis. Thank you again."

Gellis curtsied. "And congratulations to you, sir. Her ladyship ordered a lovely supper for us belowstairs last night and it was much appreciated, particularly as none of us had to serve."

Arthur spun. "What is this? There was no dinner last night?"

Gellis flushed. "Her ladyship chose to have a tray in her room, sir, and your lady wife agreed to the same."

Patience had eaten alone in her room on their wedding day?

He was a cur and a louse and nothing he could say could repair that damage.

He thanked Gellis and fairly ran back into Patience's

room, scanning it for clues. He leaned back against the door even as Tar wound around his ankles.

Where would she go?

If not her father's home, what might be her destination on a Sunday? She might have gone to church, as he so seldom did. Did she have other friends in town? She might have gone to Bettencourt's home. That was where he had encountered her before, after all, and the sisters might well be close.

The baroness had given her that page from the book of advice, the one about secrets.

Patience had gone to collect the book. He would wager his soul upon that.

Arthur returned to his room, rang for Taylor and dressed quickly. It turned out that Patience had not requested the carriage or coach that morning, which did give him pause. It was a considerable walk to Trevelaine House and again, he was stymied by a lack of knowledge of his wife's inclinations. Would she walk so far as that? He hated that he did not know.

Arthur's luck held from the night before, though, for the carriage no sooner arrived before the steps of the baron's house in town than the door opened and Patience herself emerged. She was carrying a large bag that might have been heavy, and Arthur leapt out to greet her.

She wore a plain dark coat and he glimpsed a dress that might have been the one she had been wearing at her father's shop on the day they first spoke after his return from Venice. Her boots were polished and plain, her bonnet graced with a single cluster of silk lily-of-the-valley. Banished were the soft curls that had framed her face at their wedding and her hair seemed to be pulled back with greater severity than ever.

Arthur had the strange sense that their wedding

might not have happened at all, and that troubled him greatly.

As was his custom, he hid his uneasiness with a smile. He jumped down, keeping a hand upon the lead horse as there was no one to hold the team. To his relief, Patience came to him, one hand upon the brim of her hat and the other clutching the bag. The rain was no more than a slight mist.

"And so I guessed aright," he said. "Did you walk all this way?"

"I did. The morning was fine."

They eyed each other for a long moment, and he was humble by the questions in her eyes. "I am sorry that we parted badly," he said, his words filled with conviction.

"As am I."

"But if you will forgive me long enough to accept the surrender of a secret, I have one to share." He gestured to the carriage. "Might I offer a ride, perhaps shelter from the storm?"

Patience smiled just a little, a sight that gave him hope, and tilted her head to study him. "Does your secret have to do with the book that is not truly a book, the one you left in the bookcase?"

Arthur was astonished and he could tell by the twinkle that lit in her eyes that it showed.

"I did not take the money," she whispered and he loved his sense that they were allied together. She frowned a little. "Though I did count that your sum was correct."

Of course, she had. Arthur found himself grinning as he took the bag she carried.

"But is it?" he countered, securing the bag beneath the seat where it would be out of the rain. He guessed that it contained the sole copy of the book in question.

"I can count well enough…"

"But I made an addition this morning."

She looked at him. "That was why you did not return home last night."

"It was only part of the reason." He raised a finger. "I was not cavorting."

Patience did not smile. "Are you certain the funds are safe there?"

"Of course. Safer than in my chamber, where a servant might expect to find money unattended." He touched her cheek. "It is as safe in your care as in the bank."

"Thank you for your trust."

"I have never met anyone more trustworthy," he said, for it was true.

"Arthur, I owe you an apology," she said quietly.

"And I owe you a greater one." He turned and gestured to the carriage, his confidence growing with every passing moment. "Let me make it."

"You did not bring the coach, despite the rain," she said.

"As you have noted previously, servants all have ears, and I would not have the driver and two footmen knowing the location of our savings or the intended destination of those funds." He smiled at her, noting that she could not hide her pleasure. "Only you will be privy to the confession of my secret, Patience."

"That hidden sum is your winnings, is it not?"

"It is the fund for our shared venture," he corrected, watching her lips part in awe. "And it was a secret from everyone until you found it."

"They are winnings, not savings," she said sternly as he handed her up. "You might lose the amount twice over the next time you play."

Arthur shook his head. "I play only so long as I win, and I leave the table when I lose." He cast his cloak over her shoulders, protecting her from the rain that might gain momentum before they reached home.

"But it is gambling," she insisted when he sat beside her. "You cannot be so certain…"

"It is mathematics," Arthur said with crisp authority, taking the reins in hand. He slanted her a glance, noting how she watched him. "I have been playing since our betrothal to win the funds we will need for our venture. Good fortune has smiled upon me, as if Providence itself would support your scheme. But let me start at the beginning."

"Please do," she replied and he turned the team away from Berkley Square, taking a quiet road so they could talk.

~

PATIENCE COULD NOT COMPLAIN, despite the rain. Arthur had sought her out, he had correctly guessed her destination, and now he would surrender a secret. She yearned to ask him questions but instead knew it was better to listen.

"Last night," he said finally. "I visited my solicitor to ask his counsel with regard to printers and publishers. Are you familiar with Fanshawe & Parke?"

"Of course! My father was saddened by Mr. Parke's demise last year."

"Friends?"

"I would consider them acquaintances. I know they liked to talk at auctions and such. Why?"

"Mr. Fanshawe seeks a new partner to ensure the continuation of his firm. I have requested a meeting, contingent upon your view."

"Arthur!"

"I expect to hear from one party or the other

shortly, perhaps so early as next week, but wished to know your view of their establishment."

"It is highly respectable, and their books are beautiful. My father and uncle often admire the skill of their tradesmen."

"Good. I have mentioned the possibility of your idea and have not been rebuffed, but it would be helpful, I believe, if you were present to argue the merit of your plan."

Patience caught her breath and Arthur smiled at her.

"Our investment will be contingent upon you gaining your desire from the partnership," he said with welcome conviction. "And you will make a good case, I am certain. You can be a compelling advocate when you believe in a matter."

She glowed at his praise.

"There is the question of an investment, which my solicitor calls substantial and which I call staggering."

She watched him closely, waiting for the disappointment she feared..

The carriage rocked as it made its way through the street and he leaned closer to her, lowering his voice. "I did not return home last night because I heard of a game with high stakes. The Earl of Queenston had arrived in town and meant to play, and he is inclined to lose."

"You played cards all night?"

"And rather well."

"Does that mean you won?"

"Nine thousand pounds," he admitted easily and watched her eyes widen.

"But you could have lost it all instead."

"No, Patience, that is not how it words."

"Gambling is an unpredictable venture…"

"It is mathematics," he said crisply, interrupting her.

"Each game is a calculation. Even given that, sometimes the cards favor a person and sometimes they do not. The trick is to walk away once the tide is against you."

"Do you not lose?"

"It is not common, and when I lose, I lose only a little. My luck has been remarkably good since you accepted me, perhaps a sign of divine favor."

"How so?"

"I play to earn the funds needed for your venture, Patience, no more and no less."

She frowned. "But you are wealthy. You have an income, I understand, and a hope of inheritance..."

"And Lady Beckham does not approve of those in trade. There will be hell to pay if I use any increment of funds that originate from her in such a venture."

"Is this why she does not approve of me?"

Arthur winced. "I fear so. I had hoped your charm would undermine her objections." She watched his lips tighten. "I heard that she declined to dine with you last evening. I am sorry, Patience. I never imagined she would be so rude. By the time I left Mr. Sommerset, I believed dinner would have been served, and she has always insisted that it is better not to arrive at all than to be late."

"I did not mind as much as I should have," she admitted and he cast her a sparkling glance.

"I don't suppose you would mind if we dined in your chamber alone tonight. We have a great deal of research to do, after all."

"Arthur! Will she not be vexed with us?"

"Perhaps. I am vexed with her." He smiled down at her. "And having botched our wedding night, I fear I must labor long and hard to redeem myself in your view."

Patience found herself flushing at his perusal. "I am not certain it will be such an ordeal, sir."

Arthur laughed. "Nor am I." He turned the horses then and she recognized that they headed toward Berkley Square again.

"I suppose you have more than one secret," she said and his smile flashed.

"I might contrive to have a hundred to keep your interest."

"I do not jest, Arthur."

"Nor do I and I apologize for my reticence." He frowned. "The fact is that I have never had a confidante." He halted the horses before the house, then turned to look at her. She saw the truth in his darkened eyes and watched him swallow, her chest tight that he confided such a truth in her. "I am so accustomed to keeping my secrets close that I was not certain how to begin."

Patience's heart clenched tightly. He had never had a confidante. That meant he had never truly had a friend. Patience had sisters, and had confided in Prudence all her life. "But you must have had friends at school."

Arthur shook his head slowly. "I was not there long." His gaze rose to hers, an appeal in his eyes. "There was an accident, a prank in truth, but a boy died. I was taken away from school immediately and had tutors at home since."

"How dreadful!"

His throat worked. "It was tragic, to be sure." He seemed discomfited by the memory and Patience did not dare to ask him about the lost boy. Had that been his friend?

"Goodness. That is two secrets in rapid succession," she said lightly, hoping to prompt his smile.

But Arthur simply raised a gloved hand to her cheek, his gaze warming in that way that made her heart nigh stop. "You have made it so easy that I fear you will soon be burdened with another confession."

He bent and brushed his lips across her cheek, his touch sending a thrill through her. "Forgive me, Patience," he whispered and she could not have refused him anything.

"Of course," she said, pulling back to meet his gaze. "But I was wrong last night as well. I must beg your forgiveness."

"You?"

It was galling to admit the truth. "I was afraid."

"Because you had no guide or instructions," he replied with a small smile. She nodded and his smile broadened. "But you have me, Patience." He sobered. "I will never hurt you and I will never demand more than you wish to give," he vowed.

Patience believed him.

Arthur kissed her again, this time upon the mouth, and she kissed him back. She felt as if they began anew and had a newfound accord.

When he finally lifted his head, his eyes were glittering and his expression bemused. "How scandalous we are, Mrs. Beckham," he murmured, his gaze flicking to the butler who stood impassively at the door, waiting for them to alight.

Patience felt herself flush with predictable ease and saw the flash of Arthur's smile. "Indeed, we are," she agreed. "Perhaps we should do something about the matter."

"Perhaps we should," he agreed, then jumped from the carriage with admirable ease. He reached back to lock his hands around her waist and swing her down to the ground, then claimed the bag she had collected from Catherine before escorting her toward the house. "Fine day, Stevens," he said.

"Indeed, sir."

"I know Lady Beckham likes to have tea on Sunday

afternoon with everyone in attendance, but my wife and I will send our regrets today."

The butler's brows rose for a heartbeat, but his tone did not change. "Very good, sir."

Arthur swept Patience up the stairs with purpose. Outside of her room, he surrendered her bag, bowed and left her there—much to her astonishment. Then he winked before vanishing into his own room and Patience understood. She went into her chamber, locked the door, shed her coat and bonnet and set the bag down. She went to the adjoining door and opened it, only to find Arthur leaning against the wall there, her book in his hand. He had discarded his jacket but looked as if he had been waiting a long while.

His eyes twinkled when she laughed. "Your book, my lady," he said, presenting it to her.

"I wish for more than a book, sir," she said, feeling audacious indeed.

"Truly? Are you my wife? Because I am given to understand that Patience Beckham née Carruthers finds the greatest of satisfactions in a good book..."

She reached up to kiss him quickly, silencing him with surprise at her move. "And I invite you to demonstrate my error, Arthur," she whispered, loving how he laughed, caught her up and fairly charged into her bedchamber.

~

THE TRUTH of the matter was that Arthur much preferred intimate interludes in daylight. There was something seductive about a lazy afternoon spent abed in amorous pursuits. He liked the light, whether it was sunny or raining. He liked the sense that time had halted. He liked feeling that whatever was done was not a secret or a stolen moment or an interval seized before sleep came upon them both.

To be sure, he also enjoyed liaisons at night, when the shadows added mystery to the encounter, but overall, a rainy Sunday afternoon was ideal.

He could think of no better time to first seduce his wife.

Patience, despite her comments, was still vibrating with uncertainty and he moved more slowly than was his wont, not wanting to startle her. The fire had been lit in her room and the cats had claimed both chairs already. He opened the bag she had brought from her sister's home and lifted out a pile of loose sheets of paper. They might have been a sheaf of letters, for the text was written by hand. "This is the book?" he asked in surprise and she nodded, an enticing flush touching her cheeks. He read the title aloud. *"The Ladies' Essential Guide to the Art of Seduction."*

He could not help but think that had promise.

Patience came to his side, her fingertips dancing over the pile of paper as she spoke. "Catherine says she is still editing it, and that new pages came this morning." There were, in fact, several sheets loose on the top of the bundle, which she claimed. He watched her read the first of them. "Oh!" she said, her gaze flying to him with surprise.

Arthur smiled as he plucked the sheet from her hand.

"Upon the importance of first encounters. Suggestions for the lady and for the gentleman," he read.

"That one is for the lady," Patience said, switching sheets with him. She evicted Tar and settled into a chair to read with enviable concentration. Arthur found himself watching the way she bit the ripe perfection of her bottom lip, the grip of her slender fingers on the sheet. Even more delightful was the exposed softness of the inside of her wrist, the curve of her neck and the loose tendril of fair hair beside her ear. If he had an ability to draw, he would have captured the sight of her in charcoal on the page. As it was, he could only stare and admire.

She cast a reproving glance at him. "You should not look at me thus," she whispered.

"How?"

"As if you would gobble me up."

"I am tempted. You look delicious." He bent and kissed the side of her neck, then grazed her skin with his teeth. She shivered in a most delightful way.

Her cheeks pinkened as he had hoped they might. "You are full of nonsense," she chided.

"You did wed a rake and a scoundrel. I would not have you disappointed to find me a sober man of honor instead, of sedate temperament and modest appetites."

She laughed aloud at that, her eyes dancing in a most attractive way. "You are wicked."

"Agreed. The question remains is whether you will reform me or whether I will lead you astray."

"We could each continue as we are and not influence the other a whit."

"And how would that be diverting, Patience? The only thing I could not abide in a marriage is mutual tolerance." Her gaze brightened at that and he wished he had not spoken thus. "There. It is decided. I must lead you astray with as much haste as possible to avoid such a dire fate."

"You should read your sheet. I have read mine already."

"But it is so much more satisfying to prompt your blush."

"Arthur!" she said in mock outrage so that he was delighted by her sparkling eyes. "Read it!"

For once, Arthur did as instructed.

His own lips curved into a smile as he read, the advice reassuring him immeasurably.

Upon the responsibility of a wedding night...for gentlemen.

I recommend that those ladies who have not as yet been introduced to the pleasures of the marital bed offer this page to their husbands in advance of that event. For there is little that can be so sweet as one's first encounter with a partner, nor are there many events that can go so badly awry. Worse, the first night of a marriage may well set the tone and expectations for all future years of such encounters, and so, the required deed should not be embarked upon without thought and preparation.

Gentlemen, you hold the power to ensure your lady's devotion and her satisfaction, by your persuasive indoctrination of said companion to sensation and pleasure. Most ladies come to their matches in innocence, and an innocence that is so complete in its ignorance of such body matters that many men fail to anticipate the breadth of the chasm between the expectations of bride and groom.

I encourage you to be leisurely, to coax her laughter in her uncertainty, to awaken her to your touch with gentle caresses. I invite you to explain what will happen, to indulge in physical comforts beyond your own satisfaction. Compliments, given in good faith, can only encourage us all when we are uncertain of our path. I urge you to remain with her afterward, to hold her while she sleeps, to whisper plans for your shared future. Confessions made abed, be they sweet or audacious, are inclined to bind a couple more closely together.

Above all, do not rush.

If you conjure your lady's response with sufficient fortitude, you may earn a lifetime of merry moments abed together, the loyalty of a devoted partner and the joy of complete trust, one in the other. The lady you introduce to pleasure may ultimately ensure that you conquer higher peaks of satisfaction than ever you dreamed—for the act of union is made more potent with emotional intimacy, and that far beyond the expectancy of many a man who seeks only momentary relief.

Seduce your wife, sir. Beguile and entice her, and you may find yourself in possession of the greatest prize of all, a match that provides such satisfaction that neither of you will ever be content with another. This is the promise of the nuptial night, and I adjure you to fulfill it—body, heart and soul.

There was a challenge Arthur meant to accept.

CHAPTER 11

$\mathcal{P}$atience watched as Arthur read the document, liking that he gave it his undivided attention. That granted her the opportunity to scrutinize him. She liked how intent he was, and how quickly his gaze flew across the lines. She liked how he returned to a passage or two, how he smiled to himself as if in anticipation of what they might do together.

She liked also how he lounged in the chair from which he had dismissed the grey cat, completely at ease with his own power. He looked both young and virile, a man whose very presence made her chamber seem smaller. She felt more aware of herself in his company, remembering not just his wondrous kiss, but the vigor of his response to her participation. She recalled the weight of his hands on her shoulders, the feeling of being swept into his arms, and understood how women were dazzled by the surety of a handsome man.

She felt herself on the cusp of being dazzled, for certain.

The cat jumped back into his lap and he was not startled. On the contrary, he stroked the beast gently, knowing its preferences so well that it closed its eyes and purred. She admired his hands, the way his gaze flicked to her when he was done, how his eyes filled with a mischief that made her smile before he spoke. He was a good companion, to be sure, but so consistently good-natured and easy-going that she wondered what he held in esteem beyond his own comfort.

He had never had a friend, but he had placed his winnings in her bookcase.

He had chosen to trust her, probably against his learned impulse, and Patience would never betray that trust.

In truth, she found it difficult to concentrate on the page she had claimed. She frowned and forced herself to read it again.

"This might have been written for my own eyes," Arthur said, reaching to capture the other sheet from her hands.

"It is not for you!"

"But I would know what you know, or what you do not know," he said so solemnly that she relinquished her grip. "Truly, the responsibility to do as much is mine, as this first sheet declares." Once again, she had the luxury of watching him, though this time, he frowned. "It is cursed vague."

"It is true that everything we are told is vague," she agreed. "But I did consult a medical volume in my father's collection."

Arthur's brows rose as he looked at her. "Your father agreed to this?"

"Of course not, but a man cannot keep inventory of all his books and his daughters at the same time."

"I shall bear that in mind and take it as a warning of future curiosity," he said solemnly, though she saw the twinkle in his dark eyes. "And what did you learn from that volume?"

She took a breath, feeling the heat of a blush rise from her very nipples. "That the first time a female is penetrated, she may feel some discomfort, as the protective membrane of the hymen is broken."

"That does not put one in mind of romantic novels."

"It does not, although the hymen is named after the Greek god, Hymen, who died on his wedding night. He was one of the sons of Apollo and a love god, who was invoked before the marriage ceremony when the bride was being escorted to the home of the groom." As was typical when she was flustered, Patience became fulsome about details that were unlikely to hold as much interest for her companion as herself. "In fact, his attendance at a wedding was deemed crucial to the happiness of the match…"

She was almost relieved when Arthur interjected a question.

"Did we invoke him yesterday?"

She shook her head. "But we are not ancient Greeks."

"There is that," Arthur said with a sage nod. "But I think there are more practical means of ensuring the future of a match. And fortunately, we have all day to pursue such objectives."

"We do," she agreed, recalling his instructions to the butler with another flush.

"And so, we will take our leisure, as this volume advises, to begin again." He offered his hand and Patience, uncertain what else to do, took it. He stood and raised her to her feet, setting the pages of the book aside and led her toward the adjoining door to his chamber.

"But surely this room suffices?"

"You do not have a mirror of goodly size so we must use mine."

"A mirror?"

"I cannot grant you a map to your beguiling spot, but I can show it to you."

Oh!

He led her across his chamber to a large mirror on a stand, one almost as tall as she, and stood before it with her. It felt both sinful and delicious to be in his chamber, with its dark hues, wood paneling, velvet and leather. The room even smelled of his skin in a most delightful way. He stood her before him and leaned over her shoulder, meeting her gaze in the mirror.

"You argue that you are not pretty, but Patience, you are mistaken in that." She parted her lips to protest, but his fingertip landed upon her lips to silence her. "Look, for example, at this mouth. I invite you to consider its assets." At his gesture, Patience eyed the reflection of her own face, Arthur looming behind her. "A more perfect and rosy bud has seldom been seen. It fairly invites a caress." He slid his fingertip across her bottom lip slowly, making her shiver to her toes. His other arm closed around her waist, drawing her against him, lifting her slightly. She could not look away from the slow motion of his finger and savored the weight of it against her mouth.

Arthur leaned closer and her heart leapt. "Such a mouth as this entreats a kiss," he murmured. "Indeed, so pretty a mouth is irresistible." He kissed the corner of her mouth slowly and she caught her breath. He brushed his mouth across hers, once quickly and then more slowly. She felt his lips ease against hers, tempting her response and once again, she kissed him back.

This time, she dared to trust in sensation. She closed her eyes and let herself enjoy the pleasure of their embrace. She also mimicked Arthur, parting her lips as he did and catching her breath at the playful flick of his tongue.

"You are wicked," she whispered when she pulled away and he laughed, untroubled. There was satisfaction and pride in his response and she could not be annoyed with him, not when he looked at her as he did in this moment.

As if she were a queen.

As if she had hung the moon and the stars.

As if…their match could be more than an arrangement. How often had he looked at another woman thus? Was it a practiced scheme to win his way? Patience did not know and could not care, not when she was so beguiled.

"And these eyes," he continued in that low voice. He framed her face in his hands and pressed a kiss to one eyelid and then the other. "Perfection indeed. Such a hue, both stormy and serene, distinct and unforgettable. Perceptive and perhaps as dangerous as a medusa's stare."

He kissed her lips again, slowly and sweetly, and Patience could not deny the tide of heat rising within her. She was being carried away by his seductive touch, and she resolved to enjoy whatever sweet torment he meant to inflict.

Once again, his fingers were in her hair, scattering pins and freeing her long tresses. "And this hair of yours," he rumbled. "You cannot guess the temptation it offers, so lustrous and golden, like a silken net over my hands." He set it loose, pushing his fingers through it, spreading it over her shoulders. It fell to her hips and Patience had never thought it particularly remarkable —Prudence's hair was a lighter hue of gold and prettier in Patience's view, but she could not dispute the admiration in Arthur's expression. He framed her face in his hands and bent to kiss her leisurely once again.

"You would seduce me," she whispered.

"I would appreciate you, and take my time in so doing. Your book advises a leisurely progress and I have no objections to that. Indeed, I do not wish to miss a single detail." He turned her before the mirror and she felt him unlacing the back of her dress. He raised his gaze to watch her reflection, no doubt noticing how her throat worked. Could he see the pulse of her heart? She was almost paralyzed by his steady progress, his smooth movements, the brush of his warm fingertips. He set his hands on her shoulders when the dress was unfastened, his hands beneath the cloth, and held her gaze as he bent and kissed the back of her neck sweetly. "You smell divine, Patience," he murmured, his lips against her neck. Again, she saw a sudden flare of heat in his eyes, a hint that he, too, was affected by these caresses.

When he eased the dress from her shoulders, Patience shook it free and they both watched it cascade to the floor. She stood before him in her sheer chemise, her stockings and garters visible through the fabric, along with a good deal more. She felt her color rise, even as Arthur cupped one of her breasts in his palm. He stood behind her, all strength and heat, and she heard him catch his breath as his thumb landed on her nipple. She watched in the mirror as he caressed the tightening peak slowly, sliding the edge of his thumb across it repeatedly, back and forth, creating a sensation that was both wondrous and excruciatingly insufficient.

He cleared his throat and she felt his other hand, the one on her waist, flex, as if he sought to muster his control and that sent satisfaction surging through her. He bent to kiss her neck at the curve of her shoulder, then inhaled, breathing deeply of her scent as if he could not get enough of it. When his gaze met hers in the glass, his eyes were deepest blue, his manner intent. She was not snared in sensation alone and she was glad.

"You cannot argue that this breast is less than perfect," he said softly, then reached to unfasten the tie of her chemise. Once again, the cloth tumbled from her shoulders but this time, the fire in Arthur's eyes could not be denied. He whispered her name like an invocation as his hand rose to cup her breast again. She felt the heat of his palm against her bare skin. She watched as he bent and kissed that same nipple with a gentle reverence that made her gasp aloud.

His tongue proved to be even more wicked than she had imagined and when he flicked it across the taut nipple, she gave a little cry.

He halted immediately. "Does it hurt?"

"No. It feels wondrous, but insufficient. I cannot explain it better."

"But you have explained it perfectly, Patience." Arthur's voice was low, intended only for her ears, and the rough sound of it was perfect. "It is the sensation of lovemaking, the temptation, the sweet torment and the anguish of anticipated release." He kissed her ear and her throat, his hands running over her and she turned in his embrace, reaching to kiss him back. "I promise you—" he said with a resolve that thrilled her "—that the reward will be worth the price."

Given the merit of the adventure thus far, Patience could only believe him.

COULD a man die when confronted with such sweetness? Arthur halfway thought it might be so. Patience was both lovely and trusting, her confidence that he would ensure her satisfaction so complete that Arthur was humbled. He had to force himself to be slow, to not hasten to the prize of release, to pace himself that she might be pleased, too.

He could smell her arousal, a most encouraging sign, and he could not find fault with this slow exploration. Would he survive a similar exploration of his own body on her part? That might kill him if this did not.

But the volume advised leisure and a slow afternoon of lovemaking it would be. The rain was pounding against the windows again, but he did not care a whit for the rest of the world. There was only Patience with uncertainty in her glorious eyes, and her unexpected audacity in returning his embrace.

He shed his jacket and knelt before her, unlacing her boots and setting them aside. Of course, they were sturdy and sensible. She had been to visit her sister and a woman like Patience would not wear satin slippers in the street. "Perfect feet," he said to her and she giggled as he ran a fingertip along the underside of one. She leaned upon his shoulder, her hands feeling delicate upon him. "Of an ideal and delicate size, and finely shaped."

"Feet cannot be perfect," she chided.

"You err in that, my lady," he said, bending to untie her garter with his teeth. She caught her breath at the flick of his tongue on the inside of her knee and he knew then that she was ticklish. He wrapped his hands around her thigh, then smoothed them downward, easing the stocking down her very shapely leg. "The legs of a lady who walks often," he said in admiration.

"Perhaps too robust," she said and he glanced up at her.

"Perhaps not," he argued gently, watching her eyes widen slightly. The scent of her arousal tempted him to bend closer and kiss the top of one thigh, even as he held her gaze. She caught her breath and flushed a little more, but did not move away.

Indeed, her eyes glittered and her lips parted. He released a slow breath, felt her shiver, then let his tongue flick against the softness of her skin again.

"Oh!"

Arthur had to avert his gaze lest he pounce upon her and ruin the mood he had himself created. The other stocking was discarded a little more hastily than the first, despite his effort, then he stood again, letting his hands slide up her smooth soft skin to frame her face once again. Her eyes were gleaming and she was on the cusp of a smile.

"My turn?" she asked in a whisper filled with welcome hope and yearning.

"I demand a kiss first," he replied.

"As payment for your assistance?" she teased and he grinned down at her.

"At that price, you may summon my assistance at any time."

"Perhaps I will," she said, her manner impish, then Arthur could resist no longer. He caught her around the waist and pulled her close. He liked the feel of her in his arms, her breasts against his chest, her hair wrapped around his fingers, her mouth hungrily upon his own. He could not restrain himself entirely but kissed her more hungrily, emboldened by her own avid response. She gripped his hair in her hands and rose to her toes, kissing him back with a demand of her own and one that made his heart thunder. Once again, he whispered her name when they parted, and he saw her smile of triumph.

Her hands landed upon his chest, her head turning back and forth as she surveyed him. She plucked the gem from his cravat first and set it carefully aside, then untied the length of smooth cotton. Her brows drew together as she figured it out and Arthur provided no guidance to the mystery, being more than content to stand with his hands locked around her waist and look down at her. The fire on the hearth crackled, filling the room with its light and gilding the fair lady before him.

Not pretty. He would spend every night arguing that

matter with her. How could a woman of such intellect not see the truth?

Her eyes lit with such triumph that he laughed when she discarded the cravat. "Should it be folded?"

He shook his head. "It has been worn and will have to be washed and pressed again."

"What a foolish garment," she said beneath her breath, but her eyes were glimmering in a thousand shades of silver and grey. They were like the sea in this moment, shifting and changing in the sunlight, disguising untold mysteries and secrets. Her lashes were long and unexpectedly dark, and when she dropped her gaze, it was as if a veil was dropped to hide her thoughts.

She had unfastened his waistcoat already and was pushing it from his shoulders. "You have to raise your hands," she said.

"But I would have to relinquish a most satisfying grip." He gave her waist a playful squeeze, liking how she smiled at him. He dared to tickle her a little and she gasped in outrage, twisting out of his grasp to retreat.

"Do not tickle me!"

He shed his waistcoat and held up his hands. "I cannot make such a promise. The temptation is too great."

She braced her hands on her hips, doubtless unaware of how alluring she looked. "The temptation to have me at a disadvantage?"

"The temptation of seeing those eyes flash." He caught her chin in one hand and bent toward her with purpose. "Perhaps you are a siren, intending to hold my heart in thrall."

"Perhaps you talk too much, sir," she replied, then kissed him of her own volition.

Arthur was startled to silence—and utterly delighted. He caught her around the waist and lifted her from the ground, deepening their kiss in a thoroughly satisfying way. When he set her on her feet again, they were both breathless and he was aroused beyond all.

Patience noticed. Her fingertips swept across the front of his breeches and Arthur inhaled at her touch. "The word penis," she said. "is derived from the Latin for 'tail', though in English, the organ was referred to as a 'yard' from at least the fourteenth century." She fixed him with a quizzical look. "Surely that is not an indication of its size?"

"Only in stories inappropriate for ladies," Arthur acknowledged, now confident that her perusal of the medical volume had provided her with some expectation of what they would do. "I am certain you will find it of manageable dimensions."

"Manageable," she repeated, then reached for the opening of his breeches with resolve.

Arthur bent in the same moment to remove one of his boots and they bumped heads and parted awkwardly. He held up a hand and retreated a step, shed his boots with haste, then hauled his shirt over his head and casting it aside. His breeches quickly followed suit, then his smalls, and he looked up to find Patience staring at him, her cheeks aflame.

"Manageable," she said again, and as if summoned by name, his arousal became more pronounced. "Oh!" she breathed, then came closer to investigate. Her eyes shone with curiosity and he was glad she was not fearful or repulsed.

"You are bold," he said with pleasure.

Her eyes danced. "You do not realize that I looked upon you this very morning." Her cheeks burned crimson at this confession.

"You did?"

She nodded. "While you slept."

Arthur thought of a detail. "I had discarded my

nightshirt." If he thought her cheeks had been red before, that had been but a faint promise of how they flushed now.

"You did," she agreed, her voice tight.

She walked around him, looking him up and down, then reached out to touch him. Arthur closed his eyes at the light caress of her fingertips on his arm, feeling desire rise within him at her touch. Her hand slid from his arm to his shoulder. Her fingertips feathered down his back, up his spine and into his hair, down his back to dance across his buttocks. She traced a line across the top of his thigh as she circled him, then flattened her other hand against his side as she came to face him.

She was a temptress, and one who would destroy his control, undermining it a little more with each soft caress. Echoing his own exploration, she slid that hand over him, from hip to chest, letting her fingertips slip through the tangle of hair there. He had one glimpse of the mischief in her gaze, then she kissed one of his nipples, her tongue flicking it to attention just as he had teased her own. He felt her hair against his erection and closed his eyes, fighting his urge to carry her off and bury himself within her.

Leisurely.

He might die this afternoon of sweet pleasure, and he would be content all the same.

"Sweet torment?" she whispered and he looked to find her watching him through her lashes.

"Precisely," he agreed and she smiled.

"Good. I should hate to be enduring it alone."

Arthur began to laugh and lifted a hand to her cheek with the plan to reassure her, but she touched him, her fingers closing around him with a gentle surety that banished every thought from his head. Her gaze was fixed upon him and suddenly he could not think coherently. There was only Patience and her curiosity, Patience and her glorious eyes, Patience and her sweet mouth that demanded his kiss.

SOMETHING CHANGED when she touched him. Patience saw the heat in Arthur's eyes and saw how he caught his breath. He moved like lightning then, sweeping her into his arms and carrying her to the bed. She might have protested, but he kissed her to silence, stretching out beside her as one hand roved over her body. She should have felt brazen in her nudity, but the admiration in his touch made her want to preen.

She arched her back when his hand cupped her breast this time and dared to squirm when he teased her nipple to a peak. She kissed him back with more enthusiasm than she had allowed herself to show so far, and when he growled approval, she reached up to tangle her fingers in his hair and pull him closer. He was partly atop her, braced on one elbow as he kissed her and slid his hand down from her breast. She felt his fingers slide between her thighs, then gasped aloud when he touched her and a surge of heat raced through her.

"Oh!" she said, breaking their kiss.

He looked alarmed. "Did I injure you?"

"No! No, far from it." She urged his hand back into place and her lips parted again when he touched her. She wanted to purr at the sensual languor that resulted, an irresistible combination of temptation and pleasure, again with the sense that there was more to be savored. She heard herself moan and Arthur settled against her again, his fingers moving more deeply against her until his thumb caressed that place with surety.

He chuckled. "It seems I introduce you to your most bewitching spot."

"I can only hope it is uncommon for it to be worn callous," she said before Arthur's thumb stole every word from her lips. She gripped his shoulder more tightly and felt her lips part with pleasure.

"You are a siren," he whispered, bending to capture her lips beneath his own. His kiss was rougher and hungrier, filled with a ferocity that made Patience want more. His hand moved against her, demanding her response with a surety she could not resist. "And you will hold me in thrall," he growled against her neck.

But Patience was the one in thrall to his caress, and she could not find fault with that situation. She felt his finger slide inside her, first one and then the second, his kiss demanding her all even as his thumb drove her to madness. She felt lost in a storm, one in which Arthur was her only anchor, and she clung to him, surrendering to the sensation he provoked, trusting in him completely. The tide rose within her, relentless and thrilling, seizing every crumb of her attention and demanding that she surrender even more. She realized that Arthur teased her, tormenting her and then retreating, taking her to the cusp of something she could not name, then relenting in his caress. Again and again, he did this until he claimed her with his most demanding kiss yet. His thumb moved against her with new demand and she felt as if an explosion erupted within her, spilling heat and light in every direction.

Patience cried out with her release, shaking with its vigor and digging her nails into Arthur's shoulder. She smiled at him even as she struggled to catch her breath, and he moved atop her with purpose. "It may pierce this first time," he warned her, his voice low in her ear, then he moved against her. His hands were on her waist now, and she knew what would replace the demand of his fingers. She gasped only once, then felt a glorious satisfaction of being filled.

She opened her eyes to find Arthur looking down at her, his gaze still hot and intent. "Oh," she said, stroking his shoulders as she smiled.

"Oh," he echoed, watching her closely as he moved. The thrust rubbed against her, sending shivers through her once again, and she knew she flushed with delight.

"Arthur!" she said softly, her voice uncommonly low, and daringly lifted her knees to give him better access. When she saw the effect of her move in his reaction, she wrapped her legs around his waist. She heard his surprise in the way he caught his breath and saw desire in the glitter of his eyes.

"Siren," he murmured, then moved again, both of them gasping at the sensation. He chuckled then gathered her close, making her feel both treasured and aroused as he moved with deliberation, conjuring the storm again. Patience felt a quickening that she already recognized, and noticed the tension in him.

"What do I do?" she whispered.

"You are doing it," he said, his teeth gritted.

Patience laughed at the very suggestion. "I am doing nothing at all! You are doing all, and that is unfair. Let me inflict pleasure on you this time."

He studied her, a welcome fire in his eyes, then moved quickly so that she was atop him. He pulled up her knees so she was seated there, then interlaced their fingers. "I am your captive, Patience," he rumbled, looking entirely content with his situation. "Do with me as you will."

Oh! There was an invitation she could not refuse. Patience began to echo his movement, rising and falling atop him and watching the need grow within him. It was thrilling to watch his desire grow, to see his pulse at his throat, to feel the tension of his body beneath her own. It was potent to feel that she had some command over this man, that she was not the sole one lost to the sensation conjured between them.

With each stroke, she became bolder. With each move, she knew better how to continue. She watched him and repeated what gained the greatest response, finding her own desire grow along with his. She rocked atop Arthur, seeing his nostrils flare and his eyes glitter, feeling his grip tightening upon her hands as he gave her free rein to torment him. She gasped aloud as her pulse thundered in her eyes, felt her skin flush as the tumult rose within her. He felt larger and harder with every stroke and she bent impulsively to touch her lips to his, sliding her tongue between his lips to kiss him as fervently as he had kissed her.

And with that caress, Arthur lost his composure. He locked one arm around her waist and seized her nape, rolling her to her back to bury himself inside her. His hardness rubbed against her in the most perfect way and she cried out in ecstasy, clutching him as she shook in her release. She felt him shudder and the spill of his heat within her, then he murmured her name and caught her close, rolling to his back and cradling her against his chest.

"Arthur," she whispered, her cheek over the thunder of his heart, and he chuckled.

"Temptress," he accused, letting a fistful of her hair spill over his fingers and pool on his chest. She lifted her gaze to find his warm and filled with stars, his smile making her heart flutter anew. He bent and captured her lips once more, kissing her so sweetly that she thought her heart might break. "And so it is done, Mrs. Beckham," he said, clearly content with that.

"It is not done, Mr. Beckham," she replied, feeling audacious. "You have not shown me my beguiling spot."

"I have located it."

"But you promised to show me."

He rose with purpose, carrying her from the bed and sat down on a stool before the mirror. As she watched with wonder, he parted her thighs and caressed her boldly. Once again, his touch made everything jump within her and she writhed on his lap. "Look at you," he growled, and she stole a glance at the disheveled and flushed woman reflected in the glass. "Ah, Patience, now we can begin to discover what you like best."

"What do you like best, sir?"

His smile twisted. "I begin to think it might be you," he whispered, then stole another slow and thorough kiss. She was beginning to think his thumb was what she liked best, but she had no chance to confess as much. This time, the tide rose quickly and consumed her, leaving her clutching Arthur as she gained her release.

He grinned down at her and stood, holding her in his arms. "A bath," he whispered and when she might have argued, his eyes shone with devilry. "Together, Patience," he added and she flushed from head to toe at the very suggestion.

It was a sight that evidently gave him great satisfaction, for he laughed aloud and did not relinquish his grip upon her as the bath was summoned. Patience found herself wrapped in his nightshirt and held fast in his grip, and truly, there was nowhere she would rather have been.

~

It was a shocking thing for Lady Beckham to be so completely aware of the pursuit of pleasure beneath her own roof. She heard Arthur's roar of satisfaction repeatedly that afternoon, and even the delighted cry of his new bride. The springs of first one bed and then the other could be heard to move in a rhythm that could not be mistaken for anything other than what it was. Feet scampered down the hall as fires were built up then as a bath was summoned, then later yet as hot water was delivered to two chambers once again. She was certain she heard a tray being delivered to sustain the lovers and ground her teeth that matters should have gone so far awry.

Not only had he wed the daughter of a tradesman, but that match was consummated so surely that everyone in Mayfair must know the truth of it.

Perhaps the girl would conceive soon—there was no reason she might not, given their enthusiasm for each other—and die in childbirth. Lady Beckham took some reassurance from that possible means of removing the unacceptable bride from Arthur's life.

She supposed the chit was better than the other one, but only just.

Why were men such ridiculous fools?

She had no reply to that question by the time she descended for dinner, uncertain whether she would be dining alone or not. To her dismay, her brother had arrived, having invited himself to dine.

"I gather your luck has not changed," she said by way of greeting. "It is a sad day that you must visit me only to ensure that you have a good meal."

"Yvonne, how can you doubt my devotion?" Reynaud demanded, striving for charm and missing his target completely. He bowed and she surveyed what had to be a new waistcoat. She shook her head and proceeded into the dining room as Arthur and his new wife appeared.

They both looked so delighted that she almost forgave him for his matrimonial error. He seated her with a consideration that filled Lady Beckham with envy. She was not to be revered or teased or honored in future. She was only to be a means to an end, a source of funds, a treasury for his indulgences.

The girl was wearing a necklace and earrings that Lady Beckham wagered had been purchased by her son.

"Are those sapphires, Arthur?" she asked, knowing she sounded waspish and not caring.

"They are indeed, Mother," he said smoothly, taking his own place. "Patience has no gems so I saw fit to repair that with a wedding gift. I thought the hue of the stones would favor her eyes."

His bride blushed prettily, her eyes sparkling as she held his gaze.

Arthur stared at her like a man besotted.

Had Lady Beckham chosen the gift, one that she surely paid for, she would have been less generous. "Amethysts might have suited as well," she found herself saying and Reynaud chortled.

"Ever frugal, my dear sister," he said. His words might have been teasing, but there was an edge to his tone that hinted otherwise. "But Arthur has been confoundedly lucky of late at the tables. Doubtless, he could have stretched to diamonds and tiaras to adorn for his wife, without concern for the expense at all."

Arthur granted his uncle a cool glance. "It is true, Uncle, that I paid for the gems from my recent gains. I did not realize that would cause offense."

It did not cause offense, but it made Lady Beckham wonder. "I did not realize you had been so fortunate of late," she said, as the soup was served. A good hot clear leek soup for a damp night. There was nothing better. She inhaled in approval.

"I thought it vulgar to discuss such a detail," Arthur said lightly.

"You have not in the past," Reynaud noted.

"I have not been so lucky in the past." He saluted his

bride with his glass. "It is clear that good fortune comes to me in all matters."

The lady smiled and tasted her soup, murmuring admiration of it that was wholly deserved.

"You might lend me some of those funds," Reynaud said.

"I think not, Uncle." There was steel in Arthur's tone.

"You have no need of it," Reynaud protested, his tone becoming peevish. "You have every comfort here while I am utterly without funds."

"Perhaps you should have left the tables sooner," Arthur said mildly.

"Perhaps you could show some kindness to your relations," Reynaud snapped.

Arthur looked up. His gaze flicked to Lady Beckham, his resolve as clear as the direction of his thoughts. Something had changed. She had an intimation of a new defiance, though he had never given money to Reynaud that she knew of.

What was he going to do?

Why did he need that money? That he had not spoken of it, not so much as mentioned it, was curious to her. She would check with her bankers in the morning about his funds, for Lady Beckham smelled a plot.

"I have declined, Uncle," he said quietly.

"And I am in dire straits," Reynaud said, casting down his napkin. "That wretched tradesman, Grosvenor, has bought up all of my outstanding bang debts and would compel me to wed his daughter!"

"This is not my situation to repair," Arthur said calmly.

"It is!" Reynaud shouted, as petulant as only he could be. "You should have married her. You were the one she wanted. Now the chit is determined to have me, the better to cheat you of any chance of inheriting the title."

"Truly?" Arthur said calmly. "She does not surrender a battle readily, does she?"

He did not seem to care about the title, but that, Lady Beckham knew, was his lineage speaking. She gritted her teeth.

Reynaud, of course, was in the midst of a tantrum and disinclined to notice anything but himself. "Worse, her father is determined to grant her desire. Instead of acting for the best of the family, Arthur, you betrayed me, abandoned your duty, and married *her*." He pointed to the new bride and all turned to consider her.

The new Mrs. Beckham put down her soup spoon. She looked pale but resolute. She did not cry, nor did she rise to Raynaud's words and reply in kind. "Lady Beckham, I would ask to excuse myself. My presence appears to be causing offense at your table."

Despite herself, Lady Beckham admired the girl for speaking thus. She quickly assessed the situation and decided that she would prefer Arthur's loyalty to that of her younger brother. Reynaud would always come crawling to her for one favor or another, but Arthur showed signs of potential rebellion.

The situation might yet be saved, and turned to her satisfaction.

Lady Beckham smiled at the younger woman. "Nonsense. My brother is the one whose manners are bad and whose comments are unwelcome. I apologize for his vulgarity." She lifted her gaze to the earl, who glared at her from the other end of the table. "And I suggest, Reynaud, that you are no longer welcome on this night. Perhaps you can find someone else to see your belly and your purse filled." She lifted a finger. "I know. Perhaps you should call upon Mr. Grosvenor and spend some time with your intended."

Reynaud swore with impressive vigor, then spun from the table, marching out of the dining room then out of the house.

"I thank you, Mother," Arthur said quietly and she smiled at him.

"Perhaps you might find me a little trinket when next you visit the jeweller's shop," she said, intending to make a jest though it did not sound like one.

Her gaze locked with that of Arthur, who did not appear to be amused, then he smiled thinly and nodded once, returning his attention to his dinner.

Something was in the wind and Lady Beckham intended to discover what it was, with all haste.

CHAPTER 12

"Of course, we must hear you play," Lady Beckham said when the horror of dinner was finally over.

Patience could have groaned aloud, but instead she smiled. "I fear, Lady Beckham, that my playing will not be of the excellence to which you are accustomed."

"You do play?" that lady said, gesturing to the pianoforte.

"Of course, but my sister Prudence is infinitely more talented and dearly loves to play. It is a matter of routine in my father's house that she plays when we are to be entertained." Patience took a seat in the drawing room as far from the instrument as possible. She also chose a chair that was not positioned to dominate the room, as she feared that might be taken as a challenge.

Lady Beckham paused beside a fine card table. "We have not the numbers for whist or quadrille, though I suppose Miss Granger could be prevailed upon."

Miss Granger, Patience knew, was the governess who tutored Amelia. She scarce had time to marvel at the magnitude of this concession before Lady Beckham continued.

"Her father was a baronet by birth, after all, though

the lands were lost when he was only a child." She fixed Patience with a stern eye. "Do you play casino?" Patience shook her head. "Piquet?" Again, Patience was compelled to shake her head. Lady Beckham sighed magnificently. "Is there any game of chance you play?"

"As a child, I played cribbage with my grandmother. Though it has been years, I might recall the game with some instruction."

Lady Beckham turned away. "I am not so aged as that," she muttered.

Arthur winked at Patience, apparently more accustomed to his mother's poor humors. "I would wager that Patience and her family are inclined to read in the evening."

Lady Beckham exhaled and took her seat, the one with the most commanding view of the room. She looked between the two of them, her dissatisfaction clear. Tea was poured for the ladies, a port for Arthur, then the butler vanished quietly. "I do not suppose you have any tidings to share?" she asked Arthur.

"I have been in my chamber all day, Mother, and it is rather early for Patience and I to have any tidings from that quarter to share. I request that you grant us a few months."

Patience felt her eyes widen that he would speak so boldly but Lady Beckham almost smiled.

"A boy," she said to Patience.

"I do not believe children are ordered like flowers for the foyer," Arthur drawled, then his tone hardened. "If and when we are so fortunate as to welcome a child, its gender will have no influence upon our delight." He sipped his port, his gaze like steel. "Mother."

Something passed between the pair of them at that last word, though Patience could not explain it. If she had been compelled to try, she might have guessed that Arthur's mother knew at least one of his secrets. She supposed that made sense, for no one else had known him longer, but she could not help but feel that she missed a pertinent detail.

Lady Beckham turned upon Patience again. "And what will you do, now that you are married, while you await that happy day?"

"I had thought to continue as I have been, if possible. I like assisting clients in my father's shop."

Lady Beckham put down her tea so hard that Patience feared for the china. "You intend to work in a shop? Like a clerk?"

"My sister, Baroness Trevelaine, did as much after she was married."

"The fact that others in your family have no sense of decency does not mean that you should follow their example."

Patience might have argued in Catherine's defense, but Lady Beckham continued forcefully.

"You are my son's wife now, and thus nearly my daughter. I am the daughter of the Earl of Fairhaven and I forbid you to return to such menial labor."

Patience did not think time spent in her father's shop was menial or labor. She straightened to defend herself but Arthur spoke first.

"What would you have Patience do?" he demanded. "Visit the sick? Shop for stockings and pastries? Leave calling cards hither and yon?" He yawned mightily, but Patience could see by the gleam of his eyes that he was deadly serious. "I cannot imagine a life more tedious for a clever lady like my wife. Discussing books all day sounds infinitely more fascinating and a better foil for her nature."

Once again, Lady Beckham glared at him, and once again, he held her gaze as if in challenge.

Lady Beckham took a sip of her tea. "I suppose it

would be too much to ask that your wife take an interest in sharing my charitable work."

"That work is your interest," Arthur said mildly. "I would not for a moment make any suggestion that might deprive you of its many satisfactions."

"Arthur!"

"Tomorrow, Mother, I propose that I will escort Patience to her father's place of business to consult with him about her future plans." He finished his port and set the glass aside. "We will return in time to dine with you, if that is satisfactory."

"I suppose it must be," Lady Beckham acknowledged.

"Excellent," Arthur said and rose to his feet. He offered Patience his hand. "If you have finished your tea, I should very much like to retire and read more of my book."

Patience bit back a smile, guessing what book that might be. She rose and put her hand in his, glad that he had come to her rescue. He bowed to his mother and she curtsied, then they left the drawing room together. Arthur cast her a warning glance and she remained silent as they climbed the stairs together.

How she yearned for her own household!

Within moments, Gellis had helped her to undress and left her alone in her chamber. She opened the door to Arthur's chamber to find him leaning there once more, a smile lifting the corner of his mouth. "Alone at last," he murmured, linking their hands and drawing her to the chairs before the fire. "Get along, Tar," he said, nudging the black cat out of one seat.

"*Catrame*," Patience corrected.

He looked up at her, then his eyes lit with laughter as he understood. "You did rename them."

"*Catrame e Piume.* Amelia and I decided that Italian cats should have Italian names."

He murmured the names beneath his breath and chuckled, then sat down and drew her down to nestle on the seat beside him. It was a cozy fit, but Patience liked the feel of him against her. "And now we scheme," he whispered in her ear, his arms closing around her.

"Is everything a calculation?"

"No, but more things are than many people believe. When my mother is vexed, it is wiser to proceed with care." He stared into the fire, clearly considering his options. Catrame took advantage of this moment to leap back into Arthur's lap and he smiled as he dropped a hand onto the cat, ruffling its fur. "I am thinking that you might seek your father's advice about our proposed alliance," he said finally and Patience understood. "He may have suggestions."

"He may, indeed. My father loves to solve matters, and I would be glad to consult him first."

Arthur nodded, then studied her. His gaze was dark and his expression made her remember all they had done earlier that afternoon. "Are you sore?" His voice was low and velvety, his concern enough to melt her reservations away.

"A little," she confessed.

"Then we will read tonight."

"I can imagine nothing better," she admitted and he smiled.

"I read one of your favorite books, now it is time for one of mine."

"Is it here?"

"Of course. Who else would I entrust with my treasures?"

She rose to retrieve the book. "Which one?"

"*The Canterbury Tales*. I had a tutor who believed all wisdom upon the human condition could be found within its pages."

Patience fetched the book, fanning through it. It was

a fine edition with several illustrations. "I have never read it all."

"I think the Wife of Bath's tale would be particularly apt this evening," Arthur said. He stretched his legs out toward the fire and opened the volume, his hand still in Catrame's fur. Patience took the other chair and Piume jumped into her lap, circling before she laid down as well. The fire crackled, the cats purred and Arthur read aloud.

Patience was certain there could not have been a more perfect evening. She must have dozed off because she awakened as she was lifted into Arthur's arms. "I fell asleep. I am sorry."

"You did not hear the moral of the tale, then."

His tone was teasing and she watched him. "Which is?"

"That what a woman desires most is her own way, of course." He grinned down at her. "And so the choice is yours, Patience. Would you sleep alone, with me in your bed or with me in mine? I feel compelled to note that my bed is larger, though your chamber is warmer."

"Which would you prefer?"

He looked down at her, smiling slightly, then bent and claimed her lips in a potent kiss. He took his time, savoring the embrace, conjuring a heat within her that made her toes curl. When he lifted his head and looked down at her, his eyes glimmered with an intent that made her heart skip. "I would be with you, here or there, but I heed the wife of Bath's counsel."

"Here, then," Patience whispered. "Tomorrow, we can sleep there."

"For a lady can only make a firm choice once she has gathered all the details."

Patience laughed, though she was concerned that she might not sleep at all. She should not have feared as much. Arthur lay behind her, his arm around her waist and his breath in her hair, his heat at her back. The fire burned down low and first one cat, then the other, jumped onto the bed. She nestled against him and he gave a little growl that made her smile, then she slept again, content in his embrace.

❧

THERE WERE WHISPERS AT CARRUTHERS & Carruthers when Arthur escorted Patience into her father's establishment. To his satisfaction, her father appeared immediately and invited them back into his office. Patience was radiant, a fact that her father surely noticed, and Arthur was glad of that man's nod of approval.

She told her father of the plan to invest in Fanshawe & Parke, which made that man's brows rise. He looked at Arthur who nodded once. "I am surprised," Mr. Carruthers admitted, fixing Arthur with a look. "I did not expect you to enter trade, sir."

"I believe Patience has an excellent idea and I would see her ambition supported."

Her father nodded, satisfied with this partial truth. "You must have a plan of what titles you would publish."

Patience visibly took a breath. "There is a volume of intimate advice for ladies that Catherine has been editing…"

Her father shook his head. "The one I declined to publish? Such a book…"

"Is needed and necessary," Patience said with resolve. "This volume helped Catherine and her husband and it has also helped me. I must ensure that it is available to a wider audience."

Mr. Carruthers was wary but Arthur had the sense

that two daughters in agreement swayed his view slightly. "And you agree?" he asked Arthur.

Arthur nodded. "I do."

"Your mother will be scandalized, to be sure."

Arthur shrugged and Patience's father studied him for a long moment.

"But then, if it succeeded, such details would not be of concern," he mused and Arthur nodded again.

Patience looked between them, not understanding as much as her father did, but that man continued before she could ask.

"One book does not a publisher make, Patience, no matter how successful that volume might be. I would suggest to you that you make it part of a larger offering. You know that the lending library is highly popular with ladies and many of them have income to spare."

"Special editions?" Patience asked.

"A special library," Arthur guessed. "All of a size, and designed to look well together on a shelf."

Mr. Carruthers wagged a finger. "And such a plan will take advantage of Fanshawe's gift. The man has a skill for ensuring the economy of a series of books the better to ensure their pricing. He can wrestle every scrap out of a sheet of paper, a bindery board or a piece of leather. He created a series of Latin and Greek works for the gentleman's library."

"They were oxblood leather with gold," Patience recalled. "All the same."

"Most attractive on a shelf," Arthur said. "Even if they were never opened and read."

Mr. Carruthers nodded. "There is good revenue in such a series. People can subscribe for two books a month perhaps, or choose them individually. Fanshawe does not have the space in his facility for a lending library, but I would buy at least one of each volume for our lending library."

"And I could write to the other lending libraries to suggest the same to them!" Patience said.

"And you could choose titles that you know to be popular with the ladies who borrow books here. I have no objection to you checking our records to make your choices."

Arthur smiled at Patience's delight. "Papa! That is so clever."

"Ah, the idea was yours, Patience. I merely packaged it up that Fanshawe might find it more appealing. The prospect of steady revenue with these books will outweigh any objection he might have to the other." Mr. Carruthers shrugged. "And if that one is destined to be as successful as you suspect it will be, then Fanshawe will be delighted."

"You might need several copies for your lending library," Arthur said and Carruthers laughed aloud.

"Such a book might tend to vanish, Mr. Beckham. I would suggest you sell the copies that you print. Now you have me intrigued, Patience. Let us consult the files. There will undoubtedly be obvious choices, but perhaps a few unexpected ones, as well."

"Yes," she agreed with delight, spinning to Arthur to kiss his cheek before she turned to the files with anticipation.

"And I would invite you both to dinner this week, at your convenience," Carruthers said. "I regret that I have been remiss in arranging such an event, though truly, I have relied heavily upon Patience to manage the house since her sister's marriage. All is less organized in her absence, to be sure."

She turned to Arthur, her eyes alight. "We should be delighted, Papa."

"Please choose the date," Arthur said. "We are at your disposal, sir."

He watched the pair as he considered what he had

just learned. Patience had managed her father's house-hold. Arthur felt foolish for not guessing as much sooner. She was sensible and organized, and probably had managed the house effortlessly. Patience would find it doubly challenging to be beneath Lady Beckham's thumb after being the one to make choices.

Yet he could not finance the publishing venture and the establishment of a household at the same time. Those of his acquaintance who found themselves in debt entered that state due to an excess of ambition and a failure to accommodate unexpected expense. He would ensure the stability of the publishing endeavor first. If the books succeeded as they hoped, they might establish their household in a year or so.

He would also continue to gamble, in hope of giving Patience her wish sooner.

~

DAME FORTUNE ABANDONED ARTHUR, just when he believed he had greatest need of her favor.

He returned to the gaming tables on Monday night, even though it was not likely to be an evening with high stakes. Enduring another meal with Lady Beckham, who made no effort to hide her disdain for Patience, had only strengthened his resolve to arrange an escape.

The difficulty, as ever, would be funds.

If he left the house in Berkley Square, he could not rely upon any financial support from Lady Beckham. There might be some, but equally, there might not be. At the same time, he was aware that those of his acquaintance who ended up in debt found that path by pursuing too many options at the same time. Given his preference, he would keep the focus on the publishing venture to ensure its success.

But that might mean several years in Lady Beckham's domain. Could Patience endure it? Would the older lady's view soften? Arthur preferred to have choices, so he returned to the tables with hope in his heart.

His desire was not to be fulfilled. The cards had turned against him with such vigor that his prospects on this night were abundantly clear. He lost ten pounds only before he left, waving off the heckles of his companions that he was distracted by his new obligations of matrimony, and returned home.

His spirits lifted as the hackney approached the house. There was a light in the window of Patience's chamber, and Arthur knew who he most wished to see.

PATIENCE WAS BECOMING convinced that she would lose her wits in this house, for lack of anything of merit to do. She had never been idle and it was not a condition she welcomed.

Though once she would have been enthusiastic at the opportunity to read to her heart's delight, several days of such activity fed her impatience to be useful. She knew that she would visit Mr. Fanshawe with Arthur on Wednesday morning, but that appointment seemed an eternity away.

Arthur had departed for his club after dinner and Lady Beckham had retired, leaving Patience to wander about her room, talk to the cats, and read.

It was not long before she heard a cab halt before the house. She wondered who might visit and peeked out her window, only to see Arthur himself approaching the steps. He glanced up and waved to her with his usual flair, an indication that nothing was amiss.

Still. Why was he home so early? It was scarcely ten o'clock.

She heard his steps on the stairs, his cheerful greeting of Stevens, and the closing of his own chamber door. When he rapped upon the adjoining door, she smiled and could not open it with sufficient speed. He had only shed his hat and gloves, his haste to reach her apparent. He murmured her name, stepped into her room and caught her in his arms, bending to kiss her so thoroughly that she was left breathless.

"I feared you might be asleep," he confessed finally.

"I am not tired." She sighed and chose to tell him more. "I do so little each day, after all."

He nodded and she noted that he did not progress toward the bookcase, to add to the sum hidden in the book-that-was-not-a-book.

"Did you not triumph tonight?"

He laughed a little. "Not at all. I chose to leave rather than linger."

"You said before that gambling was all mathematics."

"And so it is. Would you like to see?"

When Patience nodded, he caught her hand in his and led her back into his own room. Taylor was there and took his jacket, the fire having already been stirred to life. Arthur dismissed his valet and guided Patience to a small table of the sort used for games. There were drawers in two sides of it and a chequered board inlaid in its top, made of polished squares of ebony and ivory. He removed a deck of playing cards from one drawer and shuffled them deftly even as he took the seat opposite her.

"In every game of chance, there is an objective, and that objective defines what the astute player must watch. Do you know *vingt-et-un*?"

"Each player must collect cards that total twenty-one," Patience said.

"Precisely." Arthur turned over the cards and spread them across the table. "You see that if you mean to have twenty-one, you will need a ten or a court card, along with an ace."

"Yes," Patience agreed, trying to find the mathematics. "So there are only twenty cards of real import?"

"Four," he corrected, pulling out the four aces. "You cannot win without one of these."

"But perhaps no one will have them."

"Perhaps not." He scooped up the cards and shuffled them again. "If we have six players and the dealer, that is seven by two or fourteen cards. What are the chances that one of those fourteen is an ace?"

"There are fifty-two in the deck, are there not?" At his nod, Patience thought about it, watching as he deftly dealt the cards, face down, two to each place as if there were seven players all together. "One in four?"

"Precisely. So, we assume there is at least one ace already in play, thus one person at the table has a chance of a winning hand. Now we wager."

"Before looking at the cards?"

Arthur nodded. "A show of bravado, for it is based on no information at all." He lifted a finger. "But it will reveal the nature of each player. Are they bold or meek? Do they assume their good fortune or do they wait to see?"

Patience smiled. "It is not just the cards you read."

He grinned. "Not at all. The better you know your fellow players, the more readily their reactions can be read. I know one gentleman whose left eyelid ticks when he has an ace. I know another who only raises the stakes when he has at least twenty."

Patience nodded understanding. How interesting that there were so many ways to anticipate the outcome, beyond the calculations he mentioned. She had a new appreciation for Arthur's cleverness, for his decisions would have to be made instantly and in the presence of many distractions. "How do you do it so quickly?" she asked. "It must be almost instinctive."

"It becomes that way. And drink must be avoided at all costs. It dulls the judgement and fuels one's optimism."

She nodded understanding, watching his hands.

"Once those wagers are made, we look at our cards." He turned over the cards from the first pile to his left.

"The player would not show them to all, would he?" Patience asked.

"No, but we are learning."

There was an ace and a deuce.

"One ace," Patience noted.

"Though no one else knows, as yet. This player is asked whether he will stand or not. Of course, he will not. He asks for another card." Arthur put the card on top. It was a three.

"Sixteen," she said.

"Some would fold, but this player demands another." Arthur snapped down the next card from the deck. It was an eight.

Patience winced. "Too much."

"And he is out." Arthur cast the cards into the middle of the table, face up. "He must pay his stake because he has lost. Now all the players know that one ace is accounted for."

The next 'player' had a jack and a nine. Patience suggested he might hold and Arthur nodded.

She was next and discovered she had a queen and an ace, much to her delight. She said she would hold and Arthur nodded.

The next 'player' had an ace and a seven.

"I would hold," Patience said but Arthur shook his head.

"Perhaps if this player was first. But by now, two players have held already. One of them must have twenty, if not twenty-one. He might as well ask for a card." Arthur tossed the card across the table face-up. It was a two.

"He will hold," Patience said.

"He will hold," Arthur agreed.

The next two players took cards until their totals were too high. Among the discarded cards were a number of court cards.

"What do you see?" Arthur invited.

"Only one ace known to all," Patience said. "Three players holding, which means at least one must have twenty, as you said. And I know the location of a second ace."

He indicated the cards before himself. "And here is the moment I see whether the cards favor me tonight. If so, this will be twenty-one." He turned over the cards received by the dealer. He winced at the two fives. "At least Dame Fortune is consistent," he murmured.

"Of course, you will take a card," Patience said.

"It can only bring me closer. Though in practice, I would not know the contents of your hand or that of the other player who held, there are still many court cards in play. I could easily reach twenty and that might be sufficient."

"What about the aces?"

"I would consider that either you or the other player who was holding might have one. That you both kept your original cards might indicate that one of you already has twenty-one."

"Two aces assumed to be gone and twenty-one cards played."

"That's not half the deck."

He tapped the top of the deck with a fingertip. "What do you think it is?"

"A court card or a ten," Patience said.

Arthur nodded. "If the cards were coming to me. I would hope for an ace." He turned over the card. It was an eight.

"Eighteen," Patience said. "You would take another card."

"I would, though it seems Dame Fortune taunts me. The proof will lie in this card."

"You would stake so much upon it."

"There are times when the cards flow, each one appearing for you as if summoned. And there are times when the cards declined to show favor. On those occasions, only fools continue to play, hoping for a change. If the die is cast, it is best to walk away." He tapped the top card. "Will it be a two, a three or a four?"

"If you are lucky."

"And on this night, I have not been. It will be a larger card." Arthur turned it over a five.

Too much.

He picked up his cards and cast them face up into the middle of the table. "And now we have another round of wagers, from those who remain in the game. Then everyone turns over their cards. Anyone who has less than the dealer will pay his stake. Those who have the same score as the dealer do not pay." He tapped her cards. "But you have twenty-one, and you have it naturally—which means it was dealt to you—and the dealer has folded, so you have won the game."

Patience considered the cards upon the table. "I can see why people are seduced. It seems so simple."

"But one must heed the cards and the message they send." Arthur tapped the eight. "If I were lucky this night, this would be an ace."

Patience understood. "That is why you are home so early."

He nodded agreement, gathering up the cards and putting them away.

She could see that he was discontent and wished she could reassure him. She did not like that he gambled, even though he was good at it and seemed to be prudent. "Will you always play?" she asked, fearing the answer.

He turned to study her, his expression inscrutable. "I must contribute something to our shared future," he said. His tone was light, but Patience knew his mood was not. "If I assisted you in the choice of new dresses each and every day, you would soon be overwhelmed by garments."

"You must be able to do other things," she chided.

His brows rose. "Not any that you would deem to be of merit."

Was she so demanding as this? She was shocked to think that he believed she might hold him in such low regard and would have reassured him, had his expression not turned wicked.

"Although," he mused. "I believe there is one activity in which you believe me to have promise." His eyes sparkled as he surveyed her and she welcomed the sight of his smile. "Will you choose a page from your book, Patience?"

THE BOOK MANUSCRIPT mocked Arthur as vehemently as the cards. Patience chose blindly from the sheaf of papers and they read the page together.

Upon the merit of disguise...

Arthur cast the page back with an excuse and chose another.

Upon the merit of surrendering secrets...

Patience eyed him, the direction of her thoughts most clear, but Arthur pulled another page from the manuscript before she could protest.

Upon the merit of leisure...

It has become routine in our busy world to admire the efficiency of haste in gaining our objectives. This, I suspect, comes from a suspicion of surfeit, that is the conviction that a limited quantity of all goodness exists and that each of us, to ensure we have our share, must lay claim to prizes with speed and enthusiasm. We fear the prospect of missing out on some lauded advantage or pleasure.

I not only adhere to the opposing view—that there is more than sufficient of all goodness to accommodate the desires of all people—but insist that each increment of the pursuit of a goal should be savored. Not only should the chase itself be enjoyed for its own sake, but victories should be appreciated. The capitulation of two parties to physical pleasures, shared affection, and even mutual ardor is a journey of many steps and stages. Each one should be celebrated as it is reached—and the best way to celebrate intimacy is with the gift of time.

What purpose is achieved in a hasty union? Perhaps physical satisfaction is gained, but perhaps not. In my experience, the delight in the encounter increases based upon the time spent in pursuit of the ultimate goal. There is little more seductive or satisfying than an appointment of some hours duration, preferably behind a locked door and without interruption, in which two partners explore each other and each learn the preferences of the other.

This is the basis of a bond to defy all others, for what begins in offering sensation and physical pleasure can readily expand to include confidences and confessions. Once that foundation is made and two partners continue to strive to provide for the happiness of the other, affection is sure to dawn, and from affection, all great loves begin. Indulge in time with your lover. Linger over the pleasure you can offer each other and learn what your partner loves best. Do not hasten to finish an interval, for mutual satisfaction is not a race, and the surrender of the heart is well worth the expenditure of time.

They read the passage together, then Patience looked up at Arthur, her eyes dark. He watched her swallow and wanted nothing more than the sweet capitulation offered by this advice.

"It is yet early," he noted and she nodded immediately.

"I have no other engagements on this evening," she said quickly and Arthur smiled.

He put down the page and framed her face in his hands, savoring her trust. He bent and kissed her cheek softly, feeling how she trembled a little. Her hand rose to cover his and he felt her catch her breath. Her eyes closed as he slid one hand into her hair, drawing her closer, and kissed her ear. "You like this," he murmured, then grazed her skin with his teeth.

"Oh yes," she confessed, her voice shaking.

"Tell me what you like best," he invited.

"Your kiss, your teeth, your breath."

He continued to kiss her, loosening her braid so he could entangle his fingers in her hair. He felt her clutch his shoulder and smiled that she rose to her toes, pressing herself against his chest so that he could feel her pert nipples.

"Your voice when you murmur to me." She caught her breath, almost laughing. "Your very wicked thumb."

Arthur smiled, lifting his other hand to her breast. Through her chemise, he teased her nipple, liking how she squirmed. "This one?"

"That one," she agreed, then drew back to look at him. Their noses almost touched, their breath mingled, and the wonder in her expression humbled him. "I like that you know what to do," she said. "And I like that you do it with me."

Arthur smiled. "How could I resist?"

He might have kissed her but she placed her fingertips over his mouth. "What do you like?" she asked, her gaze searching his.

"I like how clever you are," he admitted. "I like how you tell me details of some pertinence when you are uncertain –" she laughed a little at this and blushed "– but mostly I like that your uncertainty does not stop you."

"It would if I did not trust you."

"Then I like that you trust me. I am honored by that." He watched his thumb slide across her nipple and felt her hair around his other hand. "I like that I can make you blush or prompt your smile. I like that you respond to me, that you heed me, and that there is this wondrous camaraderie between us."

"It is wondrous," she agreed, flushing so that he wanted to devour her.

"I like that you chastise me," he said, for it was true. "And I like that you surprise me."

"There is much that you like then," she said, her tone teasing.

"More than I ever imagined possible, and this in a matter of days." He smiled down at her. "In no time, Patience, you will hold me utterly in thrall." Even as he said the words, Arthur recognized that they were already true. He loved her, heart and soul. And if the way to capture her heart was with leisurely lovemaking, then he would spend every moment seducing his bride.

But on this night, he wagered he would surprise her.

250

CHAPTER 13

*P*atience knew Arthur well enough to recognize that he had a scheme, and his fleeting smile indicated that it was a mischievous one. She did not doubt that it would also be a seductive one, and perhaps a surprise. He kissed her before she could ask and she kissed him back, wanting to show that she found encouragement in the passage they had just read. This time, she strove to abandon herself to sensation, no longer fighting against a loss of control, choosing to trust Arthur completely.

That he was as aroused as she made her capitulation simpler. She was thrilled at his incoherent groan of satisfaction, of the urgency she felt growing within him. He was taut and demanding, his kiss so possessive that it nearly made her swoon.

It seemed that she had a power to excite him that might even equal his ability to make her forget her usual reserve. The notion was a thrilling one and she caressed him, loving how he responded to her touch.

Wonder of wonders, her own body responded to him and she found herself clutching his hair, her mouth open as she kissed with as much savage demand as he showered upon her. She felt him swing her into his arms with purpose. In a heartbeat, she was upon the bed on her back, still kissing him, Arthur bent over her. She reveled in the warm strength of his hands in her hair, and the way he pressed her into the mattress, his solid strength holding her captive to his caress.

He broke their kiss and whispered her name, looking down at her with a marvel in his eyes that made her smile. She untied his cravat and cast it aside, then worked loose the buttons on his waistcoat. He moved to facilitate her efforts, a smile curving his lips as she tugged his shirt free of his breeches. She unfastened his cuffs and pushed the cloth over his shoulder, not hiding her admiration as she surveyed his bare chest.

She landed a fingertip upon the scar, which curled over his shoulder. She knew it was deeper upon his back. "A secret?" she asked.

He shrugged. "Souvenir of a duel. It was the sole time I was injured, and I vowed I would never be so again."

"Do not tell me that you always win."

"I usually do." He stole a kiss. "Partly because I do not take a wager I am doomed to lose."

She laughed, then he silenced her with a kiss that left her gasping with need. He rolled her over with ease and unfastened her dress, kissing her bared shoulders as he pushed it down along with her chemise. She rolled back, arching toward him for his kiss, and his hand cupped her bared breast. He teased the nipple to a taut peak with an ease that should have alarmed her but Patience found herself arching her back, wanting more and more and more.

When his mouth closed over that same nipple, she jumped in surprise. But then he flicked his tongue across the tight bud, sending sensation surging through her and she fell back against the pillow, content to let him do whatsoever he desired. She was on fire with need, but trusted him completely to guide her on this new adventure. The graze of his teeth made her gasp aloud, then he turned his attention to the other breast, his hands locked around her waist and pushing her garments steadily downward. She playfully lifted her buttocks off the bed to aid in his quest, earning herself a wicked upward glance that made her laugh aloud. Then Arthur swept her dress and shift aside, cupped her buttocks in his hands and kissed her most bewitching spot.

Patience fell back in astonishment at this caress and its effect. She gasped as he settled to teasing it with gusto and heard herself moan in unbridled pleasure. Indeed, she could not have stopped herself—and the last thing she wanted him to do was stop. As before, he took his time, making her blood quicken, then pulling back, teasing her repeatedly with the prospect of release then cheating her of it. Each time, the tumult built a little higher until she gripped his shoulders, almost incoherent in her desire. She entreated him to grant her release. She writhed beneath him. She seized a fistful of his hair and he laughed, the fan of his breath against her only increasing her agitation. The next time he drove her toward the summit, she was certain he would draw back again—but he continued, pressing onward, demanding more and more of her until finally, he cast her over the abyss and she shouted with her final release.

He drew himself up beside her, his eyes glimmering with satisfaction, and Patience reached for his chausses. "Now," she urged and a flame lit in his eyes. He stood up and shed his remaining garb with haste, wiping his face with his shirt, then returned to the bed. Patience wrapped herself around him, welcoming his weight atop her and his heat within her. It was easier this time, smoother and simpler, more familiar and more wonderful. She rolled her hips beneath him and watched him inhale sharply, then he rolled to his back so that she was perched atop him once more. This time, she leaned down and kissed him, loving the wicked taste of him, driving him onward, then cheating him of release as he had done to her.

And when finally she ceded, pushing him to the climax he had earned, Arthur roared with satisfaction. His arms locked around her and he drove deep inside her, shuddered with the power of his release, then kissed her shoulder, her neck, her ear and finally her lips.

He whispered her name with a reverence that Patience could understand, and she found herself drifting asleep, still wound around his strength.

This union was a marvel indeed and one that improved each time. She smiled in anticipation of their next attempt, even as Arthur pulled the covers over them both. "I need a rest before I divest you of those stockings," he murmured into her hair and she laughed before he kissed her to silence again.

$\sim$

PATIENCE WAS PERFECTION.

Arthur sat in the offices of Fanshawe & Parke the next morning, watching Patience explain the details of her venture to Mr. Fanshawe. The older man was clearly skeptical when they arrived, but Arthur deferred to Patience in the discussion. She spoke decisively and with conviction, showing a passion for her plan that Arthur found most compelling. Her discussion with her father had only buttressed the original notion so that she had not only a scheme but a reply to every question posed by the older gentlemen.

Arthur fought against his smile as he watched Mr.

Fanshawe's reservations be steadily overwhelmed, then a glint of enthusiasm dawned in the other man's eye. By the time, Patience had answered all of his questions, he sat forward in his chair, apparently intent upon beginning the venture with all haste.

She cast him a glance, her eyes sparkling as if they were filled with stars, and he reached to take her hand. As Mr. Fanshawe and Mr. Sommerset retired to review Arthur's offer, he kissed Patience's hand.

"Was I too forthright?" she whispered.

"You were perfect," he said with conviction, and held her gaze until she flushed with pleasure. He was glad to be fulfilling his pledge to her and excited about the possibilities of this new venture. The agreement was made, and Mr. Sommerset declared that he would draw up the necessary contracts. They would meet in a week to seal the partnership.

Patience almost floated to the carriage, her satisfaction so great that it was impossible to disguise. Arthur shook hands with Mr. Sommerset, and handed her into the coach, wishing he could give her even more.

"Oh, Arthur, even Lady Beckham cannot sour my mood on this day," Patience said. "Thank you!"

"I made a promise and I kept it. Surely that is not so remarkable."

"You have another to keep," she reminded him, placing her hand upon his thigh in a most distracting manner.

"I do," he agreed, forming a plan even as he met her gaze. "I would visit my club again tonight," he said, watching the light in her eyes dim a little. "The tide may have changed and more is always better."

She heaved a sigh. "Will it ever be enough?" she asked, her gaze searching his own.

Arthur was the one to look away first. He feared he

would never be able to do enough to win her heart, but he would use every available moment to try.

If he could win enough to establish their own household as well, she might surrender her heart to him. He could only try.

~

THE HOUSE on Berkley Square echoed with silence when Patience returned alone. Arthur had helped her out of the coach, then returned to it, waving a jaunty farewell as he departed for his club. Stevens was as impassive and somber as ever, only volunteering that Lady Beckham was out for the afternoon when Patience asked. Upon being pressed further, he confessed that Miss Beckham and her governess were also absent, having chosen to attend a lecture at Lady Beckham's suggestion.

It was remarkable to Patience that a house could even be so quiet. She climbed the stairs to her room, not feeling sufficiently audacious to sit in the drawing room alone, and smiled when she realized the cats were following her. The three of them settled into her bedchamber, Gellis hastening to light the fire and tend to Patience's coat.

She could not help but feel let down to be alone after the triumph of that morning. She picked up the book she had been reading but could summon no interest in it at all. She had read it too many times.

Perhaps one of Arthur's books would provide a distraction, or at least keep her from worrying about his habits. Would he ever relinquish those expensive pleasures? Would she always be awaiting his return from his club? She could not bear to imagine a future of endless waiting upon her charming wastrel of a spouse.

Once again, she was impressed by the variety of languages represented in even this small collection of books. She wondered if he was as analytical about languages as he was about cards. Her hand fell on the book-that-was-not-a-book and she picked it up, reminding herself that there was some benefit to his unfamiliar skills. He had provided for their venture and she had to remember that some good did come from his gambling.

Then she opened the book for a reassuring glimpse of the banknotes and their tally.

The box, so cunningly shaped to look like a book, was empty.

Patience caught her breath and spun to survey her room, then realized the simple truth. Arthur had taken the money to fund his gambling. He had confessed the night before that he had lost, and he had need of some money to place a stake.

He had won the money. It was rightfully his and she could not argue with that.

But all she could see was that his compulsion to return to games of chance might cost the future of their planned venture. His need to gamble might lead him to break his promise to her.

Unless there was worse to be known. Unless the truths he had not shared with her included an expensive mistress, or a secret life, or another demand upon his purse that he knew she would not find compelling.

How could he do this?

How could he so disappoint her?

What was she going to do?

~

"WILL you change the name to Fanshawe & Beckham?"

Arthur halted on the stairs of his club. It was close to midnight and he had been headed for Berkley

Square. Luck had flirted with him on this particular night, taunting him with small gains that were subsequently diminished. He was not ahead more than ten pounds after hours of playing and had decided to relinquish the fight for the moment.

Then he heard the mocking query from the Earl of Fairhaven. He turned to find that man watching him from the doorway of the club.

"Uncle Reynaud," he said with a slight bow. "What an unexpected pleasure."

"Is it?" The earl came down the steps to confront him. He smelled of brandy and insolence. "I saw you," he said. "I uncovered your scheme, and I would discuss the matter with you before sharing the tidings with my sister."

Arthur bristled but hid his reaction. "I should be pleased to call upon you tomorrow."

"No," Reynaud said. "It will be now, for I will never wait upon a tradesman." He pivoted and marched up the stairs of the club, leaving Arthur to follow.

He considered his options for a moment, then chose to follow. If Reynaud meant to make trouble, he would likely have Arthur barred from the club, which might make this the last time he entered the place.

He checked his watch, reasoning that he could still return to Patience before midnight, no matter how long-winded the earl might be, and followed the other man into the club.

～

PATIENCE CLOSED her eyes in relief when she heard Arthur speak to Stevens in the foyer. It was after dawn and she had sat awake all night, uncertain which possibility that rose in her thoughts was worse.

Arthur might be an inveterate gambler.

Arthur might have lost all the funds he had previously won.

Arthur might have a mistress whose pleasures cost him dearly.

Arthur might be drunk. He might be dueling. He might be racing horses and living recklessly, while she sat alone and fretted for his welfare.

Arthur might have come to harm during the endless night.

The cats had both settled in her lap around midnight, as if sensing that she had need of comfort. She eased them aside now as she heard Arthur's tread on the stairs. His steps were heavy as if he carried a great burden, which only fed Patience's anger.

He must have lost.

He must have lost it all.

No doubt he remained out to drown his sorrows. That would have been on credit, which meant the lost funds were not the sum of the debt. Oh, if only she could shake sense into him!

The door to his chamber closed softly and she heard the low murmur of him consulting with Taylor. Was he drunk? She could not hear clearly enough to tell. She rose to her feet and smoothed the dress she had not removed the night before. Her hair was still up and she did not doubt that her exhaustion showed.

Her fury was probably also evident.

There was no flinching this task, though. She took a deep breath, strode to the adjoining door and rapped hard upon it. She did not wait for a reply but charged into Arthur's bedchamber, hauling open the closed drapes on her way. Pale pearly light flooded into the chamber and she spun to find Arthur wincing at her from the bed, one hand before his face.

He was still dressed, his cravat loosened and his shirt opened along with his waistcoat. He still wore his boots and his jacket, but sat on the edge of the bed, looking like a man still under the influence of his revels. She could see the faint shadow of his whiskers on his chin and a bit of the dark hair on his chest. His hair looked as if he had run his fingers through it repeatedly, his boots were scuffed and he positively reeked of brandy.

Patience seethed. She had never had greater evidence of his rakehell habits than his own appearance on this morning. If he suffered from his indulgences, he deserved as much. She hardened her heart against the sight of him and braced her hands upon her hips, prepared to grant a lecture.

"Patience," he said without surprise, a weariness in his tone that convinced her that every one of her suspicions was correct.

"How dare you?" she fumed, keeping her voice low that the servants might not hear. "How dare you stay out all the night long, carousing and gambling and drinking—"

"Cavorting?" he asked with a hint of his usual playful manner.

Patience was not to be diverted. She continued heatedly. "—indulging in who knows what manner of egregious behavior while I sit and worry about your welfare? You are a wastrel and a scoundrel of the worst order, a blackguard and a ruffian, a man whose charm does not excuse his choices…"

"You worried?" he echoed as if she had said nothing else. His eye glinted as he considered her from behind his hand. "You cede that I have charm?"

"Arthur! This is no jest. Of course, I worried! You did not return for dinner, nor in time to retire to bed. And your charm is beyond dispute, though I cannot condone the fact that you use it as a weapon."

"And are you disarmed by said weapon, Patience?"

He smiled at his own jest and she yearned to strike him for finding the situation amusing.

They would never agree upon his choices! Her life would become a sequence of mornings similar to this one and she would be condemned to stand and watch as he gambled away every thing of value to either of them.

She realized his sapphire pin was missing and was struck by how much she regretted its sacrifice to his games of chance.

She returned to her tirade with gusto. "We spoke before about your decadent indulgences and I had understood that you meant to abandon such pursuits in favor of a sensible and prudent life. But no, you lied to me about your intentions."

"Patience…"

"The worst of it is not that you willfully deceived me, but that you stole funds to indulge your habit."

He looked up and she was shocked to silence at the sight of his face when he braced his hands on the mattress. "Stole?"

With his hand before his face, she had not been able to see that his eye was swollen almost closed, the skin around it turning vivid hues of purple, black and blue. He had indulged in fisticuffs, as well!

"Goodness, Arthur." Patience took a step back, the discussion of his gambling completely forgotten. "Your eye!"

Gambling. Drinking. Brawling. Was there no end to his degenerate habits?

"Is blackened, yes," he said without interest, his tone tinged with impatience. "I might insist that my opponent looks worse, but I am not certain that is the case. Fear not, Patience, I am otherwise uninjured, and sufficiently whole to survive your chastisement." He frowned, wincing at the pain it caused him and she realized he had other injuries, too.

"Do not mock me, sir!" she fumed. "Do not feign ignorance of what only you could have done. I will not stand by and watch you cast your life aside, to abandon every asset, to surrender every shred of decency simply to play your wretched cards. What will become of our venture now that the funds are gone?"

Arthur rose to his feet in alarm. "What funds are gone?"

"The ones intended for Mr. Fanshawe!" she replied in a heated whisper. "Gone, and doubtless forever." She gestured to the chamber. "I see no pile of banknotes in your chamber and I doubt you would leave them in your pockets for Taylor to count. The money is gone, spent likely as soon as you put it down on the table in some gambling den…"

"Gone? Are you certain?" he demanded, now looking to be wide awake.

Patience was startled. "Of course, I am certain. It is gone. You took it."

"I assure you, I did not," Arthur said crisply. He strode to her room, opened the bookcase and crouched down before it. He lifted out the false book, as if hoping to prove her mistaken, and she knew from his expression when he looked within it that he told her the truth. He stood for a moment, staring at the empty box with a dismay that surely equalled her own, then raised his gaze to her. "You do not make a jest upon me to prove your point?"

Patience folded her arms across her chest as her doubts grew. "No. I would not find such a jest amusing in the least."

"I cannot imagine that Gellis would even find it," he mused. "Much less that she would take it."

"No," Patience agreed, moving to his side. "Then you did not take it?" She had to be certain.

"No." Arthur shook his head and replaced the box in the bookcase. They both stared at it for a long moment, then Arthur turned aside, moving past her, and swore with a vigor she had not known he possessed.

"I am sorry, Patience, but I did not take the money. I know you did not take it, but it has vanished nonetheless." He spared a glance over his shoulder at her and she caught her breath at another view of his eye. "I am sorry to break my promise to you."

"I am sorry that I blamed you," she said. "I should have asked you instead of making an accusation and assuming your guilt."

"Why, Patience? Because I have told you all of the truth?" Arthur shook his head. "No, it was fair that you thought the worst of me." He grimaced and she urged him back toward his own chamber.

"The eye is not the sum of it, is it?" she asked.

"Not nearly," he acknowledged.

"How much brandy did you drink?"

"None." He almost smiled when she looked up at him in surprise. "I do not drink when I play, Patience." He lifted his shirt away from his chest and she saw the golden stain upon it. "This was a waste of good brandy, for no one enjoyed it." He grimaced again when he sat down on the bed once more and looked so defeated that her sympathy rose.

She perched on the mattress beside him, placing a hand upon his arm. "Where were you? What happened?"

He spared her a glance. "Am I no longer assumed guilty of every debauchery, then?"

Patience flushed. "I am sorry. You look terrible and you smell like a distillery. You were out all night. What was I to think?"

"Only what you did." He sighed and frowned, then considered her. "I would tell you of it, if you would listen."

"I would like to know. Who struck you?"

"The Earl of Fairhaven," he ceded. "He saw us at Mr. Fanshawe's and has learned the truth." Patience caught her breath, for Arthur seemed to view this as very bad tidings. If the earl had told Lady Beckham, she imagined it might be. "He demanded a discussion, considering our choice to be an insult to his family name, and I returned to the club in the hopes of placating him. In truth, he did not wish to talk. No sooner had we retired to a quiet room alone than he assaulted me. He and his companions took me by surprise, and gave me a pummeling. Perhaps he meant to teach me a lesson, or urge me to reconsider." Arthur shrugged, raising a hand to the back of his head. "I remember feeling my head strike something and I fell, then he cast the contents of a glass of brandy over me."

"Arthur!" Patience whispered, horrified that he should have been so abused. She found herself feeling the back of his head with gentle fingertips and located a small bump.

"I awakened at dawn or near to it, to find my pockets had been emptied." He patted the place where his sapphire pin should have been, his expression rueful. "I liked that pin. It matched my eyes."

"It did indeed," she ceded and he smiled at her.

"Shall you add vanity to my crimes?"

She could not halt her own smile. "I could call it honesty instead of vanity. You are a handsome man and would have to be blind to be oblivious to it." He grinned and she dared to continue. "I like that you take pride in your appearance, for I find you most attractive."

"Patience," he murmured with surprise and she found herself flushing again.

"Did he even take your coppers?"

Arthur almost smiled. "He did, the wretch. Every one of them. I am surprised he left my watch, but perhaps he was interrupted." He shrugged. "Without a single coin to my name, I knew I could only walk back to Berkley Square. I waited for the sounds of the workers in the street, then did as much." He raised his hands. "And so you find me returned, if somewhat more disheveled than is my custom."

"Did you lose last night?" Patience found she hated the notion of the earl absconding with Arthur's winnings more than the prospect of Arthur gambling.

"No, but nor did I win." He turned to her, his expression haunted. "But it is in this moment that I stand to lose all of import, if you have come to despise me, for your choice would not be without cause." He was so earnest that a lump rose in her throat.

She touched his arm. "Arthur! Do not lose hope. We will find a solution. We might find the funds themselves. Or perhaps Mr. Fanshawe will grant us a loan."

Arthur gave her a hot look. "Based upon what principal? My boots are not sufficiently fine and as you have noted repeatedly, I possess no skills or expertise."

She had never yet seen him despondent and it troubled her. "Arthur, we will find a way together, somehow. We are bound together for better or for worse, after all, until death us do part." She had thought to provoke a smile but he frowned.

"Are we?"

Patience blinked. "Of course, we are. We stood before the vicar and exchanged our vows just last Saturday…"

"You pledged yourself to Arthur Beckham. I know that man has been dead these twenty years."

Patience could only stare at him. "But," she managed finally.

He held her gaze and even if she ignored his blackened eye, he had never looked so much like a stranger to her. "My name is Charles Arthur Leighton."

Patience felt her mouth drop open.

There was a gentle rap at the door then and Taylor appeared. "Sir? I would not interrupt."

Patience rose to her feet with purpose. "Please, Taylor, my husband has need of you. If you might summon a hot bath, I think he would welcome it as much as a change of clothing. Please have the fire laid, as well. I suspect you have a better notion of how to care for his injuries than I might."

"Ma'am?" Taylor came into the room, his expression turning to horror as he looked at Arthur's blackened eye. "Sir!"

Arthur stood up and shed his jacket with some effort. "My wife is right, Taylor, save that I would also like breakfast after that bath."

"Of course, sir."

Arthur fixed Patience with an intent look. "You might bring that to my wife's chamber, for she and I have much to discuss this morning." He raised a brow, lowering his voice as Taylor hastened away. "There is no point in withholding the tale any longer. You will have your truth, Patience, and you will have it this very day. Perhaps you will see why I did not hasten to share it with you. Not only did I mislead you, but I am not even the man you believed me to be. Perhaps the truth is the only thing of merit I can offer you." He looked saddened by this and as much as she yearned to reassure him, Patience knew she had to hear his confession first.

～

ARTHUR FELT MUCH RESTORED by his bath, and his stomach growled when he proceeded to Patience's chamber in his dressing robe. He admired how she had directed Taylor's efforts with a minimum of discussion, seeing proof in that of her experience in managing her father's house. Her hair was done by the time he joined her and she had changed her dress. The fire was crackling and the cats, once his loyal companions, had clearly chosen Patience as their new guardian.

He could not blame them.

She rose to greet him and took his hand, ushering him into one chair while she claimed the other. It was sweet torment to touch her and suspect that he would likely never do so again. Even the weight of her hand within his seemed infinitely precious and he mourned his own failure to defend what was of import to him.

He had betrayed her and she would not forgive him. The sole thing she could not abide was a deception, after all, and his life had been a lie for twenty years. He would tell her the truth, simply to clear his debt to her, then nothing else would matter. He knew the earl would ensure that his membership at the club was revoked and he suspected that Lady Beckham would soon hear of his unacceptable choice. With the funds having vanished, he could not finance Patience's goal or keep his promise to her.

All was lost and Arthur did not see how any of it could be made to rights.

He saw no reason to evade the facts. "I have lied to you, Patience, and in fact to all the world," he admitted when they faced each other. Her expression was neutral and he knew she hid her thoughts. "My name is not Arthur Beckham, though I have pretended to be him for over twenty years."

She surveyed the chamber with a frown, as if the

answer to her obvious questions might be lurking there, then met his gaze again. "But how can that be?"

"It is a long story," he said.

"Then start at the beginning," she instructed, her practicality making him smile a little.

Indeed.

"Once upon a time," he began softly. "There was a boy who lived with his parents in a small village in England. They were not rich but neither were they poor, for as the mother said, they had each other and that was sufficient for anyone's happiness. It was sufficient for the three of them, until the day the mother died."

Patience let out a breath, as soft as a sigh. To Arthur's surprise, she reached out and took his hand in hers. She gave his fingers a squeeze, as if to encourage him, and to his astonishment, it did.

"Both father and son were bereft without the lady, who had been not just wife and mother but the very focus of their lives together. She had been the one to know when one of them was ill, she was the one who knew what to do in any situation, she was the one who cooked the meals they loved and tended to their garments. She was a sweet and generous woman, much inclined to kindness but not averse to a stern word when one was needed."

"She sounds lovely," Patience said and he nodded agreement. He felt his throat work, but he continued. "Without her, their lives spun into disarray. The man began to spend what few coins he possessed at the public house, and often he missed days of labor, which meant their resources steadily diminished. Bills were left unpaid and the larder was often empty. The boy sold what he could. He took to doing tasks for others for coin or to begging, though there was little opportunity for either in their small village. He was hungry and dirty, his clothes ill-fitting since there was no one to patch or replace them, when he saw the fancy coaches on the road."

"That explains the pennies then," she said quietly and he looked at her in momentary confusion. "The ones you give to children."

He winced. "That coin might provide their first meal in days. I know how much it can matter, but for Arthur Beckham, giving away a hundred pennies a day makes no difference at all."

She tightened her grip on his hand and looked to be blinking back tears. He could not bear that he might have made her cry, so he frowned into the embers of the fire.

"The coaches came each year at regular intervals for the school terms, though the boy had never paid much heed to them in the past. They were from another world, one more affluent and privileged than his own. As he watched them this time, he recalled his mother saying that each coach carried a wealthy boy to school in Shrewsbury. She had said the boys came when they were at least ten years of age and he realized, with some surprise, that he was that age himself. It was early October and they arrived for Michaelmas term. On impulse, he followed the carriages, drawn to them by a fascination he could not explain. When one stopped at the tavern in the next village, he persuaded the coachman to let him ride along with a tale of his ailing aunt in Shrewsbury. He had never been more than a quarter mile from the house where he had been born, but there was so little for him there that he did not even look back.

"Shrewsbury was enormous and busy to him, confusing and thrilling. His efforts to fulfill a task for a penny or two were more successful here than in his home village, for it seemed not only that there were many minor tasks to be done but that people had much more coin in their pockets. He found himself lingering near the school, fascinated by the lives of these boys born to advantage. They had wealth and clothing, horses of their own even, and lessons. What would it be like to live thus? To never be hungry? To know that your future was assured, and would be one of comfort and indulgence?"

He shook his head at the very thought.

"The boy found favor in the kitchens of the school and worked long days, hauling supplies, shovelling manure, doing whatever had to be done. The cook let him sleep by the hearth, purportedly to ensure that he was always available, but she was a more kindly woman than she wished others to know. He eavesdropped on lessons whenever he could and watched the students with fascination, marvelling that Fortune could make lives so different for no apparent reason. A coachman taught him to play draughts, then cards, showing him how to anticipate the play. He was fascinated by the suggestion that chance could be foretold."

Patience's grip remained steadfast, though he knew at some point she would be troubled by his tale.

"There was a group of new boys seemingly determined to find trouble. One day, they schemed that they would escape in the night, and the boy heard of this plan. They chose to challenge each other to a feat of bravery. The wind was up, a sign that a storm brewed, but they were accustomed to having their way and paid no heed to the weather. The boy watched them creep out of the dormitory at midnight and considered whether he should tell anyone. Instead, he followed them.

"They all had insisted they could swim, but several could not. The boy could swim, though, and when he heard their cries of distress, he did not pause but jumped into the river himself. Two made the shore alone. One he saved. The fourth, name of Arthur Beckham, he reached too late."

Patience inhaled sharply.

"The cook had noticed her missing charge and had him followed by a groom. In a school of boys, she doubtless had learned to smell mischief in the making. By the time the boy brought the third boy to the shore, there were half a dozen men from the school there, bundling up the survivors and carrying them off to the infirmary. In the chaos and the darkness, only the boy and the headmaster knew Arthur's fate and the boy was sworn to silence. The headmaster took custody of Arthur and the boy was returned to the kitchens, where the cook fussed over him. He returned to his customary tasks and held his tongue.

"The boys were severely punished for their breaking of the rules and kept isolated from each other, as well as the other students. The dead boy's father, Viscount Meadstone, was summoned at once. The sound of his arrival echoed through the halls and his roar of fury left more than one shaking in fear of repercussions. I was terrified when summoned to him."

Arthur fell silent, realizing belatedly what he had confessed.

Patience bent to kiss his hand. "You were the orphaned boy," she said, smiling up at him so his throat tightened.

"I was." He exhaled, his vow finally broken after so many years of silence. He felt he had put down a burden, one that had become more weighty with every passing year, one he had never desired to pick up in the first place. He nodded once more, conviction growing in his voice. "I was."

CHAPTER 14

*P*atience was honored that Arthur shared his story with her. An earlier promise had kept him from surrendering it sooner, and doubtless, Lady Beckham had some influence in that choice as well. She was surprised to realize how little she cared what his true name was or what his origins had been. The man before her had claimed her heart completely. His nature was the reason she loved him, not his name. "Tell me about Viscount Meadstone," she invited, because he seemed to be lost in his memories.

He stirred and took a breath, his gaze fixed on the coals of the fire again. "I expected him to chastise me for failing to raise the alarm sooner, thinking that might have saved Arthur."

"You did not expect a reward?"

The quick flicker of surprise was the clearest answer she could have been given.

"Not from the viscount. From the cook, I had my bit of beef." He shrugged, his gaze drifting to the distance as he remembered. "I found the viscount terrifying but knew better than to show my fear. I met his gaze and told my tale without wavering. I remember how he turned to study me when I said that his son was the one who could not swim. He lied, you see, about his abilities, and the others smelled it. His lie was the reason for the challenge, for they taunted him to prove he spoke the truth. He could not back down and admit he had lied, and so he jumped first into the river and he died."

Patience shivered.

"I soon realized that the viscount did not mourn his son overmuch. In later years, he confided that Arthur had always been a brash fool and one he feared would never overcome his early inclinations. On that day, I stood, wondering, until the viscount turned to study me. 'Do you not fear me?' he demanded and I shook my head, well aware that the schoolmaster lingered in the shadows, listening. The viscount indicated that I should speak. 'Why should I fear a father who grieves for his son?' I asked. 'What of your own father?' he demanded. 'Would he grieve for your early death?' I wager he had guessed that I was an orphan within those walls, or perhaps he had been told as much. 'He grieves for my mother and has forgotten his son,' I said without thinking. 'Charlie is one of many lost children,' the schoolmaster said. 'But more biddable than most.'

The viscount walked toward me, I can see him yet, as he crouched down before me. 'Your hair is dark, like his,' he said but I shook my head. 'No, sir, my father is fair. I favor my mother.' And he smiled for the first time, then shook his head and fixed me with a look. 'Do you like it here?' I had no notion what the correct reply might be, a startling realization for one who lived by his wits. The master was watching me in silence, which did not help. 'Cook is kind to me,' I ceded and the viscount straightened, folding his arms across his chest as he looked down at me. I feared a pronouncement of some kind, but his question astonished me. 'What if I were kind to you?' he asked softly. 'What if I gave you everything Arthur had?' The master caught his breath, understanding before I did. 'You must want something in return,' I said, thinking he made a joke at my expense. He nodded. 'Your name,' he said in a murmur, his gaze clinging to mine, even as the schoolmaster caught his breath. 'Your promise until your dying breath that you will never admit the truth.'

Patience caught her breath. What a demand to make of a child! "How wicked," she murmured.

"The schoolmaster protested at this point, but was reminded of the scandal that would erupt at the revelation that the grandson of the Earl of Fairhaven had died while under his care. He paled then and retreated, his agitation so clear that I knew a rare opportunity was before me. 'I will take you,' the viscount said to me. 'I will make you into Arthur Beckham. You will become my son and whoever you are now will cease to be forever. You will not write to your father ever again. You will not reveal yourself to anyone, for this will be a secret you and I take to our graves.' I looked at the schoolmaster. 'As will he,' the viscount confided. 'If he has his wits about him.' I was tempted, sorely tempted, but had to ask. 'Someone will know,' I said. 'His mother will know.' The viscount smiled. 'Leave his mother to me.' And he offered his hand, as if I were a man and not a ten-year-old boy."

Arthur shook his head. "That was the first time I had the sense that Dame Fortune rode with me, that opportunity was within reach and that if I did not seize the chance, it would slip away forever. I can still see his hand. His nails were trimmed short and clean beyond anything I had seen before. In that instant, I wanted to live a life in which my hands were always smooth and clean, a life in which I was always warm and never hungry, a life in which my clothes fit and I knew I would be safe all the night long while I slept, and I wanted it enough to surrender whatever the viscount asked of me. I put my hand in his and I remember his nod of satisfaction, then my life changed forever."

He fell silent then, perhaps reliving the details of that moment, and Patience studied him while his attention was diverted. She hated to imagine him alone and hungry, a boy with only his wits to rely upon, a child who did not hold his own name to have any merit. She could understand why he would make such a choice—indeed, she could not imagine anyone making a different one.

She wondered what it was like to know with such certainty that no one valued you for your own self.

"Charles Arthur Leighton," she repeated.

His smile was sad. "That was the ironic detail. I had been christened Charles Arthur, though I had always been called Charlie. The viscount took that as a sign that his idea had divine approval."

"Was he religious?"

"When it suited him."

"What happened next?"

"We left in the night, the tale being that the viscount would not leave his son in a place so careless with the boy's welfare. 'Charlie' was doubtless buried in the potters' field with no one to miss him."

"Save the cook," Prudence insisted, giving him a little poke. He smiled, to her relief.

"She had to set her own fires until she found another urchin, to be sure." He cleared his throat. "We went to the viscount's country house, which Arthur and his mother had not frequented, where the servants were loyal and of long service to the family. And there my education began." His brows rose. "I was scrubbed and trimmed and tutored seemingly all day and half the night. I had to learn to ride properly, not to sling myself across a horse's back like a peasant, to eat, to dress myself, to dance, to make conversation, to remember names and titles and family history. It was grueling, but it was also a challenge beyond anything I had ever done before."

"You loved it," Patience guessed and was rewarded by his grin.

"Truth be told, I did. Languages. Mathematics. I could not get enough of it. The viscountess soon arrived, took one look at me, and retreated to a private chamber with her husband. Their battle was spectacular, noisy and furious, doubtless tinged by a mother's grief. They raged all the night at each other, the servants exchanging glances as they went about their tasks. I did not sleep that night, for I believed all had been for naught and that they would cast me out." He frowned. "It is curious how fearful I was that I should lose what I had only recently gained."

"You liked affluence. I cannot blame you."

"But such a gift creates an uncertainty in the heart that would not be there otherwise," he said. "I sometimes feel I have lived that night over and over again for twenty years."

"What is given can be taken away."

He nodded, meeting her gaze. "And one tires of the possibility. One yearns for resolution, one way or the other, instead of the endless prospect of loss without warning."

Patience nodded understanding. How curious it was to realize that so many envied Arthur Beckham while no one knew his truth or his torment.

"I was summoned after breakfast to her chamber. Lady Beckham was more terrifying than the viscount, for it was clear this notion had only been granted her approval with reluctance. 'My husband decrees that my father, the earl, cannot be without a grandson,' she said without preamble. 'I do not like it and I see no reason to disguise that truth from you. You have not a drop of decent blood in your veins. Disappoint me and I will defy him, without a single regret.' And I was dismissed."

"Goodness," Patience found herself whispering. "She was never soft, was she?"

"Lady Beckham is formidable, to be sure, and it was whispered that she did not welcome the viscount again to her bed for almost a decade. She blamed him for the loss of her beloved boy, though the more I learned of Arthur, the more I became convinced that he had disappointed his parents."

Patience turned to look at him. "Did you think you might one day be earl?"

"I did not care. Truly!" he added when her skepticism must have showed. "I lived the life of a prince. I could do whatsoever I wished, go wherever I desired, spend what I wanted. My life was finer than I might ever have hoped it to be and I was more than content with my lot. The viscount, though, often commented upon the possibility."

Patience had to believe that her husband would make a better earl than the man he called his uncle, but she knew her loyalty had been fully claimed.

Arthur frowned. He was more serious than she had ever seen him. "Every person has something he or she cannot abide, and thus that person cannot be blamed or chastised for acting in accordance with something key to their nature. The viscount, for example, had an aversion to a title passing out of use. He was a great advocate for the merit of the aristocracy and I believe he felt it as a personal blow when a nobleman died without issue. His wife's younger brother was notoriously unhealthy as both a child and youth, but was the sole male issue of the earl. Arthur was the earl's only grandson, and thus, by the viscount's reasoning, no price was too high to pay to ensure that there was an heir and a spare. In time, I am proud to say, he came to favor me, the spare, over the heir." He smiled a little. "I liked him well. He was a better father than my own had been."

There was a hint of more than he had thus confessed in that last declaration.

"Did you ever return to the village where you were born?"

"Once," he admitted heavily. "I made a detour on an expedition, and asked after Charles Leighton. I offered a tale that his services were recommended to me by an ostler of no name."

"Your father tended horses?"

"When he was sober. He had a touch with them." He cleared his throat and straightened. "They said he had died some years before, just after his wife." He looked away, blinking back tears that seemed to have surprised him.

"I am sorry."

"As was I." He stirred himself. "But, to return to the tale and its import." He met her gaze, his own solemn. "We were speaking of faults that people cannot tolerate. You, by your own admission, cannot abide deception. Whatsoever you did in response to learning of a falsehood told by someone within your acquaintance would be completely justified, especially as you make no attempt to hide your feelings about dishonesty."

She parted her lips to speak, but he silenced her with a touch. "Patience," he entreated. "This confession is long overdue. Let me finish it." His gaze was so intense that her mouth went dry, but she nodded. "I would not blame you for spurning me now that you know the truth," he continued with quiet heat. "You are wedded to a man long dead, and if you chose to step away from me now, all fault would be mine. If it is of any import at all, impulse led me true, for I soon fell in love with you." He smiled wryly. "Perhaps it is a kind of justice for me to lose my heart to a woman who thinks love a folly for others. Know that I would do whatsoever is in my power to ensure your every happiness."

Patience's heart contracted so hard that it hurt. She wanted to reassure him in the most fundamental way possible, but there was a crisp knock at the door to her chamber before she could speak.

"Sir?" Stevens said from the corridor. "Lady Beckham requests your presence in the breakfast room with haste."

Patience met Arthur's gaze. He placed his lips against her ear and murmured. "Go." The single word was filled with insistence. "Go to your father's house. Take the book manuscript and go as quickly as you can. I will tell Stevens that you mean to make a visit and will order the carriage."

"But what is wrong? Why does she summon you at this early hour?"

"The earl granted me this injury," he said with quiet resolve. "That was the beginning and this will be the end. Arthur Beckham is finished."

Patience wanted to argue with him but he rose with purpose and strode toward his own chamber. "Go," he mouthed from the threshold of the adjoining door and Patience could not ignore his urgency. He closed the door behind himself and she heard him ring for Taylor.

Go. Patience would leave this house without regrets, but she would not abandon her husband.

She loved him, no matter what his name, and she knew they would find a future somehow.

Patience donned her coat and bonnet with haste, shoving the book manuscript into the bag Catherine had given her. She took the gems Arthur had given her, too. She was tugging on her gloves when she noticed the two pairs of eyes watching her from the rug before the fire, one pair green and one pair golden.

If Arthur was to be cast out of this house, Patience

must take everything of import to him. She could only hope that Lady Beckham would send her books to her, for they were too heavy for her to carry. If not, Amelia would cherish them in her absence.

The satchel was a generously proportioned one. Patience put a shawl on top of the book manuscript and beckoned to the cats. They seemed to understand for they leapt into the bag, one after the other. Patience stroked their heads, urging them to lie down. "Quiet for just a moment," she urged them, then strove to carry her bag as if it weighed nothing at all.

She met Arthur in the corridor and he lifted the bag from her hands gallantly. He wore his navy jacket and buff breeches, his boots polished to a gleam once more. She could not help but note his eye, but otherwise, he looked as perfectly groomed as ever. He certainly showed no lack of confidence. "Stevens, my wife will consult with her father this morning. Please have Morris take her to Golden Square in the coach."

"But, of course, sir."

Patience drew him to a halt and met his gaze steadily. "I hope you will join us shortly," she said and saw his slight inhalation.

"I would not impose..."

"But you must. My father will so enjoy your company." She pressed his arm when he did not reply. "Promise me."

Their gazes locked and held for a potent moment, then he smiled and nodded. "As you know, madame, your wish is my command." He spoke lightly but she trusted him to keep his pledge.

Within moments, Patience was on her way out of Berkley Square. She placed the bag on the seat beside herself and opened it, so both cats peeked out.

Arthur had said she would consult with her father. That had been an excuse but it was precisely what she would do. She would tell her father everything, and together they would seek a solution.

He loved her. Patience gripped her hands together and felt her cheeks heat with pleasure.

There had to be a way.

~

LADY BECKHAM WAS NOT ALONE.

She sat at the head of the table, her brother standing behind her. There was no doubt what the earl had told her, for his eyes gleamed with anticipation for this interview. Lady Beckham's features might have been carved of stone. It did not appear that either of them had eaten, although there were two full cups of tea on the table.

"You summoned me?" Arthur asked as soon as the door was closed behind him. He did not sit down for he suspected his audience would be short.

"You have defied me," Lady Beckham said in a low voice. "You have disregarded every principle you have been taught in this house, and you have done as much at the instigation of that common chit."

"I have challenged only one of your edicts, in wedding a bride whose family are in trade. To be sure, Uncle Reynaud was determined to wed me to another such bride a mere fortnight ago." He met the other man's gaze. "How fares your courtship of that lady, Uncle?"

The earl's eyes flashed but Lady Beckham waved him to silence before he uttered a sound. "I am not interested in Reynaud on this day, but with you. You are my son. You are my heir. You are to be my pride and my joy, but according to my own brother, you have dishonored me by choosing, secretly, to abandon your birthright and become a tradesman." She almost shuddered at the last word.

Arthur took a chair in that moment, crossing his legs as he regarded her. "Forgive me as I consider which detail to challenge first."

Lady Beckham's lips tightened. "We will not speak of origins," she said and the earl frowned in confusion.

"But I believe we must," Arthur said. "You fear that my natural tendences overwhelm all of my education and the influence of your example, do you not?"

The earl's frown deepened as he looked between his sister and her supposed son.

"And perhaps you are right," Arthur continued. "I find myself with the very good fortune of a lovely wife, one who is much enamored of honesty, and admires those who make an effort to improve the world around them, rather than simply entertaining themselves. I find her views persuasive. In fact, the lady is a delight, and there is little I would not do win her happiness."

"Do not confess that you are in love," the earl muttered.

Arthur smiled. "But I am, and I believe, Lady Beckham, that you know as well as I how love can change one's view of the possibilities." The lady in question flushed a little. "I believe that you might best understand how such affection might persuade one to defy convention."

"But you cannot do this. I forbid it!"

"And it may not be done, but not because of your disapproval."

"You are defiant and ungrateful," Lady Beckham said. "You would discard all that has been given to you, all the dignities that have been bestowed upon you, and you would stain the honor of my name and my household..."

"Never that," Arthur said. "Such a stain lies entirely within your own power to bestow or withhold."

She ignored him and continued with barely restrained fury. "You insult me and the memory of my husband, and I will not stand silently while you do as much. You must choose before you leave this room. You must choose either to resume your former habits and remain my son, or you may leave with your humble bride and never cast your shadow upon my door again. I will deny you in every quarter if you choose her, and you may be sure that I will not relent."

The decision was remarkably easy. Arthur had been impoverished before and he had survived. He had possessed nothing but his name, and survived in its absence. But he could not willingly survive without Patience.

If she denied him, that was another matter, but he would not surrender all chance of happiness simply for financial security—and the satisfaction of a person who had never truly valued him for himself.

He thought of Patience's expression after his confession and he dared to hope that she felt some fondness for him. Perhaps her reluctant heart could be won in time.

He could think of no more noble pursuit.

As so often he did, Arthur made a calculated gamble.

"Alas, Lady Beckham, my choice is both evident and made." He rose smoothly to his feet and bowed to both of them before stepping toward the door.

"Yvonne, you go too far in this," the earl whispered. "He is your son!"

Arthur paused to survey the other man when Lady Beckham did not speak. "But I am not her son, Reynaud. And thus, you are not my uncle. Perhaps you finally understand why I would not cede to you arranging my nuptials for me. There was a limit to how much I was prepared to surrender for the good of the Tattingers, and you exceeded it."

The earl opened his mouth and closed it again, his eyes so round that he resembled nothing so more than a gaping fish.

"You will regret this," Lady Beckham insisted when Arthur reached for the door.

"No, I will not. I thank you for your generosity over the years, but I believe my balance to you has been paid in full." He glanced toward the earl. "If you could see your way to returning the sapphire stolen from me last night, I would appreciate it. I have always been fond of it, and it will not sell for a sufficient sum to make a difference to your finances."

"Reynaud? What is this?"

"You do not think I contrived to blacken my own eye, do you madame?" Arthur asked, then took his leave as the siblings glared at each other. Her heard their voices rise in argument when he was in the foyer, but he did not care. He claimed his hat and gloves, his walking stick, then nodded a farewell to Stevens. The butler's expression was as impassive as ever, but there was a glint in his eyes that hinted at understanding.

Arthur smiled at the conviction that Stevens was likely the only one who had not been surprised by the revelation.

"I would speak to Miss Beckham before I leave," he said and the butler inclined his head. Arthur hurried up the stairs to Amelia's chamber on the third floor. Adjacent to her room was the nursery where she took her lessons. He tapped on the door and entered, finding her at work. The governess excused herself, a hint that all in the household knew at least part of what happened this morning.

"Is it true?" Amelia demanded, casting herself into his embrace. "Are you leaving?"

"I am, but I will send word to you of my circumstance." He kissed the top of her head. "I could not abandon my only sister."

"But they said…"

He lifted her chin with a fingertip. "And I say that you are my sister in deed if not in blood and that you always will be."

She hugged him tightly in her relief, then studied him. "You look awful."

"I thank you for that."

"Does it hurt?"

"Less than it should for such a spectacular display."

"I want to see it when it turns yellow and green."

Arthur shook his head, then his gaze fell upon a book Amelia had been reading. He was certain it was the third volume of the novel that Patience had been reading, the one that he had borrowed and read himself. "Does that book belong to Patience?" he asked and Amelia nodded agreement.

"I had the first volume from Carruthers & Carruthers, then she loaned me the second one from her own collection on Saturday. I had to finish the story, though she was out yesterday, so I went into her room to exchange the second volume for the third one."

Arthur looked down at her as he had a sudden notion. "Did you take anything else?"

Amelia smiled. "The lark sings at dawn," she said quietly.

"The crow calls at sunset," he replied in an undertone, looking around the nursery with apparent suspicion.

"The sparrow chirps at noon," Amelia confided.

"And the owl hoots at midnight," he concluded and she swatted him.

"You would make a terrible spy," she said. "For you do not know the first thing about hiding anything of import."

"You took it," Arthur whispered, optimism rising hot within him.

"Of course, I took it! Even I know that anyone could find it there, and Patience would never have a book without a legible title on the spine." She went into her chamber and lifted a doll from her cradle. He watched as she opened the end of the doll's bedding, and removed a fistful of banknotes. "Anyone might expect you to have hidden funds, and thus they might believe Patience had some. In contrast, everyone knows that I have no money at all." She smiled and handed the clutch of banknotes to him. "I checked your tally, but your sums are always right."

"Amelia!" Arthur caught her up and swung her around, kissing her cheeks in turn. "You are an angel."

"Not often," she ceded with a frown. "Not *literally*."

"But I am beholden to you all the same. Thank you!" He kissed her again, then secured the funds in the inner pocket of his jacket. Patience would be able to publish her book after all. He was unaccountably relieved that he would be able to keep his pledge to her, and he would do it, regardless of her choice for their future.

"I cannot see them at all," Amelia said, then indicated his empty buttonhole. "My brother would not consider himself to be properly dressed thus."

Arthur grinned. "I will remedy the situation before the greater world can take note of my error."

"You will write me?" she entreated and he hugged her again.

"Before tomorrow. I promise."

The governess cleared her throat then, and Arthur looked up to find her in the doorway. He bid them both farewell then descended the stairs with a light step. In the foyer, he helped himself to a yellow rosebud from the arrangement on the table and fitted it to his button-hole. He nodded to Stevens as he left the house, then stood on the steps and surveyed Berkley Square.

It was a fine day for a walk, in Arthur's view, and not so very far to Golden Square.

He could not help but hope that Patience could be persuaded to give him a second chance.

"A CALLER FOR YOU, MA'AM," Wentworth said as he opened the door to the library.

Patience was there with her father, the cats now curled together upon a small settee that was graced by a sunbeam. She had confided the entire tale to her father and they had reviewed every pertinent detail. As she had hoped, once he knew of her regard for her hus-band, her father was determined to set all to rights.

She spun to find Arthur entering the room, a wel-come glimmer of mischief in his eyes that made her heart skip. Perhaps he had realized that she loved him, regardless of his finances.

"Arthur!" she said and hastened to him, reaching to kiss his uninjured cheek. Then she frowned. "Or should I call you Charles?"

He smiled. "I have been called Arthur for so long that I should think you summoned another if you called me Charles."

"Then Arthur it will be," she said. She might have drawn him toward her father but he claimed her hand and placed it upon his chest, his eyes glimmering all the while. There was something secreted in his jacket, something that crinkled when she moved her fingers.

No!

He bent and put his lips to her ear, setting her afire

with the low murmur of his voice even before she heard his words. "Amelia was very critical of my choice of hiding place. She is very interested in becoming a spy, but finds my inclinations sadly lacking."

He had retrieved the funds. Truly, Patience could not have imagined a better resolution.

"They are yours," he continued. "To fulfill the pledge I made to you."

"Arthur!" she whispered and stretched to brush her lips across his. "But I have a better solution," she said. Patience put her hand through his elbow and led him to her father. The men greeted each other with welcome pleasure. "We have conferred, as you advised, and have contrived a solution."

"Indeed?"

Her father gestured to the various books opened on his desk. "I have been consulting various references, and it seems that you and Patience might yet be legally wed. Marriage is the sole sacrament that does not require the service of a priest, as I am certain you know, but there is always the question of legal clarity, and in the case of offspring, I believe it might be prudent to have witnesses of your union…"

"But the lady may not wish to have me," Arthur said and Patience nudged him.

"I will have no other," she vowed, watching him smile. "The vicar is coming within the hour," she informed him. "We sent for him immediately that he might arrive once you were here." She watched as Arthur began to smile. His eyes lit in the way she loved, a sparkle lighting in their depths. It was wondrous to watch him realize she wanted him for his own sake, and that even penniless , she would have willingly put her hand in his forever. "If you would repeat our vows."

"I should be honored." He lowered his voice. "Are you certain, though, that you would see your life bound to a man who did not surrender his truth to you immediately?"

"I am," Patience said, her gaze locked with his. "For I love you, independent of what your name might be. And I know that situation to have been an exception, not a rule."

"You are correct in that, Patience." His eyes darkened with a satisfaction that made her heart skip, then he brushed his lips across her mouth. It was a tantalizing reminder of how they would celebrate this nuptial night and Patience flushed to her toes, knowing that he watched her closely.

Her father cleared his throat. "I also have taken the liberty of inviting Patience to return to this house, along with you, sir, and to resume her former responsibilities in managing the household. As a widower with only one daughter remaining unwed, I have considered the prospect of shortening my hours at Carruthers & Carruthers, that I might indulge more regularly in reading. My brother would like to bring in his sons as apprentices to the trade, and I thought that having you and Patience in residence here would be ideal."

Patience had the satisfaction of seeing Arthur astonished. "That is most generous of you, sir," he said, his voice husky. "I would be delighted, if Patience finds the situation acceptable."

"I do," she said. "Which is why the house is in uproar, for we shall have the room that was formerly my mother's."

"There is only a small dressing room adjacent," her father informed Arthur. "With insufficient room for a bed of the dimensions you undoubtedly find customary. I could move from my chamber..."

"No, Papa, there is no need." Patience smiled at Arthur. "I was hoping that you might not mind sharing my chamber as a matter of routine."

"There is another sizable chamber down the corridor," her father interjected, but Arthur was already smiling.

"I cede to your arrangements, Patience, with great pleasure." His eyes fairly glowed as he looked down at her and she could not believe how much she adored this man.

That he loved her as well was more than she could ever have hoped.

"The vicar has arrived, sir," Wentworth intoned from the doorway. "As have Mr. and Mrs. Carruthers and their sons, along with a generously proportioned hamper."

"We cannot simply appear and demand a meal," Aunt Elizabeth declared, hastening forward to take Patience's hands. "I had two chickens set aside for our dinner and they should not go to waste. I was certain that Mrs. Frobisher would know precisely how best to bring the meal together, for there was no chance of our missing your second wedding within a week, dear. Praise heaven that both matches are to the same man!" She beamed at Arthur, who looked bemused.

Patience heard Prudence come racing down the stairs, for she had been banished from the discussion in the library and was clearly curious. The bell rang again as Catherine and the baron arrived, one of their footmen carrying a flagon of wine into the house and the other delivering a fine fresh salmon. Wentworth directed them toward the kitchen and Patience saw two shadows slip from the library, one black and one silver, as the cats followed the progress of that salmon. There was a veritable crowd in the foyer as everyone greeted each other with the enthusiasm of long lost friends, then a fierce rapping at the door.

"Oh, Mrs. Oliver," Catherine said. "I thought she had come inside already."

"Mrs. Oliver?" Patience whispered as Wentworth opened the door to a crooked old lady dressed in the fashions of forty years before, a vast collection of veils hiding her face. She feared she had recalled the name of the author incorrectly, for this lady looked unlikely to have composed such a volume.

"She is the author of the book you intend to publish, of course," Catherine said. "When we heard from your father today, I thought this an ideal opportunity for all of you to become acquainted."

"Do not tell me that you are among those families who declined to appreciate spirits?" Mrs. Oliver demanded, peering at the group of them. "After such an impromptu invitation, I should expect at least a glass of ratafia." She moved closer to Arthur, looking him up and down. "Were you not formerly the son of Lady Beckham, a notorious rake and scoundrel?"

"I am such a wastrel no longer, Mrs. Oliver. My affection for my wife has redeemed me."

"Ha! It was not your wife, sir, who tamed your wild impulses. It was my book!" The old woman cackled as she headed for the best seat, the plumpest once closest to the fire. "The baroness has told me of its triumph in her conquest." She settled into the chair, accepted a glass of ratafia, and saluted Patience with such gusto that half of it spilled onto her glove and dress. "We should give a copy to the wife of every rakehell in London, the better to ensure it is favorably reviewed."

They all laughed together at the notion as she drained the rest of the beverage and set the glass down with a thump. "Now what is this about a wedding? If there is to be one, let it commence, as I am famished."

Patience and Wentworth directed the guests, ensuring that everyone entered the library for the second exchange of vows, but Patience caught Arthur watching the older lady with a puzzled expression.

"Do you know her?"

He shook his head. "I am certain we have never met, but there is something undeniably familiar about her."

That mystery would have to wait to be resolved, for the vicar called for their attention. Prudence seized a flower from the hall table and thrust it upon Patience, who faced the man she loved for the second time in rapid succession. Arthur's gaze flicked to the noisy gathering of guests when the vicar cleared his throat portentously, then met Patience's gaze again. Goodness, how she loved that he always looked to be on the verge of laughter.

She realized that he was unaccustomed to such a raucous gathering and might have apologized for her family and their enthusiasm, but he shook his head and bent closer. "You bring me another gift, Patience. I had lost my name before you. I had no purpose before you granted me a commission. And I had no family before you claimed my heart and shared yours with me." His eyes twinkled. "I shall have to live long indeed to have the time to properly demonstrate my appreciation.

"You might begin this very night," she whispered so mischievously that he laughed aloud. Then they stared into each other's eyes as they pledged again that their two hearts would be one.

ARTHUR COULD NOT BELIEVE a man could be so blessed. Patience chose him, her words clear and filled with conviction as she made her vows again. Her family gathered around to celebrate their happiness. The publishing venture would be launched and against every expectation, they had a warm and welcoming home. He could not have contrived a better resolution himself.

There was but one outstanding detail to resolve.

When the ceremony was completed (again) and congratulations had been exchanged (again), he asked Patience's father if he might write a note. "I promised to tell my sister where we might be found," he confessed and found himself with a stack of fine paper, a new quill and a pot of ink. As he wrote to tell her of his situation, he realized another detail, though it was Patience who noticed his consternation.

"What is amiss?"

"Taylor will lose his post," he said. "Lady Beckham may dismiss him this very day, and I know he keeps very little of his income for himself. He sends much of it to his mother in Sussex."

"And you fear for his welfare, of course." Patience crossed the room and spoke to her father, who nodded and listened as Arthur finished his letter to Amelia. What could he do? He would offer Taylor a post, but he had no notion of the Carruthers household finances—nor even did he know what income he and Patience might expect from their venture.

"You must ask him to join us here," Patience said, appearing by his elbow again.

"I would not impose…"

"But Papa does not have a valet and you will need Taylor's services. I will write also to Gellis and invite her to follow us here, if she so desires." She smiled. "The household could use another man and another maid. We had a couple leave at the end of the summer, and I had not advertised for replacements before you so distracted me."

And so Arthur wrote to Taylor and Patience wrote to Gellis. Wentworth assigned the delivery to the baron's footmen in the baron's coach, and Arthur had to admit that Lady Beckham would be more inclined to receive any tidings from footmen in livery.

The boys then demanded that he teach them how to

win at cards, and while Arthur demurred, they suggested he might teach them to fight instead. Their mother urged the cultivation of their dancing skills, their father spoke of increasing their commitment to reading while Patience's father discussed the merit of skill at bookkeeping. Prudence insisted that Arthur find her a husband. He teased her with the suggestion of Mr. Fanshawe.

"But he is old, as old as Papa!"

"Older yet," that man said mildly, ushering them all toward the dining room.

"You are a fiend," Prudence said and Patience scolded her even as Arthur grinned.

"I meant his son, of course."

"He has a son?" Prudence demanded.

"But on further consideration, he is a handsome and diligent man of responsibility, almost as old as me." Arthur shook his head. "You would not like him at all."

"I will come to the shop," Prudence declared. "I will come every day until you introduce me to him." Truly, she reminded him of Amelia in her determination to have her way.

Then someone somewhere shouted that a wretched cat had claimed the fish's tail.

Patience and Arthur exchanged a knowing glance. "Catrame," he said with assurance, certain he had not enjoyed an afternoon more. "The better thief, although he shares."

"If he mouses in exchange, Mrs. Frobisher will ensure he has his fill."

The afternoon culminated with the arrival of Taylor and Gellis in the baron's coach, the vehicle packed with Patience and Arthur's clothes, and the new bookcase, as well as Patience's books. Gellis herself rode with the coachman and a grinning Taylor hung onto the back between the footmen. There was much laughter as everything was unpacked and brought into the house, and Arthur smiled when Gellis dropped into a deep curtsey before Patience.

"Bless you, my lady," she said with a broad smile. "Nothing will be right in that house soon and I could not be more glad to be away." Her gaze slid to Taylor, who offered her a quick wink, and Arthur guessed there was a greater inducement to the move even than that.

They were then summoned to a very crowded dining room, and a table and sideboard burdened with food. He felt the cats winding their way around his ankles and held Patience's hand fast within his own as everyone raised a glass to toast to their future welfare.

Patience had brought him everything he desired, and more.

It was late when a chattering Gellis finally left Patience alone. The room that had been her mother's was still in some disarray, the bookcase still empty in one corner and books piled on the floor before it. The cats had chosen their perches in this smaller room and purred contentedly, their bellies full of fish. She could hear Arthur and Taylor in the adjoining room, and the occasional burst of male laughter, as well as the sounds of the others in the house.

Carruthers House was more than an abode. It was her home and she had not realized how much she loved it until she left. It was wonderful to be back.

She considered the book manuscript she had removed from the bag and set upon a table. She smiled, closed her eyes, and riffled through it to choose a page.

In the bedroom, in privacy with one's lover, a lady can reveal her own urges as nowhere else in the world. Be bold in your caresses, and forthright in your demands. Instead of lying back and accepting whatsoever your partner deigns to offer, tell him what you wish of him. Make the first address. Touch him as you wish—or touch yourself as he watches. I have written of boldness before, but the combined power of audacity and surprise cannot be underestimated, nor can its ability to change the foundation of a relationship be overlooked...

Goodness. Did she dare?

Patience heard Taylor leaving the adjacent chamber. She barely had time to cast aside her robe before Arthur opened the door. She turned to face him, wearing only a welcoming smile, and watched a thrilling heat light his eyes. He murmured her name with reverence and crossed to her side more quickly than she might have believed possible. His kiss was more potent than ever it had been and there was a new and irresistible fire between them.

Audacity and surprise, indeed. This volume would be worth its weight in gold.

EPILOGUE

*L*ondon in December was festive, with garlands of greenery hung over the shop windows and carolers in the streets. Patience and Arthur had chosen Saturday the twentieth for the launch of Mrs. Oliver's book and the shop was bustling with enthusiastic customers. They also had the second volume of their Ladies' Library, an edition of *The Canterbury Tales* with numerous illustrations, for sale. Patience was initially gratified at how quickly Mrs. Oliver's books were selling, then increasingly worried that they might sell out before the holidays. Arthur had invited many of his former acquaintances and their wives and sisters, and Patience could not have hoped for a better endorsement by the ton.

Mrs. Oliver had sent her regrets that morning, which was both disappointing and a relief. Patience did not like to say as much, but she could only think that some of the potential customers might have found it alarming to discover that such a wizened old lady was the source of intimate advice.

Everyone caught their breath as a singularly glamorous lady swept into the shop. Her red hair and brilliantly green eyes could not be mistaken for the features of anyone other than the beautiful Miss Es-meralda Ballantyne. A ducal coach awaited her outside the shop, which also could not influence trade badly.

She bought thirteen copies and loudly declared that her Christmas shopping was complete before leaving the shop. Chatter broke out immediately and those who had been undecided surged forward to claim their copy of the book in question.

Patience heard Arthur shout a welcome and turned to see Amelia searching the crowd for a glimpse of him. She smiled as the pair embraced, then Arthur brought Amelia toward her. "I hope you do not mind an early present," Patience said, offering the wrapped package to Amelia.

The girl bit her lip. It was clearly a book, but just as clearly, she wished to know which one it was. "I came to buy the new book," she confessed. "Mother says that I can."

"And you will have it," Arthur said, "but add this one to your collection first. You were the inspiration for its publication, after all."

Amelia looked between them then opened the package with a care that Patience would never have shown for a new book. She eyed the cover of the Ladies' Library edition of the *Lais of Marie de France*, which would be the January offering, then opened it with care. The book had the original Breton on the left of each page and an English translation on the right. Amelia went through the entire volume, page by page, her expression solemn, running a fingertip across the flourishes and studying the illustration for each story. She stroked the marbled paper end pages, then closed the book and ran an appreciative hand over the foiled leather cover.

"It is beautiful," she said in soft wonder. "But it is not signed."

Arthur took the book into the back and Patience watched as he inscribed the front page. He wrote quickly, for he evidently knew what he would write, blotted the ink, then presented the book to Amelia again.

"For Amelia, Christmas 1817, with love from Patience and Arthur." Her eyes welled with tears and she cast herself at him, earning a tight hug. "I miss you," she said.

"Then you must come to dinner this week," he replied. "I know Lady Beckham does not wish to come, but I will send a carriage."

"Yes, please," she said, then there came the tap of an umbrella.

Lady Beckham stood surveying the pair of them, her manner unwelcoming. Amelia hugged her book and returned to her mother's side, eyes downcast. Lady Beckham turned to Patience. "I should like to acquire a subscription to the Ladies' Library for my daughter. I assume you can arrange that for me?"

"Of course, Lady Beckham." Patience retrieved her ledger, well aware that Arthur and Lady Beckham stood considering each other like adversaries.

Lady Beckham reached into her bag and retrieved a small box, which she handed to Arthur. "Yours, I believe," she said crisply.

Patience watched him open the box and his brows rose. "It was." She saw the blue glint of a sapphire and guessed it was his pin.

"I took it from him immediately," Lady Beckham confessed. "Reynaud had no cause to relieve you of a valuable, much less to see you assaulted, and I chastised him severely for his regrettable behaviour. You may have heard that he and Miss Grosvenor are now married."

"I read of it," Arthur said.

Lady Beckham looked to be pained for a moment. "I am embarrassed that he was the one who showed himself common, he who had been born to better manners than that." She straightened. "You were a better son than he ever was."

Arthur considered the box. "Yet you did not return this until now."

Color flared in the older woman's cheeks. "I hoped you would return to Beckham House. I hoped you would miss it and its luxuries, that you would regret your choice and return to entreat my favor."

"But I do not," Arthur said easily, his tone such that his resolve could not be doubted. "Is that the price of this token's return?" He offered her the box again but she did not take it.

She shook her head and swallowed. "Reynaud is suddenly in possession of more funds than even he knows how to spend. Perhaps it is fortunate that his new wife has many ideas. She plans to expand his country house, so that it exceeds the grace of mine."

"I doubt that is possible, Lady Beckham," Arthur said politely. "You could sell your house to him, if you are less fond of the neighbors than once was the case. You might even be able to buy it back in five or ten years, at a discount, when the earl finds himself lacking in funds."

Their gazes met as Patience watched and a glimmer of humor passed between the two of them.

"You think he will spend it all."

"I think he will not be able to help himself."

"He wants to buy the house in Berkley Square," she confessed. "I thought to make it your legacy instead."

"You owe me no legacy."

"You once were my heir. Indeed, you still are, for I have not visited the solicitors to make a change. You are missed, Arthur. I would leave matters as they are, if you would grace me with your presence on occasion."

But Arthur shook his head. "You do not have to buy my attention, Lady Beckham. I would have called upon you already if I had believed you would welcome me."

"I would," she said quickly and Patience felt a lump rise in her throat.

"Then I will come," Arthur said easily. He took her hand, then bent to kiss her cheek. He murmured something, but Patience heard his words. "Make the house Amelia's legacy. Give her the ability to choose her fate, just as you were able to choose your own."

Patience's heart warmed that he showed such concern for the young lady he had so long known as his sister. Lady Beckham blinked rapidly, then glanced at Patience. Her gaze flicked down Patience before meeting her gaze. "Are you?" she asked softly.

Patience smiled and nodded. "June, if all is well."

"Good," Lady Beckham said, her tone decisive. "I am past due for a grandchild to spoil." And then she smiled as she had not yet, and reached to kiss Arthur's cheek. They eyed each other for a long moment before she nodded satisfaction, then she and Amelia turned to leave.

"You should come on Sundays," Amelia said. "And Patience must come, too. And we will talk about books."

"Of course, we will," Arthur and Patience said in unison, and Patience waved as the pair left.

She would have spoken to Arthur but a woman stepped toward her with purpose. She was breathless, her expression revealing her excitement, and she placed a large sheaf of papers on the table between them. "My name is Eurydice Montgomery," she said hastily. "Countess of Rockmorton. I have written a book and my friend, your sister, recommended that I bring it to you in the hope that you might publish it."

"Has the baroness read it?"

"She says it is perfect." The countess gripped her hands together.

Patience eyed the stack of paper. "What is it about?"

"It is a novel and a tale of two sisters," the countess began even as Patience reached to turn the first page.

"But that is the very best kind," she said and they shared a smile of complete understanding. "Leave me your address and I will write to you when I have read it."

The countess smiled. "And I must have a copy of Mrs. Oliver's book. I was there when she began to write it, you know, as was your sister."

"Truly?" Patience had not heard this tale.

"It was a year ago, at Rockmorton Manor." The countess glanced over the crowded shop. "You are busy today but I will tell you of it when we speak again."

Patience could scarcely wait.

THAT EVENING, Miss Esmeralda Ballantyne reviewed her diaries, her journals and her notes regarding clients past and those men with potential. She compiled a list of twelve men of promise who were, nonetheless, notorious womanizers. Several were inveterate rakehells. All were possessed of wives of beauty and grace beyond what they deserved, but none were so dissolute that Miss Ballantyne believed them incapable of reform.

She packed and dispatched twelve of the books she had purchased, reserving the thirteenth for her own shelf.

Twelve aristocratic ladies received an unexpected parcel in the days before Christmas. They did not realize that their package had eleven identical siblings, each without a sender or return address. Every lady surrendered to curiosity and opened the anonymous gift. All were astounded and fascinated by the book and its contents. Most read the small volume twice. Four read it three times. One read it seven times. Another used a mirror to verify the details provided in the illustrations, and all realized that the return of her husband for Christmas offered an opportunity that was not to be missed.

Eleven of these ladies celebrated a very joyous Christmas Eve. The twelfth found her husband besotted that evening, so had the brandy hidden on the following day. She invited him to embark upon the challenge of finding the key that night in her chamber, thereby adding a playful element to their intimate encounters that—unbeknownst to the lady—had been the reason her husband sought such entertainments elsewhere.

All twelve ladies enjoyed a merry Christmas night and a very happy new year year—precisely as Miss Esmeralda Ballantyne had planned.

~

THE DUKE'S DESIRE

THE LADIES' ESSENTIAL GUIDE TO THE ART OF SEDUCTION #5

The Duke's Desire is book six of *The Ladies' Essential Guide to the Art of Seduction* - it is Miss Esmeralda Ballantyne and the Duke of Haynesdale's story. These two need their own book, and it will be published in 2025. Watch my website for more details about the story, and pre-order links once they're available.

The Duke's Desire
Coming Spring 2025

~

ABOUT THE AUTHOR

Deborah Cooke sold her first book in 1992, a medieval romance called **Romance of the Rose** published under her pseudonym Claire Delacroix. Since then, she has published over ninety novels in a wide variety of sub-genres, including historical romance, contemporary romance, paranormal romance, fantasy romance, time-travel romance, women's fiction, paranormal young adult and fantasy with romantic elements. She has published under the names Claire Delacroix, Claire Cross and Deborah Cooke. **The Beauty**, part of her successful Bride Quest series of historical romances, was her first title to land on the *New York Times* List of Bestselling Books. Her books routinely appear on other bestseller lists and have won numerous awards. In 2009, she was the writer-in-residence at the Toronto Public Library, the first time the library has hosted a residency focused on the romance genre. In 2012, she was honored to receive the Romance Writers of America's Mentor of the Year Award.

Currently, she writes paranormal romances featuring dragon shape shifter heroes under the name Deborah Cooke. She also writes medieval romances as Claire Delacroix. Deborah lives in Canada with her husband and family, as well as far too many unfinished knitting projects.

Visit Deborah's websites to learn more about her books:

DeborahCooke.com

Delacroix.net

THE CRUSADER'S BRIDE
THE CRUSADER'S HEART
THE CRUSADER'S KISS
THE CRUSADER'S VOW
THE CRUSADER'S HANDFAST

The Rogues of Ravensmuir
THE ROGUE
THE SCOUNDREL
THE WARRIOR

The Jewels of Kinfairlie
THE BEAUTY BRIDE
THE ROSE RED BRIDE
THE SNOW WHITE BRIDE
The Ballad of Rosamunde

The True Love Brides
THE RENEGADE'S HEART
THE HIGHLANDER'S CURSE
THE FROST MAIDEN'S KISS
THE WARRIOR'S PRIZE

The Brides of Inverfyre
THE MERCENARY'S BRIDE
THE RUNAWAY BRIDE
<u>THE STOLEN BRIDE</u>

The Bride Quest
THE PRINCESS
THE DAMSEL
THE HEIRESS

THE COUNTESS

THE BEAUTY

THE TEMPTRESS

Christmas at Tullymullagh

Easter at Airdfinnan

Harlequin Historicals

UNICORN BRIDE

PEARL BEYOND PRICE

Time Travel Romance

ONCE UPON A KISS

THE LAST HIGHLANDER

THE MOONSTONE

LOVE POTION #9

Short Stories and Novellas

BEGUILED

An Elegy for Melusine

∾

To learn more about Deborah's contemporary and
paranormal romances,

please visit

DeborahCooke.com

∾